Circle of Death

A Warren Temple Mystery

Novels by Gary Kassay

Eric Logan Series

Under My Thumb

Best Served Cold

Seven Stones

Warren Temple Series

He Who Laughs Last

Out of the Abyss

Circle of Death

Inspector Duke Becker Series

Murder in Silence

Murder by Prophecy

Classic Murder

Murder by the Invisibles

Murder by Blood

Circle of Death

A Warren Temple Mystery

By Gary Kassay

Dedication

I dedicate this book to all of our furry pets who bring us laughter and joy, every single day. They give us unconditional love and it is our responsibility to give them the same.

My pets alive and passed are always in my heart.

Gibor, Poe, King, Prissy, Miss Apple, Bogie, Mickey, Crimson, Peter and Gordon

"The act of murder not only ends a life

but also shatters the lives of those left behind"

Mary Higgins Clark

"Murder is a reflection of the darkness that exists within society, a reminder of our own capacity for evil."

Unknown

"A murderer may escape the law,

but they can never escape the guilt

that haunts their conscience."

Edgar Allan Poe

Prologue

The rain was falling with a fury, as if it was trying to wash away all the dirt and grime from the streets and buildings. Anyone looking at the city would think all the color in the world had been wiped out. The sky was gray, the buildings and the streets also without any color. It was a rundown, drab and dirty part of the city. This part of Newark, New Jersey would never be clean, at least not from all the pain and depression suffered by the people who lived in this slum.

The apartment complex was made up of ten six story buildings and was ironically named Sunshine Manors. The poverty stricken people who lived there had a better name for it, Shithole Manors. The apartments within were small, hot in the summers and cold in the winters. There were infestations of insects and rats, and the battle to keep any apartment clean was a losing battle. The crime rate was high and the morale of the tenants low.

In building 3, Apartment 402, Peggy sat on the edge of her bed staring at the suitcase near the closet door. In it were the only things of value to her. Pictures of her parents now long deceased. A birth certificate belonging to her son John, soon to be three years old, now playing in the second smaller bedroom. A small snow globe depicting the statue of the Lincoln Memorial, from a school trip when she was only 13. Finally, buried within some of her clothes, wrapped in an old shirt was six hundred and thirty eight dollars which she had managed to scrape together, little by little, for more than two years.

Sitting there slightly in a daze, she looked around the room with its peeling paint, the color of dried puke.

On each side of the bed were the two dressers picked up from a thrift store, chipped and cracked and missing one drawer. Sheets hung over the cracked and filthy windows, hiding the view of the other buildings, and the skyscrapers further away.

Looking at her wedding picture hanging on the wall near the door, Peggy thought back to when she had met her husband, Anthony Blake. They had met in high school when Peggy was a sophomore and Anthony a senior. He had been a handsome man back then, romantic, sweet and respectful. He wouldn't even try to kiss Peggy until their fifth date, and then only on her cheek. When she graduated, she and Anthony married. Remembering her wedding day brought back how optimistic and foolish they had been.

They had little money and moving into Sunshine Manors, at first, didn't seem so bad. Anthony had a job working for the city, as a mechanic at one of the city bus depots. At first, they had been happy in their little apartment. They had made plans to move out of Newark, maybe to Red Hook or Manalapan. They were saving every dime and nickel, and the future had looked bright. Until the accident.

They had been married only three years when it happened. Anthony had been under one end of a small van the city used for some of their less traveled routes. Nearby, two workers had been having an argument. Soon it broke out into a fistfight, with both men tussling and throwing punches. Big Rick finally landed a right cross to Billy Lee's face, causing Billy Lee to fall onto the jack holding up the van. It fell and the van landed on Anthony's legs.

After a week in the hospital and three months of physical therapy, Anthony had been told the bad news. He would never walk normally again, but with the use of two canes he could still get along. The city kept him on for another six months , but finally stating there were cutbacks, had let him go. It was an obvious lie, but the city needed an excuse. The truth was Anthony couldn't keep up with the other mechanics.

He had found work in a small garage not far from their home, but things changed. Anthony began to drink heavily, staying out some nights at one of the local bars. His salary barely covered their expenses, and Peggy had gotten a job at a supermarket as a cashier. Together they were barely getting by. Anthony became sullen and depressed with each passing day. He also began to hit Peggy.

At first it was a small push, then a slap and then he would punch her. He had blackened her eyes, caused bruises all over her body, broken two ribs and one fateful night while drunk, had raped her. The result had been John. Somehow after he had been born, things just got worse. That's when Peggy decided the only way to save her, and her son's life, would be to leave for good. Three times she had left, gone to a woman's shelter, only to give in. She would forgive Anthony and return home.

Peggy began stashing away any money she could. Soon pennies, nickels and dimes had added up. And now as she stared at her wedding picture, she knew it was time to go. She glanced at her watch and seeing it was close to 7:00 p.m., she stood. Anthony would be home soon, and she wanted to be gone before he arrived home. She had to wait till now because she didn't get off work till 5:30, and she needed her last check. She had picked up John from Mrs. Galloway, a nice older lady who babysat him. Standing up and picking up the suitcase, she walked into John's room.

Taking him by the hand, she walked to the front door. Then it opened and Anthony stood there, leaning on his canes, staring at her. He saw the suitcase in one hand, their son's hand in the other. Hobbling inside, he slammed the door, causing a few knick-knacks on a shelf to fall to the floor and break. John began to cry, and Peggy moved him behind her. Without a single word, Anthony took two steps toward her and punched her in the face. She went down, pulling John with her. Anthony moved slowly past her, into the kitchen and returned with a beer in his hand. Leaning on one cane, he took a large swallow and then pulled his son from her hand.

He turned toward John's bedroom, and said, "You stay in your room," and pushed him into it. Then he closed the door.

With his back to her, Peggy knew what she needed to do. He hadn't seen her stand up or see her grab the Louisville slugger from where it stood by the door. He didn't hear her yell out or see the bat coming at him. He just went down, out cold as she hit him in the face. She had wanted to hit him in the back of his head, but Anthony had turned at the last second. Peggy saw the blood and thought she must have killed him. Peggy grabbed John and together they hustled past Anthony, lying on the floor.

About an hour later, Anthony came awake. Pushing his thinning hair away from his eyes, he tried to remember what had happened. His head was pounding. He couldn't remember. He grabbed his canes lying at his feet and stood up slowly. He needed to go and wash his face with some cold water. He took two staggering steps and then saw the bat with some blood on it, lying on the floor. He reached down to grab it, got dizzy, and fell flat on his face, banging his head, causing stars to appear before his eyes. He blacked out again and then after a short time opened his eyes. Cursing loudly, he again looked at the bat.

Suddenly it came back to him. She had been waiting for him in the living room, dressed, and holding the brat in one hand, her suitcase in the other. She was going to leave him, again. Take the brat too. He remembered hitting her and throwing the brat in his room. But nothing after that. Could she have hit him with the bat? Looking at the blood on it, he surmised she must have.

He swayed into the bathroom and splashed his face with some ice cold water. The water seemed to help, clearing the cobwebs from his pounding head. Looking into the mirror he didn't like what he saw. A twenty-six year-old man, looking closer to sixty. He had stubble on his face, some of it gray. His eyes were red and watery. His cheeks sunken and drawn. Blood had dripped from a gash on his forehead. At least it wasn't still bleeding, it was dry. Hesitantly, he felt the gash. There was a huge goose egg there and touching it caused his head to explode again.

He slowly made his way back to the living room and sat down on the couch. Shaking his head his anger began to swell. "Well the hell with her and the brat," he called out to the empty home. He was glad she was gone. He knew where she had fled to, just like she had done several times before. Maybe in a day or two he would pay her a little visit. Maybe do more than just mess her up a bit. Yeah, maybe a lot more.

He heard a cuckoo. Looking up at the stupid clock she loved so much, he saw it was nine. Damn, he had been out a long time. Getting up slowly, he walked over to the clock. He ripped it off the wall and threw it hard against the floor. Pieces flew and the damn cuckoo came out and announced the time, again and again. With each *cuckoo,* his head pounded. He walked over and stomped on it, shattering it and quieting the damn noise. Fucking cuckoo clock.

He made it into their bedroom, now only his, and stripped off his dirty clothes. Making his way back to the bathroom he went into the shower. As usual, the water was only lukewarm, but it still felt good. Twenty minutes later he was feeling a little better. Opening the medicine cabinet, he looked for some aspirin. "Too much of her damn crap in here", he thought, as he began throwing things out. Finally he found some ibuprofen and after struggling with the cap, downed a half dozen caplets.

He began to bandage his head and then decided, fuck it! He got dressed and on his way out he passed their wedding picture. He picked it off the hook and tossed it in the trash. Exiting the building he saw the usual thugs standing around, looking for trouble. He glared at them, and they slowly moved away.

"Damn right", he yelled after them, "you better move!"

He slowly made his way to where his car had been parked but it wasn't there.

"That bitch took my car!" he yelled. "Well I'll get my car back too bitch!"

He began walking toward the bar, thinking once he had a few drinks he would grab a bus and go downtown to a strip joint and enjoy himself. As he walked, one of his nosy neighbors leaned out of a first floor window and called out to him.

"Going out Mr. Blake?" she asked.

"Why don't you mind your own damn business bitch?" he called out. "Go inside Mrs. Rodriguez and make some more of your damn cookies! Then stuff them in your big nosy mouth. That's something your mouth might be good for!" Then he flipped her his middle finger.

His neighbor huffed and turned beet red. She slammed the window shut and Tony heard a loud crack. The window had broken. That made him feel better.

He began to walk to his local bar when he stumbled, going down on one knee. His head was pounding and for a second he thought about going to the hospital instead. He thought he might have a concussion or something. Then shakily standing, gathering up his canes, he moved on.

He saw the lights of the bar up ahead, the drab sign hanging out front announcing the name as *Chippy's*. Tony thought again as he had many times in the past how much the name fit. The sign, the tables, the floors and walls were all chipped. Taking a deep breath and gripping his canes, he began to walk the final few feet.

Just then he thought he heard someone call out his name. He stopped and cocked his head to listen. It sounded like it had come from the alley next to the bar. He was in no mood for some asshole, probably looking to mug him. He began to hobble toward the front door. Again he heard his name.

Looking into the narrow dimly lit alley, he called out, "Who's there?"

"Come here Tony," someone whispered in a low, hoarse voice. "I have a message from your wife."

"Oh yeah? Who the fuck are you?"

"Come here and you will see, unless you are afraid?"

Angry now, he slowly stumbled toward the alley, ready to bust up whoever was in there. He knew he could cause someone a great deal of pain swinging his canes. He had done so numerous times before. As he stepped into the dark alley, he heard a buzzing noise, felt his body go stiff and fell to the filthy ground.

For the third time this night, he awoke, his head pounding and groggy. As his vision cleared, he saw he was still in the alley. He was on his feet, the tips of his shoes barely touching the ground. Both hands were pulled up and out, secured by rope above him, tied to the security bars of a window.

"Cut me loose right now asshole," he shouted, and struggled to get free. His vision was fuzzy, everything swirling around. In front of him was someone in a hooded jacket. He couldn't make out who it was.

The figure smiled, pulled on some black gloves and then hit him in his stomach, knocking all the air from him.

As he was trying to catch his breath he heard, "These are weighted gloves Tony, lead lined. They hurt a lot more than just bare hands."

Before he could recover, he was hit again, and again. Tony was pounded on his face, his chest, and then a vicious blow to his balls. The pain exploded within him. But the beating didn't stop. He was bleeding from his nose and he felt some of his teeth falling from his mouth. The gash in his head had opened and blood flowed into his eye. His breathing hurt, feeling his broken ribs scraping against each other. He wasn't standing now, instead hanging by his arms tied above him.

Barely able to speak, he said, "Why? Who the fuck are you?"

"I'm nobody, nobody at all. But you aren't going to hurt anyone again."

He was barely able to whisper, "What the fuck does that mean asshole."

"Just this."

Tony saw a long blade coming toward him. With one swipe, Tony's throat was sliced from ear to ear.

"Never gonna hurt anyone again," the killer said, and then walked out of the alley.

Chapter One

I was sitting on one of the matching deck chairs out back on the patio, staring up at the stars in the sky. I was searching the skies for some guidance on what to do. I was close to turning fifty and I wasn't sure what direction my life, and of course Tracy's life should take. I had a beer in my hand which had gone warm, so I set it down on the table next to me. My wife Tracy, who I called Trace, had gone into bed a little while ago, and I had told her I was going to have one more beer and then be in. She had kissed me and gone inside. I didn't want to worry her, and I hoped she hadn't realized how confused I was about our future.

I got up and went into the kitchen, then retrieved a cold beer from the fridge. I glanced over to a small stool by the back door and saw the water can I had painted for Trace years ago. Funny how something so simple could trigger such good and bad memories in me. I had never told her how the Laughing Man had stolen it and then used it to almost drive me crazy. He had lured me to a warehouse where he wanted to kill me. Using the stolen water can, he tried to convince me Trace was dead. Seeing it had caused a rage and despair in me I had never felt before. I had almost given up and let the Laughing Man kill me, but it wasn't my time to die. In the end I had killed him, leaving him to rot. That had been the worst and best day of my life. Killing the Laughing man and then coming home and finding Trace alive.

A few months later my friend and now one of my

partners in the FBI, Special Agent Dave Anderson had appeared at our home. I had met him while working the Laughing Man case. He was a typical FBI agent, 6'2", 200 lbs. clean cut, white male, dressed in a simple black suit, white shirt, and black tie. He was married to Melissa, his wife of four years. He hadn't planned on falling in love with Melissa who had been a witness to a bank robbery, but he had. He only asked her to marry him after he realized he couldn't live without her. He was a real stickler for the rules. At first I hated him, had even punched him in the jaw, knocking him down. Somehow we worked well together and after a while had become friends.

On that day, he had taken out of his pocket several spent bullets and cartridges. Then he told me how a body had been found in a warehouse. The place had been the scene of some kind of shootout. My heart was pounding, believing this might be the end of my career, my life. When I asked him if he had run the bullets through ballistics, he smiled, pocketed the bullets and said, "What bullets?" It was at that moment I knew I had a great friend and someone I could rely on. A partner and a brother in arms.

Returning to the deck chair, I opened the beer and took a large gulp of it. Once again I looked to the night sky, seeing it full of twinkling stars. But I knew the answer wasn't up there. I sat there thinking back on my life. I had joined the NYPD two days after turning 21. Soon after I had met Trace, and we had married only a few months later. She turned out to be the love of my life. We had moved into a nice home on Long Island, in the town of Huntington. We had never had kids; Trace was unable to get pregnant and it had never bothered me. I loved Trace with all my heart and was devoted to her.

I made Detective after several years and had moved

into working homicides in Midtown North, one of the busiest precincts in Manhattan. With strong determination, imagination and a bit of luck, over the years I had solved somewhere in the neighborhood of 300 murders. I soon was promoted to Senior Detective First Grade. But time had moved on, and the bosses above me had decided it was time to move me somewhere less stressful and quieter. I was moved to the 111 Precinct, located in Bayside, Queens to finish out my career.

At the one-eleven, I was happy to be partnered once again with Tom Delaney, another First Grade Detective. We had worked together at Midtown North and Tom had been put out to pasture at the one-eleven, just like me. We made an odd couple, me being 6'2", 210 lbs. bald, with a silver and gray goatee. I loved puzzles, reading murder mysteries including Sherlock Holmes, Agatha Christie, and anything by Connely and Patterson.

Tom on the other hand was shorter than me and had a gaunt face, clean shaven and was thirty pounds overweight. He still had all of his hair, though it was turning gray. Where I liked to move at a brisk pace, he moved slower, worked with more deliberation, but had a keen mind. Always the detail guy, using the computer and writing on the boards the information we collected as each case advanced. Together we made a great team.

He always called me War, the only one I would allow to do so, other than Trace. While working The Laughing Man case he had finally asked the Medical Examiner, Sarah Nelson out for a date. I think he had fallen for her several years before at first sight. It turned out Sarah had a thing for Tom and things were moving fast. Tom was going to ask Sarah to marry him, and nothing could have made me happier. Just before asking Sarah for her hand, Tom had died of a heart attack in his garage. I had found him, and in his pocket had been an engagement ring for Sarah. I never stopped believing the stress of the Laughing Man had been the cause of his death. The Laughing Man had killed Tom as surely as if he had put a knife in his heart.

After the Laughing Man case, I was assigned a new partner. He was a young third grade detective named William Groat. Of course unfortunately for him, he was nicknamed Billy Goat. He was a decent detective, but he still had a great deal to learn. I was assigned to teach him all I could. Most of the time he only slightly annoyed me.

Billy was close to six feet tall, weighed about 190 lbs., had light brown hair parted on the left side, brown eyes, and no facial hair. He wasn't married when we met but I had a feeling his single status may change. The thing which bugged me the most was when he would call me War. Usually one look from me made him realize he had done it again. Tom and Trace were the only ones I allowed to call me that, and I couldn't handle my new partner doing the same. I had told Billy several times not to do it. Maybe the kid just couldn't get it.

A few months later, Billy and I found ourselves working with Special Agent Dave Anderson. At age ten, Dave's family had been slaughtered by the killer known as The Destroyer. His family had lived in a small town in Iowa, where people thought they were safe. In reality I had learned no one is ever really safe, and Dave had learned it at an early age.

Killed were his father, mother, two brothers and one sister. At the time, no one knew why the Destroyer would always leave one member of a family alive, and Dave had been the one. The killing of his family had led him to the FBI, but the case had never been solved. When the Destroyer or someone copying him, again began killing families years later, Dave had asked for Billy and me to help him out. We finally put the case to rest, catching the current Destroyer and finding out who the original had been.

When Billy and I had been temporarily assigned to work with the FBI on the Destroyer case, Captain Terry Jackson had smoothed the way with our fellow detectives about the temporary assignment. Most people did what Captain Jackson said. Jackson was a big African American, almost 52 years old and still was made of mostly muscle on his 250-pound frame. He had about 30 years on the job and in the time I had spent at the one-eleven, I had come to like him, something I usually never did with the bosses. He soon retired and a new Captain, Andrew Westman, became my boss, but it didn't last too long.

As for our two fellow detectives on my team, they accepted the extra workload with a minimum of griping. Those two should have been as different as expected, what with Victor Robles being from Puerto Rico and John Maguire a second-generation Irishman. But, they were like two splinters from the same piece of wood.

Both detectives had a good solve rate, Robles being the smooth talker of the two and Maguire being the bad cop in interrogations. Robles appeared to be a ladies' man, dark and handsome in a way that most women would open up to. It was funny because he was a dedicated married man with four kids at home.

Maguire, on the other hand, was as Irish as the day was long, with a big barrel chest and two fists the size of small boulders. He loved to fight and had taken the heavyweight title for the NYPD against the FDNY the last three years in a row. While Robles was dark...Maguire was pale, white with freckles and flaming red hair.

After solving the Destroyer case, I had been thinking about retiring. Then one day soon after the case was closed, Dave had come over to the house and he asked to speak with me and Trace.

"What's up Dave," I had said.

"Warren, I have been offered a new job," Dave began. "I will be in charge of a specialized unit, working serial killers all over the United States. I will still be working out of the NY office."

"Wow Dave," Trace had said. "Congratulations."

"Uh huh," I said, knowing there had to be more. "And?"

"You always were smart Warren," Dave said. "ADD Teller has spoken to Captain Westman as well as the Commissioner. We want you on the team, as a very special agent of the FBI."

I looked to Trace, and she nodded.

"Well, I'm not sure. Who else will be on the team?"

"It will be the same team we had on the Destroyer case Warren. Including Billy if you want him."

I only thought about the offer for a few seconds.

"Hmmmm, looks like I won't be retiring anytime soon," I had replied. "Okay Dave, I'm in! Only one thing."

Dave had shook my hand and said, Anything you need...Partner."

"Ummm when do I get my new Shield?"

Billy had jumped at the opportunity to become a Special Agent of the FBI. After a short time with Billy and me training at Quantico, the FBI Academy, we had gotten our new shields, as well as an office next to Dave at the New York FBI headquarters.

Our team consisted of Special Agent Louise Carmichael, a tall redhead with a great body. But most criminals were too attracted to her to realize she had a superior mind and was a great interrogator. She always knew the right questions to ask. She and Billy were having a fling, at least I thought it was a fling but them two getting married someday was a bet I would take. So far it hadn't caused any problems, but Dave and I were watching the two of them closely.

Next was Special Agent Arron Devlin. He was a large African American man, actually a small mountain of a man. At least 6'6" tall and weighing in at 260 pounds, none of it fat. His hair was cut short, and he usually wore a gray suit, white shirt with a red tie. Before joining the FBI, I had bullshitted him the first time Tom and I had visited the FBI headquarters. Devlin had been on security in the lobby, and he had let Tom and me pass. He had received a reprimand, but when I joined the team, he held no grudge.

Finally, there was Special Agent Carl Walkin. About 6' tall, but so skinny I was sure a strong wind would blow him over. He wore steel framed glasses, was clean shaven and was married. He had an open face, and he usually wore a big smile. I had liked him immediately. Carl's biggest asset was he was one of the best minds when it came to computers, or any other type of technology. He could hack into any place in the world, legally of course.

So here I was, almost fifty and trying to decide whether I should finally hang up my career. I knew I was lucky to have a great team to work with, and in the past two years we had worked well together, solving several serial killer cases. But I was tired. Tired of the red tape I had to deal with, tired of some of the bosses, tired of the time I didn't have with Trace, and definitely tired of all the bodies.

I drained the can of beer and got up. Looking up to the stars, I looked for an answer. Not getting one, I went into the house to go to bed with the love of my life. Maybe something would come to me in a dream.

Chapter Two

Monday, FBI Headquarters, New York City, 8:15 am

FBI headquarters in New York City was located at 26 Federal Plaza. It was a large rectangular building, gray in color with large stone blocks encircling it. They were there to stop some terrorist from driving a car or truck filled with explosives through their lobby. Nearby were the United States District Court, NYPD Headquarters known as 1PP, the Tweed Courthouse and numerous other Federal and Municipal offices. The new Freedom Tower could be seen and on 9/11, the dust from the towers falling nearly reached this far.

I was sitting in the office I shared with Billy , on the fourth floor, Room # 4303, one door down from Dave in 4301. He had his office all to himself, which I figured he deserved, being the head of our team.

I was looking over a report about a case we had just closed when ADD, (Associate Deputy Director) Harold Teller strolled by and then stopped. He was in charge of the Special Serial Killer Squad, known now as the SSKS, (Like the military, the FBI loved acronyms).

Teller was about 57 years old, with over thirty years with the FBI. He was in good shape, always eating right, no smoking and no drinking. He didn't micro manage our squad, letting Dave do what he wanted, mostly. He was a good boss, and I liked and respected him.

"Good morning Special Agent Temple," he said. He always used everyone's full title.

"Good morning sir," I replied.

"Good work on the Blind Killer case."

The Blind Killer, so named because after he killed a woman he would carefully take out her eyes. When we finally caught him, we had found eight jars with the eyes floating in formaldehyde. Not the most gruesome thing I had ever seen, but it came close.

"I'm just wrapping up my report sir," I said. Teller wanted every agent involved in a case to write up his or her own report. Each of us made sure to include all the details as well as the mistakes which might have been made.

He replied, "I have the reports of Special Agents Andersons, Devlin, Carmichael and Walkin. Still need yours and Special Agent Groat's. Be sure he gets it done. Have a good day."

He walked away and I thought his use of everyone's title sure made it tough to listen to him. But I guess it was just a quirk, and I knew we all had them. I got back to finishing the report when my young partner came in.

"Good morning Billy," I said. "Teller was just here, and he wants the report on the Blind Killer."

"Good morning War, ummm Warren," he said. "I was going to finish it this morning. But don't you think calling Derek Hampton the Blind Killer is a bit misleading? I mean, he wasn't blind, and his victims really weren't blind because he took their eyes after they were dead."

"What would you call him?"

"Ummm, maybe The Eye Taker Killer?"

"Uh huh. I think you better keep that to yourself Billy and get to work."

Billy sat down and began finishing his report. I was about finished with mine as well. He handed it to me after printing it out, asking me to check for any grammar problems. Teller was a stickler for professionally written reports. I would've had him check mine, but I usually went over my own reports three or four times.

As I began reading I thought back to how we had almost lost Louise, or Lou as most of us called her as long as Teller wasn't around. She had volunteered to be a decoy. Everything had gone right except for when it didn't. Lou was wearing a wire and all of us had been in different close locations. Hampton had outsmarted us at the last minute.

Lou had met him at a bar where we had figured out he had hunted for his victims. Lou being a good-looking woman with red hair, a fact all of his victims had matched, he had gone straight for her. They had talked a bit, and then Lou had accepted his invitation and gone with him to his house.

When they got to his home, he had led her to a small den. Then he had given her a drink. We knew from tox reports on the victims, Hampton always slipped them a knockout drug, so Lou had been prepared. She had made him look away and then spilled the drug out quickly in a potted plant. Then she faked passing out.

We were ready to move in, but there was something we hadn't counted on. Hampton had a sliding panel in his den which led to a small room where he killed his victims and took their eyes. Lou had faked being unconscious and Hampton had moved her into this room.

Two minutes later we had breached the house, rushing into the den but finding it empty. The only thing which saved Lou was the fact she was far from a damsel in distress. When Hampton had laid her down on a table and put his hands around her neck to strangle her, she had sat up. Then she neatly swatted his hands away, and delivered a swift jab to his chin, knocking him back. Jumping off the table, Lou had hit him with a sidekick and a follow up roundhouse. He was out cold when she opened the sliding panel. Lou was proud of her black belt, and she loved using her skills on perps when necessary.

We all looked on in astonishment and she had said, "Care to join the party boys?"

I was sure Teller was going to go over the entire case in a review meeting. What he was going to say about most of the team being caught flat-footed, all the men as it turned out, we were waiting on.

I made two quick corrections to Billy's report and handed it back to him. I then went to give Teller my report.

I knocked on Teller's office door and was told to come in. Dave was in Teller's office, and I began to say I could come back, when Teller told me to take a seat.

"No rest for the weary Special Agent Temple," he said. "I just received a report from our field office in Boston. They have been working on a homicide in their city. Turns out it might be the work of a serial killer. I want you both to read the report and follow up. See if this is a serial killing or a separate homicide. Then report back to me. That is all."

I left my report on his desk and Dave, and I stood up and left his office.

"Let me make a copy and then we can both go over it at the same time Warren," Dave said. "And good morning."

"Yeah right," I replied. It looked like my decision to retire or not had been taken out of my hands. At least for the time being.

Chapter Three

I had read the report from the Boston field office. The report detailed a homicide two months earlier, of an African American male, age forty three, found in a vacant lot on the outskirts of the city. He had been beaten badly. Busted face, ribs, both arms and one leg, But the death had been caused by his throat being cut, ear to ear. His head had been nearly decapitated.

The Boston Agents had been called in because there had been a similar body found in Sheffield, Massachusetts, eight months earlier. The body had been found with similar damage and the throat slashed as well. But the kicker which had alerted the FBI had been one more body found in Connecticut, one and a half years earlier from the most recent case. Again the same broken bones and bruises, and the throat slashed once again. No one had connected the homicides till now.

Dave had gathered the team together into the conference room. The room had one long mahogany table, with plush comfortable chairs around it, (nothing but the best for the FBI,) a large computer screen at the front which I had no idea how to operate, three large white boards, a coffee maker along with our own particular mugs on a shelf and various notebooks, pens and other necessary tools.

Dave had made copies of the Boston report and had even gotten the reports on the three initial police reports from Boston, Massachusetts and Connecticut. Fast work I thought as I grabbed my NYPD mug, filling it with coffee and sat down.

Lou was sitting opposite Billy trying not to make their romance obvious, something I'm sure Dave appreciated. As AIC, agent in charge, he could have made one or both of them leave the squad. Up to now he had decided to just let it ride. But I had no doubt if there was a problem he would act quickly.

Aaron was next to me, then Carl and near the front, Dave.

"No one thought to get any donuts?" Aaron said.

"I thought you were on a diet, big man," Carl said.

"Yeah right."

"Okay gentlemen, lets settle down and read these reports," Dave said. "Once we have read them, we will begin to put up the facts. Lou, will you do the writing?"

"How come Lou always does the writing?" Aaron said.

"Because you write like a caveman Aaron," Lou said.

"Awww, but Lou...."

"Can we get to work...please?" Dave said.

The conversation stopped and we all began reading the reports. As I read I had already decided we had a serial killer on our hands. When everyone was done, Dave started by asking for all the pertinent facts. Lou grabbed a marker and started writing on the white board. She started by writing Location, Victims, Injuries, Date of Homicide and COD, the Cause of Death, on top.

We began calling out the locations and Lou wrote them down. She added the dates the bodies had been discovered next to each location.

LOCATIONS

Kent, Connecticut – November 3rd, 2022
Sheffield, Massachusetts (The Berkshires) – September 14th, 2023
Bolton, Massachusetts – May 23rd, 2024

"So far it looks like once every eight or ten months," Billy said. "But most serial killers begin to kill with less time in between each kill."

"True Billy, but let's get all the information on the board before we start dissecting the info," Dave said. "Lou, continue please."

"Okay," Lou said, "Names of our victims with their ages please."

VICTIMS

Jerry Baxter, age 37 – Bolton
Robert Heller, age 29 – Sheffield
Cary Tomlinson, age 41 – Kent

"Can we add their race, if they were married or single and occupations please?" Dave asked.

"Got it," Carl said and began to state them. When he was done the board now read as follows:

VICTIMS

Jerry Baxter, African American, age 37, married, lawyer– Bolton
Robert Heller, Hispanic, age 29, married, construction – Sheffield
Cary Tomlinson, White, age 41, married, Doctor – Kent
"Injuries?" Lou asked.

"They look a lot alike," I stated, "but here goes." I read them off and Lou put them up.

INJURIES
Jerry Baxter – Broken nose, jaw, left orbit, four left ribs, two right ribs, left shoulder, left clavicle, burst stomach, groin crushed.
Robert Heller - Broken nose, jaw, left orbit, two left ribs, left shoulder, left clavicle, groin crushed.
Cary Tomlinson - Broken nose, jaw, left orbit, three left ribs, left clavicle.

"Damn!" Billy said. "These guys were really worked over. Looks like the injuries were caused in a rage. Which means our killer was probably easily angered."

"Let's keep the analysis to ourselves until we have it all up there," Dave said. "It looks like cause of death on all of the victims was having their throats slashed. Lou, add that please."

INJURIES/COD
Jerry Baxter – Broken nose, jaw, left orbit, four left ribs, two right ribs left shoulder, left clavicle, burst stomach, groin crushed. Throat slashed, nearly decapitated.
Robert Heller - Broken nose, jaw, left orbit, two left ribs, left shoulder, left clavicle, groin crushed. Throat slashed.
Cary Tomlinson - Broken nose, jaw, left orbit, three left ribs, left clavicle. Throat slashed.

"I think it might be easier if we combined all of our facts Dave," I said.

"I agree," Dave said.

"Okay boys, give me a few minutes," Lou said.

While Lou put everything together, we all grabbed some more coffee. Just as Lou was finishing up, ADD Teller walked in.

"Special Agent Anderson, what do we have?" Teller asked.

"See for yourself sir," Dave answered.

Lou had finished and Teller stood in front of the board, taking it all in.

Jerry Baxter, African American, age 37, married, lawyer– Bolton, Massachusetts.

Broken nose, jaw, left orbit, four left ribs, two right ribs, left shoulder, left clavicle, burst stomach, groin crushed.

Throat slashed, nearly decapitated.

Robert Heller, Hispanic, age 29, married, construction – Sheffield, Massachusetts.

Broken nose, jaw, left orbit, two left ribs, left shoulder, left clavicle, groin crushed.

Throat slashed.

Cary Tomlinson, White, age 41, married, Doctor – Kent, Connecticut

Broken nose, jaw, left orbit, three left ribs, left clavicle.

Throat slashed.

Teller stepped back, looked at each of us one at a time, and said, "Get on it." Then he left.

Chapter Four

Monday, *A Safe Place*, 11:30 am

People passing by 21-10 Grange street in Bellerose, Queens never looked twice at the slightly run down three story home. The grass out front was mostly green with a few bald spots. The house was painted a very pale beige color, and the shutters on the windows a light yellow. The front door was a solid looking wood , and all the windows were covered with thick drapes. In the backyard which had a six foot fence surrounding it, were a few tables with benches and an old gas grill on a cement patio. There were a few toys around, a small slide and a playhouse big enough for two or three toddlers.

Most of the neighbors knew what the house held and who lived there. But they never talked about it out of a sense of privacy needed for its occupants. What they didn't know was that the wooden door had a steel plate inside it, the windows were double thick glass, and it had a top notch security system. Rarely was there any trouble at the house and very few people came and went. One regular visitor was Dr. Malcolm Winters.

Dr. Winters was a psychiatrist who specialized in the treatment of battered women and abused children. He was a tall man, almost 6'3", 46 years of age. His hair was black, but his full beard had begun to show areas of gray and white. He kept it trimmed short, and he believed it gave him a distinguished look. He always wore three piece suits, usually gray or blue, with shoes that always had a good shine on them. In a vest pocket was a watch given to him by his mother upon graduating medical school. It had a small gold chain attached to it, and he had a habit of pulling it from his pocket, opening it and glancing at the time.

Dr. Winters had dedicated his career to helping women and children who had been abused by husbands or boyfriends. He never discussed his reasons for his choice of patients. Over the years he had seen countless women with black eyes, split lips and bruises of all kinds. He had treated children as old as seventeen and as young as three. He had heard every kind of atrocity men committed against their so-called loved ones. It never ceased to amaze him.

The most unusual thing about Dr. Winters was he had no office. Originally he had an office in Manhattan, but he found treating such a small number of patients didn't suit him. He then began seeing women in a few shelters and safe houses in the Tri-State area. Then he began traveling within several states along the east coast, seeing his patients at shelters, and safe homes.

He had started out visiting and treating women and children going on eighteen years and had over fifteen shelters he serviced. He didn't charge them exorbitant fees because he knew they couldn't afford them. Most of the time he treated the victims of abuse for free. Luckily, he was very wealthy, having inherited a small fortune when his parents had died in an automobile accident when he was twenty.

He had his pilot's license and his own jet, although he employed a pilot to fly him around. He had the same pilot, ex Air Force, for almost twelve years. He also had several cars he kept garaged at a few airports. This way he could travel to any one of his shelters within a few hours. He would visit at least fifteen on a schedule, seeing each one at least once every month or two. Of course when necessary he would show up as needed for any special cases. He also made a trip once or twice a year, seeing all of them within two weeks. More and more shelters and safe houses were added every year.

He had several small apartments, including one in Manhattan, one in Boston, in Tampa, Maine and one in Marlboro, NJ. These he kept as places he could stay when visiting his shelters. His main home was on Long Island, in Great Neck. It was a large home, almost what one would consider a mansion, on several acres of wooded and land-scaped grounds. There his wife of 19 years lived with their fifteen year old son.

He had met Jocelyn while doing his residency at Johns Hopkins Hospital, in the psych ward. It was a typical doctor nurse romance, and they were married within a year. Then, a few years later, along had come their son Brandon. Jocelyn gave up nursing as soon as they were married, never really loving it. She took care of Brandon, Malcolm and her home, was a member of several clubs, charities and a country club. She would sometimes accompany her husband on his trips, shopping in the diffcrent cities and making sure the apartments were well stocked. She was faithful to her husband and life was good for the Winters family.

Today, Dr. Winters was at the shelter in Bellerose, called *A Safe Place*. Of course there was no name out front or any indication the old house was a shelter. When a woman came to the shelter she needed to feel anonymous and advertising the name would not only be wrong, but dangerous. Doctors, nurses, ambulance drivers and other women's shelters had the location, and would readily pass it on. Most of the time, husbands and boyfriends had no idea where their battered women and abused children went. If one of them did show up at the shelter, a quick call to the police usually took care of them. Plus, breaking through the steel front door or the double glass windows was almost impossible.

Dr. Winters walked up to the front door, rang the bell and waited for a response. He knew he was on camera and after only a few moments, a voice came over the speaker.

"Is that you Dr. Winters?" a female voice said.

"It is Mrs. Caruthers," Dr. Winters replied.

A buzzer sounded and Dr. Winters entered the shelter. He stepped into a foyer where Mrs. Caruthers greeted him. She had been one of his first patients. She had been married to a wealthy lawyer who took out his frustrations once in a while on her. At first, he had started with only a slap. Then he began abusing her by raping her as often as he wanted to, burning her with cigarettes and a few black eyes. When she finally ran away to a shelter in Manhattan, Dr. Winters had begun treating her. He had helped her see she had done nothing wrong, that her husband was a brutal animal, and she needed to leave him. It had taken a few months, but finally she had divorced him.

She had received a great deal of money in the divorce, using a threat of revealing his abuse to his partners. The first thing she did once she had most of her ex-husbands money was to purchase the house. It was gutted and set up with twelve small bedrooms, a small medical suite, a large group area for meetings, and a play area for younger children. Of course there was a kitchen, bedroom and living area for Mrs. Caruthers on the upper floor. An office for Dr. Winters' interviews was also added. There was a staff of five volunteers who worked on rotating schedules, as well as two nurses who split their time at the house. Both were paid a good salary and were on call every other week.

"Good morning Dr. Winters," she said. "You are looking well."

"As are you my dear Mrs. Caruthers," Dr. Winters replied. "You said there was a patient in immediate need. Please fill me in a bit and then I will see her in my office."

Mrs. Caruthers took a deep breath and then said, "Her name is Carol Trent, and she has two small children aged two and five. She said she killed her husband."

Chapter Five

Dave had asked us to look over the information for a short time and then we would all say what we thought. We had ordered up food and were just finishing up.

"Okay team," Dave began, "who wants to start?"

"I believe our killer is escalating in the amount of damage he or she is doing?" I said.

"Explain."

"If you notice victim Cary Tomlinson had a broken nose, jaw, left orbit, three left ribs, left clavicle and his throat slashed. The second victim, Robert Heller, the damage was mostly the same but this time his groin had been crushed. Finally in the most recent victim, Jerry Baxter, the damage added was two right ribs, burst stomach and the throat was slashed with such force, he was nearly decapitated. Whoever our killer is, is escalating."

"You said he or she," Aaron said. "Do you believe a woman could have caused such physical injury?

"I do. Afterall, we have no idea if the victims had been somehow incapacitated or if a weapon was used. Also I believe our killer is right handed. Most of the damage to our victims is on the left side, which indicates being struck by a right handed person."

Dave said, "That seems logical Warren. Okay, what else?"

"As I said earlier, I believe the killer is in a rage when the murder is committed," Billy said.

"But the killer has gotten away with three murders

"

that we know of, which speaks to a controlled and thoughtful killer," Lou said.

"It does seem to be a contradiction," I said. "Maybe the reason for the murders is personal somehow but the killer carries out the crimes with planning and in a cool headed way."

"Lou, would you mind putting up on another board the main ideas we are coming up with?" Dave asked.

Lou replied, "No problem boss. So we have damage to victims escalating, rage possible in the murders but a cool headed killer as well. And probably a right handed killer."

Carl said, "Maybe the places they were killed have some hidden meaning, like the Destroyer did. Remember, he spelled out his actual name with the names of the places where he committed his murders. I can run something on the computer to see."

"Good idea Carl," Dave said. "Any other thoughts?"

I said, "There has to be a reason why these three men have been murdered, and in such a brutal way. We have to do a deep dive into their backgrounds and see if anything matches."

"Exactly what I was thinking," Dave said. "Carl, see if you can get anything about each of our victims. Also you can check if there have been any other killings on the eastern seaboard which match our killers MO."

"Why the eastern seaboard only?" Billy asked.

"So far we have two killings in Massachusetts and one in Connecticut. Let's keep to the east first and expand later on if we need to. Carl, go back three years."

"You got it boss," Carl said.

"Once Carl has worked his magic and we all have a bit more to go on, we will split up. Warren and I will take the most recent murder. Carl and Arron take the second victim in Sheffield and ummm, Billy and Louise can take the one in Kent."

"Can I have a word Dave," I said, and left the room.

Although I had been a Special Agent for the FBI only a bit over two years, I was an experienced homicide detective. I was basically second in command and as far as I knew, no one on the team minded.

When we had moved away from the door, I said, "Do you think it is a good idea to have Billy and Lou together?"

"I know they are a couple, but they have been teamed up before with no issues," Dave said. "I think we can trust them. Besides, if there is any problem, one of them will have to leave the team. I don't want to do that, but I think if I trust them and keep testing them, I won't have to remove either of them."

"Okay Dave, you're the boss."

We walked back in and before anyone could ask what that was all about, Dave said, "Okay Carl, get cracking. The rest of you get some rest. We will all meet back here in the morning. Then after reading what Carl digs up, we will head out."

"Do we get the jet?" Billy asked.

"I think you and Louise can drive to Connecticut Billy. Carl, Aaron, Warren and I will fly into Boston. Then Carl and Aaron will get an agency car to drive to Sheffield."

Everyone left and as I got to the door, Dave said, "How about briefing ADD Teller with me Warren?"

"Sure thing," I said.

As we walked down to Teller's office I thought about the killer. What was the reason behind the killings?

Could the killer be a woman, even though male serial killers far outnumbered female killers? How long would it take to catch him or her? And finally, how many more people would die?

Chapter Six

Mrs. Caruthers had taken Carol Trent's two children with her to a playroom. Carol Trent entered the office hesitantly and took a seat across from Dr. Winters. Dr. Winters did a quick appraisal of her. She looked to be in her late twenties. She was thin, but athletically built. Tall, maybe 5'10" with long strong legs and long arms. A thin gold band on her left finger and no other jewelry. She was wearing a tee shirt with the Rolling Stones on the front, a small spot of blood on Mick Jagger's nose. Black leggings showing off her legs, and running shoes which appeared worn, so she liked to run. Her hair was a mousy brown and so were her eyes. She had been crying and her mascara had run down from her eyes, making her look like a raccoon. The black eye and split lip were swollen. She was sobbing and her breaths were in short bursts of taking in and letting out.

Dr. Winters didn't say anything, wanting to let her calm down a bit. There was no point in talking to her while she was close to hysteria. He watched her closely as she tried to gain control of herself. Finally, after a few minutes, she took a deep breath and looked a bit more composed.

Dr. Winters stood and, taking her hand, led her to the bathroom next to his office, instructed her to wash her face and then come back in. He then sat down behind his desk. Dr. Winters didn't believe in having a couch for his patients to lie down on. He always felt with both he and his patient sitting eye to eye, the session would go better.

He liked looking them in the eye to judge whether they were hiding something or lying. Dr. Winters made sure his recorder was working. It was in his breast pocket of his suit. Later on his wife would transcribe it for him.

Carol Trent walked in, her face washed and composed and took a seat.

"I am Dr. Malcolm Winters," he began. "I am a psychiatrist, and I try to help women and children who have been abused. I work with many shelters and safe homes and have been doing so for many years. Anything you say to me will be kept in confidence and there is no fee for you to worry about. Now, why don't you tell me a bit about yourself before we get into why you are here please."

Carol Trent took a deep breath and said, "I'm not sure what you want to know?"

"How about you start with where you grew up, any brothers or sisters, your marriage and your children," Dr. Winters said.

"Okay. I'm an only child and I grew up in Bayside, Queens. My mom never worked, and my dad was a mailman. We lived in a Veterans co-op, a small apartment with two bedrooms, one bathroom and the usual rest. I went to high school, Benjamin Cardozo, got my diploma. I went to work for an accountant, a CPA in Little Neck, when I graduated from High School."

"A very good start Mrs. Trent," Dr. Winters said. "Do you mind if I call you Carol?"

"No, not at all."

"Very good. So Carol, were you happy in your childhood?"

"Yes, I mean mostly."

Something there, Dr. Winters thought to himself.

"And where did you meet your husband?"

"Sam, my husband, was a client, and he had come in several times when I first started working for John. That's John Roberts, the CPA I work for. Anyway, Sam always talked to me before he saw John and usually after. Sam is.....was...a....a"

"It's okay Carol. Relax and take a deep breath."

Dr. Winters poured Carol a glass of water and handed it to her. She took a drink and then continued.

"Sam was a photographer with his own studio, not too far from where I worked. Sam was tall, about 6'2", big, not fat but kind of muscular. He had blue eyes, a nice black beard, and a nice smile. He asked me to model for him and I turned him down. But he kept on asking and finally I gave in. I modeled for him in some dresses, some short skirts and then a swim suit, ummm, a bikini. Then he asked me out to dinner."

"Did you fall in love with him?"

"Not right away, but Sam was so kind and nice to be with. Then one day he told me he loved me, and I realized I loved him too. We married soon after."

"Were both of your parents at the wedding?"

"Just my mom. My uh, my dad couldn't be there. Sam's mom, dad and sister were there. It was just a small affair with only a few friends and of course John and his wife."

"I see. And when did you have your first child."

"It was about a year and a half after we were married."

"Did you want a child?"

"Well, not at first. But after Tim was born, I couldn't have been happier. And then three years later Rebecca, we call her Becky, was born."

"How did Sam react to having two children? Was he happy?"

"Oh yes. Sam loves, I mean loved our kids."

"So would you say life was good?"

"I guess so. I mean, every couple argues and, and Sam was under a lot of pressure. The studio work was slow, and he had to get a part time job. But things were getting better."

"Okay Carol, I can hear some hesitation in your voice. Remember, everything you say stays with me. I'm going to ask you a few questions and I would like for you to be very honest. Can you do that?"

"I'll try Doctor."

"Very good. Why did your father not show up at your wedding?"

"My mom and he split, and she didn't want him invited. I didn't want him there either."

"Why?"

"My dad had a bad temper. He sometimes drank too much and then he would hit my mom. Me too sometimes."

"What about Sam? Did Sam hit you or the children?"

"Never the kids!"

"But he hit you?"

Carol began to cry, a tear tracing its way down her cheek. Dr. Winters handed her a tissue and then she got up and paced around the room.

"The first time he hit me was just after Tim was born. He had colic and was crying all the time. Sam had been woken up and he lost his temper and slapped me. He was immediately sorry, and I figured it was just the lack of sleep and stress about money. But then he began hitting me more and more. A slap, then a punch in my stomach. Once a bad black eye and a broken wrist when he grabbed me. And then, last night…"

"Take your time Carol. What happened last night?"

"Sam came home, and I could tell he had had a bad day. When he walked in, he kicked some of Timmy's toys, breaking one of his favorites. Timmy began to cry, and I quickly grabbed him and Becky and got them into their bedroom.

When I came out of their bedroom he was standing there. He began to yell at me, saying things like I never clean the house, and I keep the kids away from him. Then he punched me. He split my lip and then he hit me again, in my eye. I went down and he kicked me a few times. Then as I was lying there, he opened the kid's bedroom door. I heard the kids crying. Then he said he was going to teach them a lesson too. I got up, grabbed a knife from the kitchen and then I ,,, I stabbed him in the back. Then I grabbed some things, the kids and got out of there. I had been here once before, and I figured it was the best place to go to."

"I know you are very upset now, and we will only talk for a few more minutes. How do you know he was dead?"

"Well, I guess I don't know for sure, but he wasn't moving. Could he be alive?"

"I don't know Carol, but I am going to find out. Now, why don't you go and find your children and try to relax. I will take care of things and then we will talk again. I want you to remember one thing, Carol. You defended yourself and your children. You did nothing wrong, and everything will be okay. Also you are very safe here. Now, go ahead and be with them."

Carol left the room and Dr. Winters made some quick notes. He would have to contact the police and an ambulance, possibly a lawyer. Thankfully he knew several lawyers who specialized in self-defense cases involving abused women. Mrs. Caruthers would have Carol's address. He would go to the apartment and meet with the police. Then maybe with an assistant District Attorney before allowing Carol to be questioned. Hopefully, Sam Trent would still be alive.

He sighed thinking about how many times an abusive husband or boyfriend had been physically hurt or killed. Alcohol or drugs were usually involved in the abusive person's life. It was a vicious circle. Most men who were abusive to their family had grown up in abusive homes. The women who were abused also grew up with abuse and somehow had found men who were abusive. A vicious circle which went round and round, sometimes leading to death.

He got up to find Mrs. Caruthers. He would have to call Jocelyn to tell her he would most likely be gone the rest of the day, maybe into the night. He hated not seeing her, but she always understood. Sighing, he left his office and again thought about the circle. A circle of death.

Chapter Seven

We had taken off and were now flying through clear blue skies to Logan International Airport. I rarely had been in Boston and didn't really like the city. Afterall, I was a native New Yorker, a big Yankees fan since Micky Mantle had played. I hated the Red Sox and everything about the city where they played. I also hated the New England Patriots.

We had all met earlier at the office and Carl had handed each of us some background information on each of our victims. Nothing had shown up on any other possible victims, but Carl assured us he was still working on it. We decided to read the info on the jet and left soon after grabbing a coffee and a donut or two. Aaron grabbed four or five.

Before we left, I pulled Billy aside.

"Look Billy, I know you and Lou have been seeing each other for a few months now," I began. "In fact, everyone knows, except for maybe ADD Teller."

Billy said, "Don't worry Warren. Lou and I know it can be a bit of a sticky situation, but we are both being professional. We only are affectionate off the clock and away from the job."

"Well, you better be, because at the first sign of any conflict, one or both of you will be kicked off the team. You might even be kicked back to the NYPD."

"We both know that, and we have discussed it. If anything ever happens, I will leave the team. But nothing is going to happen. I promise."

"Okay Billy, I believe you. Now get going."

As we had been getting ready to leave the office, Dave had said to me, "You talked to Billy?"

"Ummm, yeah Dave, I did," I had said. "I hope I didn't step on your toes."

"Nah. He was your partner first, so I guess you have the right to look after him and try to keep him in line. As a matter of fact, I also talked to Lou."

Now as I sat looking out a small window at the clouds below us and the deep blue sky, I thought about how lucky I had been in having a friend like Dave.

Dave called us all to the rear of the jet where there was a small table . The four of us sat down, well actually three of us sat down and Aaron squeezed into his chair.

"Looks like you might need to shed a few pounds big fella," Dave said and laughed.

"Are you kidding?" Aaron answered. "This is all muscle my friend."

"Uh huh. The pilot wasn't sure we would be able to take off."

We all had a good laugh and then pulled out the sheets with the information on our victims.

"Let's start with Robert Heller," Dave said. "Carl, since you pulled all of this and probably read it, why don't you fill us in."

Carl said, "Okay guys. Heller was born in Puerto Rico. His father, Barry Heller had married his mother Gloria in Puerto Rico. They lived in Puerto Rico until Robert turned twelve. Robert worked for a construction company, ummm, Howard Construction. He was married to Maria Narvaez when they were both eighteen years old. Together they had two kids, both boys aged nine and seven. The boys were named Barry, after Robert's father and Hector, after Maria's father."

"Sounds like the families must have gotten along, naming both boys after the fathers," Aaron said. "I for one would never name a kid of mine after my dad."

"You would first have to find a woman willing to let you get on top of her," Carl said.

"Can we continue...children?" Dave said.

Carl continued, "Nothing in the police report as to a reason he had been killed. Nothing about his family life so I suppose Aaron and I will have to interview his wife and fellow workers.

He was found in a field not far from his house. Fully clothed, lying in the dirt. I couldn't get the Medical Examiners report or any pictures of the body. That's about all, for now."

"Okay Carl," Dave said. "Any thoughts Warren?"

"Not much there really," I said. "We'll know more after some interviews are conducted. I suggest you guys also talk to the first officer on the scene, and whoever had found the body. Also the Detective assigned to the case. Oh, and the medical examiner."

"Anyone else?" Aaron asked. "We're gonna be here for days tracking this down."

"Once we land a car will be waiting from the Boston FBI office, and when you get to Sheffield, get a couple of hotel rooms," Dave said. "If we get done before you, we will send back the jet, or you can drive back. Just play it by ear and be thorough."

"Aren't we always?" Carl asked.

"Uh huh," Dave replied with a smile. "How about our victim Warren?"

I had looked it over quickly on the ride to the air-port, so I just glanced at the report as I spoke.

"Jerry Baxter, African American, age 37," I began. "Married to Halley Baxter, age 36, and they have three children, all girls. Girls are Melissa, age 16, Debbie, age 14 and the youngest, Francine, age 9. They live in a wealthy suburb of Boston, in Bolton. Baxter was a lawyer; criminal defense and he has two partners, Don West and Terry Carpenter."

"Criminal defense," Dave said. "Might be a reason why he was killed. Could have lost a case or won the wrong one. Looks like Warren and I will be in Boston for a few days as well as you guys. What else Warren?"

"Again, nothing on his home life or about his partners. Nothing from the ME, and the police report is pretty thin."

"Okay Warren. Looks like we have a lot of people to interview as well. If anything pops from your interviews Carl, which you think might be a motive, give us a call right away. Also call Billy and Louise to tell them what you find. They will be keeping in touch with me. I guess that's all for now. We should be landing soon."

We all went back to our seats, and I once again looked out the window. I wondered what could be the motives for three men killed that we knew of. They lived far away from each other, had different occupations, and they all came from different backgrounds. Hopefully we would be able to come up with something. If not, the only thing which would move the case along would be another murder.

Chapter Eight

Billy and Lou met at FBI headquarters early to pick up a car for their ride to Kent, Connecticut. They had picked up some coffee and bagels at a deli around the corner from the garage before they left. Now as Lou drove, Billy ate and started to describe the town of Kent.

"Mmff...," Billy mumbled.

"How about swallowing before you choke," Lou said with a laugh.

Billy swallowed and said, "Sorry Lou, but this bagel is awesome!"

"How about telling me about where we are going, or just finish the bagel?"

Popping the last bite into his mouth and sipping some coffee, Billy said, "Okay Lou. Now where was I? Kent is in the county of Litchfield. It's along the border with New York, so it shouldn't take us too long to get there."

"What about the town itself?"

"Here's something interesting. Henry Kissinger and Seth MacFarlane used to live there. And there is the Shag-tic-oke, Schaghticoke Indian Reservation within the town borders. Population around 3,000."

"Well if Henry Kissinger lived there, I would think it's probably a very affluent town. Anything interesting to do there, if we have the time?"

"You mean besides the bed in the room, if we stay over?"

"Knock it off Billy. We have to be professional."

"Yeah I know," Billy said with a sigh.

"And Dave will be looking to see if we booked two rooms."

"Right."

"But that doesn't mean we can't share one."

"Absolutely!"

"Now, anything else of interest?"

"Let's see," Billy said as he looked at his phone. "There is the Macedonia Brook State park with numerous hiking trails and the beauty of the Catskill and Appalachia mountains. I suppose we could go and get lost in the mountains. Might be fun."

"Hmmm, I think we won't have time for getting lost. Look up where Police Headquarters is in the town."

"It's located at 232 Fourth Avenue south, just south of City Hall. I'll enter it into the GPS. Says we should be there in about another 45 minutes."

The rest of the ride was spent going over what they knew about Cary Tomlinson.

"We should be able to get plenty of information from the lead detective and Tomlinson's wife," Billy said.

"If she still lives in the town," Lou replied.

"He was a doctor, but I don't know what kind."

"We will find out from the detective. We should be there soon."

Lou followed the instructions on the GPS and shortly they pulled up in front of a new looking police building. There was a sign which read parking behind the building, so Lou drove around. There were five guest parking spots, and she pulled into one of them. The others were empty.

"I guess this place doesn't have too much crime," Billy said.

Lou replied, "We will see. Let's go in."

They walked in through the back door and down a short hallway to the main lobby. Like most police stations, there was a large desk, raised up with a sergeant sitting behind it. He was busy looking at some papers. Lou looked him over. He was about thirty-five years old, with blonde hair, a large open looking face with a big moustache. In other words, a cop.

Looking around for a second, Lou saw several pictures of previous chiefs, a plaque with three names on it, cops who had died in the line of duty, and one larger photo of the present chief. She read the name and then she and Billy took out their ID's and presented them to the sergeant.

"Good morning Sergeant, ummm, Black," Lou said reading his name tag. "I am Special Agent Louise Carmichael, and this is my partner Special Agent William Groat."

"Good morning to you," Sgt. Black replied in a deep baritone voice. "What can I do for the FBI?"

"We are here looking into a homicide which took place here in Kent," Lou said. "We'd like to talk with Chief Doring first, if he is available."

Sgt. Black picked up a phone and said, "Chief, there are two Special Agents from the FBI to talk with you...if you are available," he said with a smile. "Chief says you can come on in. It's through that door, down the hall to the end, make a right and you will see his office."

"Thank you Sgt Black."

Lou and Billy followed the Sgt's instructions, passing photos of police officers from many years ago. Arriving at the Chief's office, Lou knocked and walked on in.

Chief Doring walked around his desk saying, "Come on in! Never met anyone from the FBI before. Sit right down."

Billy and Lou tried to hide their surprise at meeting the Chief. He was about four and a half feet tall! Lou gave Billy a nudge and he held out his hand for the Chief. The small hand disappeared in Billy's and then Lou shook his hand as well.

Before they could say anything, the Chief let out a laugh.

"Boy, if I could record all the looks I get when people first meet me!" he said.

"Ummmm..." Lou began to say.

"No worries, no worries. Have a seat and tell me how I can help you."

"We are from the SSKS, the Special Serial Killer Squad. We believe a homicide which was committed in your jurisdiction about two years ago might be the work of a serial killer."

"The SSKS huh? You people in the government sure like to abbreviate everything."

"I suppose that's true Chief Doring."

"Call me Charlie, everyone does. Do you have the name of the victim?"

"Dr. Cary Tom..."

"Dr. Tomlinson. Yeah, it figures. We don't have too many homicides in this town. I figured you might be talking about Doc Tomlinson. Let me get Detective Stone in here."

Chief Doring picked up his phone and said, "Terry, can you come to my office please? And bring the Tomlinson file with you. He hung up and said, "Terry Stone was the lead detective on the case."

A minute later a tall, long haired blonde with an amazing figure walked into the room. She was wearing a red silk shirt, with the first three buttons open, with a short black skirt and red very high heels.

Lou looked at Billy as his jaw dropped open. She gave him the look of death and he closed his mouth.

"Detective Terry Stone, these are two FBI agents," Doring said.

"Special Agent Louise Carmichael and Special Agent William Groat," Lou said and stood up. She shook her hand and when Billy went to shake her hand, Lou moved in front of him. "We are here investigating the Tomlinson homicide."

Detective Stone looked Lou over and then said, " Let's go to my office. That okay with you Charlie?"

"Sure thing Terry," Doring said. "Just let me know if you need anything else."

Lou and Billy followed Terry down the hall to her office. Lou thought there had to be a reason for Detective Stone's attire. She couldn't wait to find out.

Chapter Nine

Tuesday, Detective Terry Stone's office, 10:30am

"Before you ask," Detective Stone said, "the Chief has me working on a prostitution ring which has been set up in our town. He also likes to see me dressed like this. Being a short guy gives him a bird's eye view if you know what I mean. Have a seat."

Lou laughed and said, "The things we women have to do."

"I can't blame the Chief," Billy said, which earned him the look of death from Lou.

"Ummm, I hope you both won't mind if I say something," Stone said. "You both better work on keeping your relationship a bit less noticeable."

"Well I guess we don't have to wonder if you're a good detective," Lou said. "But our boss knows. He's a bit more modern in his thinking. As long as we don't let it affect our work."

"Wow, I'm surprised. I heard all FBI Agents walk around with a stick up their ass."

"Just the men, mostly. So can you tell us about Dr. Tomlinson?"

Opening the file and taking a quick look, Detective Stone said, "Dr. Cary Tomlinson was originally from Boston. Moved here back in 2001 with his wife. No kids. At the time of his death he was 41 years old. He was a gynecologist, and had a practice with one other doctor, Dr. Barry Jones. He and his wife Gwen lived over on Rose

Street. It's a part of town where all the streets are named after flowers."

"Does his wife still live there?"

"As far as I know. He was found in a parking lot behind his office. M.E. puts his death at around 9:00 pm. He usually worked till about seven. Found by a couple of teenagers passing through the lot at about two in the morning, so he had been out there for a few hours."

"Did you have any suspects?"

"Not a one. Doc was pretty well liked around town."

"Could we get a copy of your report and maybe the M.E.'s report? Photos too if possible."

"Sure. Can I ask you why the FBI is interested in a local homicide?"

"The way Tomlinson was killed appears to be similar to two other killings. We think he might have been the first one. The others were on the east coast as well."

"Do you have any leads?"

"Not yet, we just started. The rest of our team are looking into the other two homicides as we speak."

"Give me an hour or so and I'll have those reports for you."

"Great. In the meantime we will go see if Mrs. Tomlinson is at home. Do you know if she works?"

"When I interviewed her she said her husband didn't believe in his wife working. Maybe she got a job since his death, but I know she didn't have to. Dr. Tomlinson was one of the richest men in town."

"Thanks a lot Detective Stone."

"It's Terry."

"Thanks Terry," Billy said with a big smile.

"You can call her Detective Stone," Lou said.

Terry and Lou laughed as she took Billy's arm and led him out of the office and to the car.

"Awww come on Lou," Billy said. "I'm not dead, you know."

"Uh huh," Lou replied. "Let's go see if Mrs. Tomlinson is at home, lover boy."

Chapter Ten

Tuesday, Dr. Malcolm Winters' home, 10:45 am

Dr. Winters yawned deeply while thinking about all that had happened since he met Carol Trent at the safe home. He was listening to his recordings, and checking all the information was correct for his wife Jocelyn to transcribe. After leaving Carol Trent, he had contacted the Nassau County Police and then drove over to her apartment. He had waited outside until a patrol car pulled up.

Two young patrol officers stepped out of the car and walked up to him.

"Are you Dr. Winters?" the first one had said.

"Yes I am Officer," Winters replied.

"I'm Officer Perez and this is Officer Boyd. We got a call about a possible dead body. Want to explain?"

"I can explain later Officer Perez, but right now there may be a man, still alive but dying while we stand here and talk. The apartment is inside this building Apartment 3c. I tried to summon a landlord or manager or maintenance man, but it appears no one is around. Please let's not waste any more time."

Perez nodded to Boyd and the three of them made their way up the stairs to Apartment 3c. Perez rang the bell and knocked heavily on the door.

"You sure there is someone hurt in there Doc?" Boyd asked.

"Very," Dr. Winters replied.

"Okay then, let's break it down."

Dr. Winters stood back watching. Unlike what he had seen on numerous cop shows, Boyd and Perez didn't try to knock down the door with their shoulders. Instead Boyd, the bigger of the two, stood with his back to the door, raised his leg and kicked backward, smashing his foot just under the doorknob. The door flew open.

"Stay here," Perez said, and with guns drawn, both cops entered the house. "Got a man down here."

Perez felt for a pulse and said, "He's got a weak pulse Jimmy. Call for a bus and tell them to put a rush on it. Doc, come here."

Dr. Winters walked in and said, "Is he dead?"

"Not yet Doc. See if there is anything you can do."

"I'm a psychiatrist."

"I don't care if you're a veterinarian! See what you can do. I'm going to check out the rest of the apartment. Don't touch anything else, like that knife lying there."

Winters thought back to how everything after that had happened quite quickly. An ambulance had arrived, taking Sam Trent to North Shore University Hospital. Then two detectives showed up along with a full Crime Scene crew. He had been forced to wait inside the cop car while the detectives and techs went over the apartment.

As he waited in the car, he phoned Mrs. Caruthers to tell her Sam Trent was still alive, barely, and had been transported to the hospital. Then he told her Carol Trent would have to make an appearance at the police station, but he would try to make it for tomorrow. Then he called his lawyer, Frederick Wells, asking him to meet him at the police station in an hour or so.

Having done all that, he thought back to what Carol Trent had told him. It was obviously a case of self-defense but sometimes the obvious was overlooked by the law. He went over in his mind everything Carol had told him and replayed the recording of their session. He would let the detectives hear the tape if his lawyer advised him to do so.

It had taken much longer than he thought it would, being driven to the police station after five. He was given some coffee and a Danish to eat and left in an interview room for another hour alone.

Finally the two detectives who were at the apartment came in. They didn't smile and both of them looked to be cops who had seen it all. One was white while the other was African American. They sat down across from him, screeching the metal chairs as they sat down. Nothing was in the room besides a scarred metal table , three chairs and two cameras recording everything.

Sitting down the first detective said, "I'm Detective Green and this is Detective Briscoe."

Dr. Winters remembered how he had laughed. Briscoe was the African American and Green was white, just the opposite of the detectives on Law and Order.

"Yeah, yeah, I know," Green had said. "Just like on Law and Order. So Dr. Winters, can you explain how you knew about the attempted homicide on Sam Trent?"

"Before I say anything I would like a minute to confer with my lawyer, who I'm sure is here," I had said. "I would also like to have him in this interview please."

They had left the room without another word and escorted his lawyer into the room.

Fred Wells said, "Don't worry Malcolm. I made sure they turned off the microphones and the cameras for the moment. Now what trouble have you gotten yourself into?"

"Not me," I had replied, "but a young woman at the safe home in Bellerose. Her name is Carol Trent. When I first spoke to her she stated Sam Trent, her husband had been physically abusing her for a long time. Yesterday, he had come home and hit and kicked her. When he went for the kids, she picked up a butcher knife and stabbed him in the back. Then she fled to the safe house. She had been there before."

"Hmmmm," Wells said. "You say she has been there before?"

"Yes, maybe once or twice."

"Good, it'll work in her favor if we can show she had run away before to the safe house. Now, did Sam Trent die?"

"Right now he is at North Shore. He was hurt badly and I'm not sure if he is going to make it. Also, I have a recording of my initial interview with Carol Trent."

"You will have to turn it over to the detectives, or at least let them copy it."

"Okay, Fred, do you think you can help Carol Trent?"

"I believe I'll be able to make a self-defense case. Now, let's get those detectives in here."

Dr. Winters went to his small bar in his office and poured himself a drink of scotch. Then he sat down and continued to remember the events of the day.

The interview with the detectives had gone smoothly, and he had agreed to bring Carol Trent in to be interviewed this afternoon at three. They had listened to his recording with Carol Trent and made a copy. Then he was free to leave.

As he was finishing up, his wife came into his office. She was a handsome woman, not what some would consider beautiful. She was about 5'9 with short black hair. She hadn't changed much since he first saw her in the hospital doing his residency. Her eyes were still a clear blue and Dr. Winters loved her dearly.

"Almost done dear?" Jocelyn Winters asked.

"Yes my dear, just finished," he replied. "There's no rush in getting this typed up. I have to go pick up Carol Trent from the safe home and take her down to the detectives. Wait until you hear their names, you'll get a good laugh. What do you have planned for today?"

"I have a meeting at the club to discuss the repair to the golf course. Remember some kids broke in and took a golf cart. Then they rode over a few of the greens and really did some damage."

"Well I should be back home by around six. Would you like to go out for dinner? I was thinking of Carmine's."

"That would be wonderful Malcolm."

Dr. Winters kissed her and then went up to shower. Jocelyn sat at his desk and listened to the interviews and the dictation from her husband. As she listened, she decided to add a bit more scotch to Malcolm's drink. Taking a sip, she began to type out the notes which would go into his file cabinet. She thought back to when he had only needed one small file cabinet. But through the years he had added several more. Then he had a custom built filing system made out of oak built and it filled one wall of the study. She listened carefully and began typing again.

Chapter Eleven

Tuesday, Bolton Police Department, 11:45 am

Dave and I had been sitting in a conference room in the Bolton PD for over an hour. We had met with the Chief, a gruff man with absolutely no love for the FBI. Why he disliked us personally or the entire FBI, we hadn't been told or figured out. After showing our credentials and asking to speak with the lead detective on the Jerry Baxter homicide, we were led to this room and told to wait.

"I hope Aaron and Carl are having more luck," I said. "Why do you think that Chief has so much love for us?"

Dave was pacing the room and said, "I have no idea but it's not the first time I've come across cops and Chief's who don't like us. As I recall, you didn't like me much when we met. In fact I seem to remember a pretty good right cross that knocked me down."

"Ummm, yeah. Sorry about that, again."

"Water under the bridge. But some cops just don't like us putting our big noses into their investigations. Don't let it bother you."

As we waited I looked around the room. It was a conference room but was probably used to discuss cases where there were several detectives involved. In fact it looked a lot like the one we had back in the One-Eleven precinct. White boards to write on, cork boards to pin up photos and info, two phones and a coffee maker with several mugs in the corner. I was just about to see about making some coffee when a very large man opened the door and walked in. He was about 6′5″ and about 280 lbs. None of it looking to be fat.

"You guys from the FBI?" He asked in a deep baritone voice.

Taking out our ID's, Dave said, "I'm Special Agent Dave Anderson and this is Special Agent Warren Temple. And you are?"

"I'm Super Special Detective Cory Nash," he said in all seriousness, standing with his hands on his hips as if he were posing like Superman. Then he burst out laughing. "Sorry guys, but I couldn't help it."

Shaking our hands we all had a good laugh.

"Why do you guys always use the Special Agent tag?" He asked. "Are there any regular agents in the FBI?"

Laughing Dave said, "It's a holdover from when J. Edgar Hoover started the FBI. He wanted his men to stand out from regular law enforcement."

"I see. Well sorry for making a bit of fun at your expense guys. Call me Cory please."

"Dave and Warren. You were the lead on the Jerry Baxter homicide?"

"I was but I don't understand why you guys are here."

"We believe Baxter's murder might be the work of a serial killer. We have two more murders we're looking into. One in Sheffield, Massachusetts and one in Connecticut. Warren and I are part of a serial killer squad. Our teammates are investigating the other two as we speak."

"Let's sit down. You guys want some coffee?"

"Great," I said. "By the way, why does your Chief hate the FBI?"

Laughing while he made the coffee, Cory said," Our illustrious Chief Henry applied to the FBI when he was younger not once, not twice but four times! Obviously he was never accepted."

We sipped the coffee and then Cory began telling us about the case.

"Jerry Baxter, age 37 at the time of his murder. African American, married to Halley Baxter, age 36, and they have three children, all girls. Girls are Melissa, age 16, Debbie, age 14 and the youngest, Francine, age 9. They live in a wealthy suburb. Baxter was a lawyer; criminal defense and he has two partners. Has an office here in town and a satellite office in Boston.

"We'll need all of his partners' names as well as a copy of your report and the M.E.'s report," Dave said.

"Of course. He was found behind his office at 6:00 am by one of his partners. M.E. figured he was killed somewhere between 10:00 pm, and 2:00 am. Couldn't get it any closer in time."

"From what we have gathered, he was beaten pretty bad." I said.

"Oh yeah. I've never seen someone beaten so completely. Let's see here...Busted ribs, right and left side. His left orbit crushed, shoulder, clavicle nose and jaw. When he was opened up in the autopsy, his stomach had been busted open and his balls crushed. Then he had his throat slit, nearly decapitating him. Someone really hated him."

"Was Baxter a big or small man?"

"Average. 5'10", weighing around 175. Not too muscular. Kinda flabby around the middle."

"Any defensive wounds?"

"None. But there was a burn mark on his neck. We figured some kind of taser was used to disable him and then the killer went to town beating him."

"Any suspects Cory?" Dave asked.

"I talked with his partners, his wife, his daughters and even the janitor in his office building. No one could think of anyone who might have had a motive or hated him. So the answer is a big fat zero."

"Okay then. I guess we will recover the ground."

"I'll have copies of the reports for you guys later on today. Have you gotten rooms yet?"

"No, we came straight here after landing in Boston. Got any recommendations?"

"Actually I do. I have a big house, and I'm not married. Why don't we meet up for dinner and then we can play a few rounds of eight ball. I have a nice regulation table at my house. Never get to play anyone."

"My boss sure would be happy if we keep our expenses down, so absolutely. Meet you back here at about six?"

"That works. See you then.

Dave and I then left with the addresses of Baxter's home and office. As we got in the car, Dave asked, "Did Cory seem familiar to you Warren?"

"Now that you mention it, yeah," I replied.

"Hmmm, it'll come to me. In the meantime let's go talk to Baxter's wife.

As we drove I thought about where I could have possibly seen Cory before. I let it go figuring it would either come to me or Dave.

Chapter Twelve

Dave and I had spent the day talking with Mrs. Baxter, her daughters, his two law partners and a few of his friends. Not one of them had any idea why Baxter would have been killed in such a brutal way.

His wife was just as Cory had described. She was a slight woman, pretty, with red hair and blue eyes, and shy. She seemed very nervous and jumpy, and I was sure she was hiding something from us. We talked with her for about an hour, getting nothing useful. When we asked her where her daughters were, she informed us they were in two different schools. She gave us directions and we said our goodbyes.

Dave and I discussed our observations of Mrs. Baxter and we both agreed. There was more to her story. Maybe someone didn't like Baxter, being black, having a pretty white woman as his wife. It was something to consider.

We were able to get the girls out of their classes at the two schools. We had to meet with them with a school advisor because of their ages. All the girls looked alike with light brown skin. They had bright red hair and very light eyes of brown. When we asked about their dad, all the girls reacted in the same way. They got nervous, biting their lips and turned away. Then they all said nothing further. There was definitely something strange going on but what it was, I didn't know.

Once again as we drove, we agreed the kids had something they were hiding, just like their mom. I had given it a lot of thought but couldn't decide what it could be. Then we spoke to his two partners, Don West and Terry Carpenter. Both of them were uncooperative, and pretty useless. They knew of no enemies and would not share any of Baxter's case files with us. Even cases which were closed.

By the time we left them and spoke to a few friends of Baxter's, we were convinced something was rotten in Denmark. But there was little we could do about it now. Maybe when we all got back together, the rest of the team would hopefully have something.

Before we met with Cory, Dave and I made calls to our wives. Trace was busy working in her garden and doing things around the house. She said she missed and loved me and ordered me to stay safe. I told her we were not having much luck and would be home tomorrow or the next day. When Dave hung up with his call to Melissa, we drove over to the police headquarters to meet Cory.

We got to Cory at six and he gave us copies of the police report, pictures of the scene and the Medical Examiners report. We definitely didn't want to look them over at dinner. Cory took us to a great steak house on the outskirts of town, him in a nice BMW and us in our shitty feeb car. He must have eaten their regularly because the Maître D as well as most of the waiters greeted him with high fives and smiles.

Dave and I ordered a twelve ounce ribeye, mashed potatoes, steak fries and scotch for me and a beer for Dave. As for Cory, the big man put away a twenty ounce tomahawk steak, with mashed potatoes, steak fries, asparagus, five or six biscuits and two glasses of whiskey, and a beer. Then he topped it off with a slice of both apple and cherry pie, and two cups of coffee. The man could definitely eat.

After dinner we followed him to his home. It was a large, rustic looking home which appeared to be made out of huge logs. The outside had some nice flowers in a well-tended garden, as well as a few trees and bushes. The property looked large and must have cost a fortune. He pulled into a three car garage, and we parked outside in the driveway. In the garage was a beautiful Harley Davidson low rider all in black and silver and a hummer.

"Wow," I said. "You on the take?"

Laughing he said, "I wasn't always a cop."

He left it at that and then we walked into his home. In the living room, I saw the reason behind him able to afford the house, cars and motorcycle.

Dave and I stood admiring the pictures and trophies and especially three Super Bowl rings he had won while playing for the New England Patriots!

"You're Nasty Nash!" Dave and I exclaimed at the same time.

"Guilty," he said with a big smile.

"Both of us thought we knew you from somewhere but couldn't figure it out," I said. "Guess centers don't get their pictures taken too often."

"Yeah, we usually have our helmets on. Let's get you set up in your rooms and then we can play a little pool."

Dave and I got our things into the guestrooms. Each had a private bathroom with a tub and separate shower. The rooms also had a big screen TV on the wall. Then we went down to Cory's playroom. A beautiful pool table with the Patriots logo in the center, video games and pinball machines. Plus a fully stocked bar, filled with every top shelf brand of booze you could imagine.

"This place is amazing Cory," Dave said.

"Well, I had a great financial advisor. He had me invest most of my salary for the ten years I played. I didn't start out with the Patriots. My first team was the Raiders which is why my bike is in silver and black. As you can see, he did a great job."

We drank and played pool for about an hour, telling cop and football stories. Then Dave's phone rang, and he put it on speaker. It was Carl calling from Sheffield.

"You're on speaker Carl," Dave said. "And you won't believe who we are staying with. Nasty Nash of the New England Patriots! He happens to be the lead detective on Baxter's homicide."

"Who?" Carl asked.

Dave put his hand over the phone and said, "Sorry Cory, kids."

Cory just laughed and I shook my head.

"Okay Carl," Dave said and sighed, "what do you have to report."

"Aaron and I spent the whole day talking to everyone we could. Unfortunately, the lead detective, a guy named Simon Cunningham, left the force. So we spoke to one of his partners. He didn't have much to tell us, but he gave us the police report and M.E.'s with pictures."

"What about the wife and kids?"

"We tracked down Maria Heller nee Narvaez at work at a local hotel. She runs the front desk. She didn't have too much to say, only that she loved her husband and missed him. But she was definitely on edge. We spoke to the two kids, Bary and Hector. They had nothing useful to say either. We finished up with some of his coworkers but that was a dead end as well."

"Okay, I guess we will get together once we all get back. Did you hear from Billy or Lou?"

"Nope, but I'm sure they are enjoying each other's company right about now."

"Yeah, I'm sure. Okay, see you back in the office. If you guys want to drive back it would be fine. Warren and I may stay an extra day to check out some of Baxter's junior lawyers he had at a satellite office in Boston."

"Okay boss, see you then."

Dave hung up and gave me a look. I just shook my head and racked the balls.

"Sounds like two of your agents are a bit more than friendly," Cory said,

"Yeah," Dave replied, "but so far it hasn't been a problem."

"So far," I said, which earned me another look from Dave.

"Let's play some pool guys."

We ended up drinking too much, playing too long into the night and finally got into our beds well after midnight. It had been a long day, and I called Trace one more time to tell her I loved her. I suppose I should have looked at the time first, waking her up. After I ended my call to Trace, apologizing about the late call, I couldn't fall asleep. There had to be something connecting the murders but what?

All our victims were from different walks of life. Two were pretty well off and one was blue collar. All were married with kids, but having kids couldn't be a connection. As far as we knew they didn't belong to the same clubs or groups like the Freemasons. They grew up in different parts of the world and their wives had never met.

I knew there had to be something and trying to come up with it would just drive me crazy. If the answer were somewhere in my brain, it would come to me sooner or later. Hopefully sooner. I closed my eyes and drifted off to sleep.

Chapter Thirteen

Thursday, FBI HQ, Conference room, 8:45 am

We got together at the office to go over everything we had collected about our three victims. Dave and I had spent Wednesday morning at the Boston satellite office of Baxter's. We spoke to three young lawyers there but gained zero insight into why Baxter had been killed. We hopped on the jet around one and I was back home with Trace by three.

When I got home we made up for lost time by spending the late afternoon in bed. We finally left our bedroom to get some dinner, and Trace suggested we call up Dave and Melissa. Soon the four of us had met for dinner at a Japanese restaurant where they cook the food right in front of you.

Trace and Melissa kept on giving each other looks and Dave and I finally had enough. Dave had said, "All right you two. What's going on?"

Laughing, Trace had said, "Couldn't fool two detectives. Go on Melissa, spill the beans."

Melissa had smiled and then said, "I suppose I should have told you alone, but I wanted some back up just in case you reacted badly."

"Reacted badly?" Dave had asked.

I had a pretty good idea what Melissa was going to say. Originally, after Dave's family had been massacred by the Destroyer, he never wanted kids. After we caught the copycat and the original Destroyer he had changed his mind, slightly. So I figured I knew what the big secret was.

Taking Dave's hands in hers, Melissa had said, "I'm pregnant!"

For a split second Dave was quiet and then he whooped for joy!

We had celebrated the rest of the night and finally when we went our separate ways Dave had pulled me aside.

"I'm really happy Warren but I don't want the rest of the team to know right now."

"No problem Dave," I had replied, "now go home and make love to your beautiful bride. Oh, and get some sleep because in about seven or eight months from now, you never will."

As we had entered the conference room, there was no mistaking the glow and smile Dave had. I knew the others would know something was up, but I figured Dave would let them in on the pregnancy when he was ready.

"Okay team," he said with a big grin on his face. "Who wants to go first?"

Lou said, "We might as well. Afterall, we got basically zip as far as a motive as to why Tomlinson was murdered."

"Well let's hear what you got," Dave said with a big grin on his face.

"Ummm, sure Dave. What's got you grinning ear to ear?"

"Huh? Oh, nothing really," Dave said and put his usual grim look on his face.

We spent the next hour going over each of the police reports, the medical examiners reports, looking and putting up on the corkboard all the photos and any ideas any of us had. Unfortunately, none of us actually had any ideas at all as to where to go next.

We all were racking our brains when ADD Teller walked in. He spent about ten minutes not saying anything. He walked in front of the boards with all the details of the three homicides. He didn't miss a thing and then he sat down across from Dave.

"Special Agent Anderson, can you tell me anything about our serial killer?" he asked.

Dave took a deep breath and then went over what we had learned. Unfortunately, it only took about five minutes because we really didn't have much.

"You and your team flew to Boston, spent a few nights in hotels, borrowed other offices' cars, and came back home with basically nothing, no further along than when this investigation had started?"

"Dave and...Special Agent Anderson and Special Agent Temple stayed in Nasty Nash's home sir at no expense to the agency," Billy said.

The look ADD Teller gave Billy would have sent most agents running from the room, but Billy just turned bright red.

"Special Agent Anderson," Teller said as he stood, "I will expect some results, and soon."

As he left the room Billy was about to say something else, but luckily Carl quickly put his hand over his mouth.

I got up and shut the door.

"Are you out of your mind Billy?" I said.

"I guess I just wasn't thinking, Warren," Billy replied. "Sorry Dave."

"No biggie Billy, but we do have to come up with something," Dave said as he wiped his hands over his eyes. "Okay team, here's what we are going to do. I want everyone to get copies of all the reports. Then each of you will go over them all. There might be something we missed.

Then Carl, I want you to go back ten years and include all of the country for any similar cases. Warren, I want you to get all of the reports over to Behavioral Sciences at Quantico to see if they can come up with a profile on our killer. We better find something and soon guys or we all may be working somewhere else. Now let's get to it."

We all left to get started and I thought to myself this is one time I was glad I wasn't leading the team. It was bad timing for Dave as far as being overjoyed about Melissa's pregnancy and having to deal with this serial killer, but sometimes it was just the way things happened.

I went to my office where Billy was busy reading over all the reports.

Before I could say anything, Billy said, "I know Warren. It was a stupid thing to say. But I just figured Teller was pissed about the cost of us going to all the murder sites."

"Billy," I said, "Teller couldn't give a damn about the cost. It was just his way of getting us motivated and not saying how bad it was that we hadn't gotten anything. He was thinking about the real possibility of another victim. But don't sweat it kid."

"Okay Warren. Why do you think this guy is killing?"

"I've been racking my brain, but I haven't got a clue. But we'll figure it out. I only hope, before there's another victim."

"Right."

I gathered up all the material and went to get it scanned. Then I would e-mail it to Behavioral Sciences in Quantico. When I was just a detective in the NYPD, the usual thought about getting a profile by most detectives was the same. A waste of time. But since working at the FBI, I had come to believe the guys who came up with profiles were more right than wrong, most of the time.

I had a fifty -fifty hope they might help the case. But it was better than what we had so far. As I scanned the material I once again thought about the motive. Why was our killer picking out his victims? And why were the beat-ings so brutal? One thing I was sure of was whoever our killer was, he wasn't done yet. We had to find something about the motive or more people were going to die.

For a second I caught myself thinking our killer was a he. But after seeing all the photos from the M.E.'s, I was pretty sure it couldn't be a woman. Unfortunately, it didn't bring me any closer to our killer, or the reasons why the killings were so brutal.

Chapter Fourteen

Dr. Winters was sitting on his patio, relaxing with a nice gin martini. As he looked out on his large estate, he thought back to Carol Trent and her children. Carol had been extremely lucky. Her husband had survived the stabbing and was recovering nicely in jail. After Frederick Wells had spoken to her, he had gone before a judge to get a restraining order. Then Briscoe and Greene had gotten an arrest warrant, charging him with Abuse and Assault of a Family Member which had a harsher penalty than just plain assault. Hopefully he would spend at least five years in jail. If it were up to him, Sam Trent would never see freedom again. Or take another breath.

Carol Trent had not been charged and she and her kids had been able to retrieve their things from their apartment. Then they received some money from a fund set up to help abused women and children. Dr. Winters had expedited getting the funds. With the money, she traveled to Arizona to her sister's, who lived there. All in all he mused, a good outcome. He had also contacted a psychiatrist he knew in Arizona to keep seeing Carol and her children. Carol would have a hard time getting over the abuse. She might never again trust a man in her life. As for the kids, hopefully they were young enough to not only get over the abuse they witnessed, but to break the circle of violence so common among victims.

Once again as he had done many times before, he thought about the circle of abuse among victims. A circle of pain and sometimes death. He had spent considerable time trying to come up with a way to break the cycle but as of yet, he had only been able to try and treat the victims to the best of his ability. Of course there were other options.

Just as he was thinking about them, his wife came out on the patio. She brought out small pastries and a pitcher. She refilled her husband's glass and then poured one for herself. Then she sat down next to him. She reached out her hand and he took it. They sat quietly holding hands for several minutes before she spoke.

"Thinking about the Trent woman?" Jocelyn asked.

"A bit, but more about the way family abuse continues on sometimes for generations," he replied. "Carol Trent had an abusive father and yet she goes ahead and marries a man who is abusive. Sam Trent had an abusive father as well and carried on in his footsteps. It seems there will never be a way to stop the circle."

"It is a horrible situation, but you can't stop it by yourself. All you can do is help the victims achieve a normal life. And as far as I'm concerned, doing that is a great deal."

"I suppose you are right dear. By the way, where is Brandon?"

"He went to Jones Beach with a group of friends and then they were going to see an open air concert there."

"How is he getting home? It will be pretty late."

"His friend Jake is 17 and has a car. He'll be fine."

"At least we don't have to worry about him becoming an abuser, at least not from anything he has witnessed here at home."

Laughing, Jocelyn said, "Oh Malcolm, I could never imagine you ever hitting me or Brandon. It's just not in your nature. Now where will you be going this week?"

"It's been several weeks since I visited the safe home in Maine. I don't get up there too often."

"Are there any new victims there?"

"No, I don't think so, but I do have a few women and children still staying at the safe house. Plus there is one who had moved out of the safe house, got an apartment and lives in the area."

"How long will you be gone?"

"I think maybe three or four days. You can come with me if you want to. Brandon can come too, and you can take him to Acadia National Park."

"Maybe next time Malcolm. I have several meetings and work to do. Plus I still have to finish up some of your recordings."

"Okay Jocelyn, but I'll miss you."

"And I'll miss you."

Chapter Fifteen

We had met back in the conference room early Monday to go over everything again, hoping we had missed something. Unfortunately, there didn't seem to be any new information we could find in all of the reports and interviews we had conducted. ADD Teller had sat in and without saying a word had left the meeting.

We all went back to work checking reports which had come in over the weekend. There was a case all the way out in California but so far the agents out there didn't ask for our help. Another possible serial killer in Wyoming. It wasn't a definite case yet because three victims could have died under normal circumstances. The local detectives were still investigating and if they needed us they would reach out.

As I sat there trying to figure out our next move my phone rang.

"Hello," I answered.

"Hi honey," Trace said. "Just wanted to thank you for the great weekend. I know you have a lot on your mind, and I appreciate you taking the time to have some fun. It was great seeing your old squad all together again."

Trace and I had hosted a BBQ at our house for my old captain who had retired, Terry Jackson and his wife Sally. Also Victor Robles and his wife Maria, and his partner John Maguire. It had been great telling old war stories and for a time, I had completely forgotten about my case.

"I'm taking Melissa out today to look for some things for the new baby," she said. "I'm so excited for them!"

"Trace, I hope you aren't too upset because we never had kids."

"Don't be silly Warren. We have had an amazing life together and I wouldn't change a thing. And I intend to be a big part of this new baby's life, so stop worrying. I'll call you later. Love you."

"And I love you Trace."

Just as I hung up, Dave came into my office and just by the way he was moving I knew something was up.

"I've gathered everyone in the conference room Warren, we might have something," Dave said.

"Another victim?" I asked.

"Let's go find out. All I know is Carl stuck his head in my office and said we better meet with everyone. Maybe he came up with a connection between our victims."

We made our way down to the conference room and I saw everyone was there, including ADD Teller. I glanced at Dave and saw him take a deep breath. He probably wanted to hear whatever Carl had to say first before Teller heard. Dave took a seat and Teller stayed standing in the corner, arms folded and an unreadable look on his face. Funny I thought, all my bosses through the years knew how to make the same unreadable expression. I wondered if they taught a class on how to make it.

"Okay Carl," Dave began, "you called us here so what have you got?"

Carl took a deep breath and said, "When you told me to go back ten years I found two more cases of brutal murders. One fits right in with our three other victims. The other one is close enough for us to check out. I'm not sure it is the same killer, but I guess it still needs to be investigated."

"Lou, will you put the info on the board? Carl, let's start with the one you think fits in with our killer's Motis Operendi."

Carl began reading and Lou put the info up on the white board.

Carl said, "The victim's name is Anthony Blake. 26 years old at the time of his death. Married but the wife was never found to be interviewed. Skipped town with a young son. She was never really a suspect. He was found outside a place called Chippy's, a local bar."

"And where is Chippy's bar?" I asked.

"Oh right, sorry. Newark, New Jersey. The victim had been beaten badly, but not as badly as our other victims. Broken nose, left orbit, one left rib, testicles had been badly bruised but not crushed and throat slit."

"Sounds similar enough," Dave said. "Okay, what about the other."

"This one was found in Maine. A guy who was camping in Acadia National Park was found inside his tent. Vic's name was Tom Strauss, age 67. He had been beaten to death. The throat had not been cut but he had been stabbed. Retired teacher living in New Hampshire."

ADD Teller spoke up as he was leaving, saying, "Check em out."

Dave said, "Blake sounds like a good possible victim but the other guy...."

"Strauss," Lou said.

"Yeah, Strauss not so much. What were the dates when they were found?"

Carl looked at his reports and said, "Strauss was eight years ago, March of 2016. Blake, June of 2021."

"So one eight years ago and one three years ago," I said. "Sounds to me like the Blake homicide might have been our killer's first murder. Same kind of damage and the throat slit."

"Yeah and the one eight years ago seems to be too far in the past," Aaron said.

"I agree with you both," Dave said. "Okay here's the plan. Warren and I will look into the Blake homicide. Billy and Lou will check out the Strauss homicide."

"Does that mean we get to take the jet?" Billy asked with the look of a kid opening presents on Christmas morning.

"Yes Billy. You and Lou get to take the jet. You will have to go to Maine and New Hampshire."

"Yahoo!"

I gave Billy a look and he immediately quieted down.

"As I was saying," Dave continued," Carl, you need to keep looking in case any other homicides which fit didn't pop up in your search. Aaron, you will stay here to collate any information we send back as we get it. Also to keep an eye open in case there are any new murders. Any questions?"

No one had any so we all filed out to prepare. I called Trace and told her about Dave and me going to Newark. Then I sat down for a second thinking about the two new murders. I didn't think Strauss was one of our killer's victims, but it still needed to be checked out. I was glad Dave put us on the Blake murder. It sounded like it fit and maybe we would find out something to tie all of our victims together. One thing was sure. If Blake had been the first victim, our killer was increasing in rage and the time between killings was becoming shorter. I figured if we didn't stop him soon, we would have another victim within a week or two.

Chapter Sixteen

Monday, Greensboro, North Carolina, 2:45pm

The killer had put off murdering... no cleansing the world of this abuser for too long. It had been over two years since this abuser had been put on the list. The killer had several more but was smart enough to know killing these men too quickly would probably get the killer caught. Still, this one is a bit too close to the last one. There will have to be a longer wait for the next one.

This monster lived in the city of Greensboro and worked at the Piedmont Triad International Airport. He worked for the TSA and worked the early shift. He usually was up by 4:00 am and worked till noon. Then he came home and did odds and ends until his wife came home at around five. Then it would be dinner, hit the wife a bit, and into bed by 7:00 or 8:00 pm.

The killer wasn't sure if the wife was still living with her husband, had been killed by him or finally had the sense to leave. There were no kids, which in the killer's mind was a good thing. One less person to be abused. The killer didn't have the time to do any surveillance and had decided to approach the man at home at about three in the afternoon. A simple knock on the door and then using the taser to knock him out.

The killer approached the home, adjusting the backpack with everything needed to rid the world of one more monster. The neighborhood was fairly neat and clean, most of the lawns appeared to be well taken care of. No fences around the front of the homes but the backyards all seemed to have one kind of a fence or another. Several dogs out in the backyards. That was something the killer didn't know. If the abuser had a dog and if so, whether it would be in the backyard or in the house. That was why the killer had brought some raw hamburger mixed with enough drugs to knock it out in seconds.

Looking at the abuser's house the killer thought again how appearances can be deceptive and what goes on behind closed doors no one knows. Look at this house, the killer thought. Painted within a year or two, the lawn neatly mowed. Two bushes on either side of the walkway, also well-tended. Some rose bushes and a few other flowers were planted around. Would anyone suspect within the walls was a man who constantly beat the woman he supposedly loved?

The killer got the taser ready and slowly looked around to see if anyone was out walking a dog or taking a stroll. There was no one in sight, the killer knocked on the door. A minute later there was a loud voice yelling to hold on. Then the door opened and standing in the doorway was a big man dressed in shorts and a tee shirt. A cigar was sticking out the side of his mouth, a can of beer in his hand. He was not obese but definitely could use a workout now and then. Balding with a few hairs combed across the top. Probably once black or dark brown but now turning gray. And the look his wife saw probably every single night. A look that read as contempt for everyone. A look of hate and disgust and of course of superiority.

Stepping forward and not saying anything, the killer shoved the powerful taser directly into the folds of fat in his stomach and seconds later he was on the floor. Moving behind him, the killer dragged him by his arms inside. Then for good measure, hit him with the taser once again.

Looking around outside to see if there was anyone who might have seen what had just happened, the killer smiled and shut the door. Waiting to see if there was a dog, and not hearing one, the killer began to unload the back-pack with all the things the killer would need.

As with the other abusers who were now dead, this one would never hurt anyone again.

Chapter Seventeen

I was driving and having no luck getting out of the city. There was some kind of a demonstration at the Lincoln Tunnel, and we turned around and tried the Holland. By the time we got through it, we hit more traffic in Newark. On the way, Dave had tracked down the lead detective from the Anthony Blake homicide. He was working another case and wouldn't be able to meet with us until about four.

So when we finally got within a few miles of the Newark PD, we stopped to get a bite to eat. Pulling into a diner, we got a booth shown to us by an older man. Soon, a young, pretty waitress came by, gave us menus and then sashayed away.

"Pretty girl," I said.

"Just look at the menu Warren," Dave said with a smile.

She came back, took our orders for hamburgers and fries, with two cokes, and this time as she walked away, it was Dave looking at her.

"What was it you just said to me?" I asked.

We both had a laugh.

"Think Blake is one of our serial killer's victims?" Dave asked me.

"I do, even though the damage done to the victim is less than with some of our victims, but if this was our killer's first try, he might have been less in a rage, maybe new to killing," I answered. "The damage done has been escalating."

"Very true. I wonder if there might be another victim before this one?"

"Well, Carl has gone back ten years so far. Of course he could have missed one or there might have been one even further back. It's also possible if there had been another victim further back, the killer might have done it differently. Then Carl wouldn't connect it with our other victims. You want him to go back further?"

"Not yet. Let's check out this one and see what Billy and Lou come up with. If we still can't figure out a motive we might have to rethink what we are doing."

"If we only had something to tie all of these murders together we might be able to get somewhere. But so far none of our victims seemed to have crossed paths."

"Well let's finish up and go and talk with Detective Sommers. Maybe he will have some information which will help us out."

The young waitress came by and said the tab was on the house.

"We always comp cops," she said.

Dave said, "Thank you," and left two twenties for a bill which had come to about twenty. I added a ten spot and Dave said, "I suppose that was because she was polite,"

"What else?" I answered and we walked out.

"Isn't it amazing how waitresses across the country can spot a cop, or in this case two FBI agents?"

"Never ceases to amaze me Dave," I said.

We headed over to the local precinct which had handled the Blake murder. Driving into the back lot, we saw the same things anyone would see behind any police precinct. A number of rundown unmarked cars, some newer ones, and some marked vehicles. A few uniformed cops coming and going, some who looked too young to even shave and some old timers with the same weary look. Being a cop aged you fast and if you were any kind of a cop who did their job, it wore you down. You saw too many things you would never be able to forget. It took someone with a certain frame of mind to do the job.

We showed our ID to a young patrolman near the back entrance and asked if he could direct us to Detective Sommer's office. His eyes got wide at the sight of our FBI badges, and he said he would take us personally.

We followed him through a maze of hallways, passing a few cops who were mostly interested in either getting out onto patrol or getting home after finishing their tour. Finally, our young officer stopped in front of a door marked Investigations.

"I guess you guys being the FBI can go right in!" he enthusiastically said.

"Ummm, thanks Officer John," Dave said, reading the young officer's nametag. "Appreciate the help," and shook his hand.

From the look on the young cop's face you would have thought he had just won the lottery.

As he walked away, I knocked on the door and opened it. It looked like almost any Investigations office I had ever been in. There were about twelve desks lined up with two apiece, back to back. So I figured there were six teams. Each had several folders on top, filled with paperwork. One phone on each desk along with a lamp. Also a laptop or desktop computer on each. On the walls were a half dozen bulletin boards overflowing with bulletins and photos of missing persons, criminals and others. In the far corner was a glass enclosed office which was where the boss sat. His name was on the outside and it turned out to be our Detective Sommers, who was actually a Detective Sergeant.

There were four men sitting at the desks and one of them got up to meet us.

"Is there something I can do for you?" the detective asked.

Dave showed his ID and said, "We are here to talk with Detective Sergeant Sommers please."

The detective turned to the man sitting in the office and yelled out, "Hey boss, you got a couple of Feebs to see ya."

The detective went back to work at his desk, not impressed with us being FBI, and we started toward the office. A tall man with a full dark beard and steely eyes met us. He looked to be about forty-five years old, in good physical shape and dressed in a white shirt and gold tie. On his hip was a Glock .45 and his badge. His shoes looked to be a bit worn and needed a shine. To me it meant he wasn't a boss who sat on his ass. He worked his own cases.

Shaking his hand, Dave introduced us.

"I'm Special Agent Dave Anderson and this is Special Agent Warren Temple," he said.

"Detective Sergeant Brock Sommers," he said and then ushered us inside the office and told us to take a seat.

I did a quick look around his office and didn't see too many awards or personal photos, no ego wall. There was a picture on his desk which I couldn't see, probably of his family. Tons of paperwork, a marksman trophy as well as a picture of him with a few others at ground zero. Two file cabinets, a computer and phone. This man worked and wasn't a showoff. I liked him immediately.

"Sorry I couldn't meet you earlier, but I was working on a double homicide at the Shithole Manors," he said. "Actually, it's where Anthony Blake lived before he was killed."

"The Shithole Manors?" I asked.

Laughing, Sommers said, "It's what everyone calls it. Its name is actually Sunshine Manors, but if a ray of sunshine ever hit that place I'd be surprised."

"I see," Dave said. "When we spoke I told you we were investigating the possibility Blake's murder had been the act of a serial killer. We have at least three more victims. Would you be able to get us the reports and run down the case for us?"

"I'll do that and more. I'll have one of my guys get you the reports and we can take a ride to Shithole Manors and Chippy's where Blake was killed. If that works for you?

"Absolutely," Dave said, "and please call me Dave."

"Brock," he said, "and I guess it's Warren, right?"

"Absolutely Brock," I replied.

Brock told one of his men what he needed and then escorted us back to the back lot. There we got into a typical unmarked car and took off.

As he drove, he and Dave chatted, and I thought about our case. Was this going to finally give us the break we were looking for, or another murder with no leads? Only one way to find out and we were on our way.

Chapter Eighteen

As Brock drove he gave us a quick rundown on the case and pointed out the neighborhoods we were driving through. It wasn't much different from the neighborhoods found in Manhattan or for that matter, any other poverty ridden city area. All along the ride were empty storefronts, kids hanging out, some smoking and I saw at least one drug deal go down. Mixed in here and there were some nicer homes trying to keep the tidal wave of despair at bay.

I saw a few cops on the beat, and they were all working alone.

"I see your patrol guys work solo," I said.

"Yeah, we don't have the money or the men to double them up," Brock replied.

"It was the same in New York when I worked for the NYPD."

"You were a cop?"

"Yeah. Maybe after we get done we'll have some time to get a beer, and I'll tell you all about it."

"That's a deal. Well, here we are at Chippy's."

Brock pulled up a bit past a rundown looking bar. There was a broken neon sign in the window, and a wooden one hanging out front which described Chippy's to a tee. It had been broken at the top and it was chipped throughout. The door hadn't been painted in years and was a puke green.

"Nice place," Dave said.

"We'll go in and talk to Chippy," Brock said. "He's owned this place for about twenty years. He was also the guy who found Blake in the alleyway on the side."

We walked into Chippy's and the smell was the same as any dive bar I had ever been in. Sweat, stale beer, smoke and a smell which could only be described as failure and despair.

We stopped just inside the door getting a look and feel for the place. There was a long bar top with stools set in front. The vinyl on the stools were once a bright red, I supposed, but now looked almost black from years of dirt building up on them. A mirror of questionable taste hung behind the bar. It showed a scantily clad blonde woman who was overly endowed. There were bottles of liquor, none top-shelf as far as I could see. The floor was uneven and stained and there were a few tables and four booths against the wall opposite the bar.

There were seven people in the bar, four on the stools, and three more at one table. The two women sitting on the stools looked to be about fifty but considering the obvious line of work they were in; they might have been in their late thirties. Both had on spiked heels, short skirts and low cut tops. When we walked in all of them looked at us, and then resumed drinking and talking.

Brock walked up to the far end of the bar where a smallish man was standing. He was about 5'5" and weighed about 100 pounds soaking wet. He had on thick glasses and sported a pencil thin moustache. As soon as Brock walked up he started to walk back the other way.

"Hold it Chippy," Brock said. "You're not in any trouble, I just want you to meet two of my friends from the F-B-I."

At the mention of the FBI, five of the seven patrons stood up and beat a hasty retreat out the door. Only the two women remained figuring we weren't there for them.

In a surprisingly high pitched voice, Chippy said, "Why'd ya hafta go and say fuckin' FBI out loud like that Sarge?"

"Come out from there and have a seat, Chippy," Brock said and moved to one of the tables.

We all sat down, and I nearly fell out of my chair because it rocked on a broken leg. I stood up, grabbed another chair and sat down.

"Now Chippy, these Special Agents want to ask you a few questions and I only want to hear the truth from you," Brock said with just a touch of menace in his voice. "You get me?"

"Yeah, I get you Sarge," he answered sullenly.

Dave looked Chippy in the eye and said, "I understand you were the one who found Anthony Blake?"

"Yeah, I did."

"Tell me about it."

"Not much to tell…sir. I was taking out the garbage and I saw him lying in the alley. Knew he was dead the second I saw him," Chippy said and crossed himself.

"Was he a regular?"

"Yeah, usually two or three times a week."

"Did he meet with anyone in particular?"

"Nah, he would sit at the bar, maybe talk to someone if they were sitting next to him. But he never met anyone, far as I saw."

"When you found him, did you see anyone in the area?"

"Nope, not a soul. I went right back in and called the cops…I mean the police."

"Anything else Warren?" Dave asked me.

"Just a few more questions, Chippy," I said. "What was he like?"

"Like?"

"Was he a good guy, a tough guy, a bum?"

"He kinda tried to be tough but with him walking with those two canes…"

"Canes? You mean he was handicapped?"

"Yeah. Had some kind of accident at work. Crushed his legs when he worked for the city. Then he got laid off. I know he used to complain about that and his wife and brat."

"Brat?"

"Yeah, that's what he always called his kid, the brat, never a name."

"Do you know where he worked before he was killed?"

"Yeah, a few blocks away at Jimmy's Garage."

"I know the place," Brock said.

"Okay Chippy, thanks," I said, and we left.

When we walked out the few patrons who had left sauntered back in. Then we made a left and walked into the alley where Blake had been found.

Brock pointed to a spot below a window with bars on it.

"Blake was lying right here," Brock said. "Forensics found some rope fibers on the crossbar in this window and some same fibers on his wrists. We figured he was tied up upright and then beaten. We never found any canes and I'm afraid him being handicapped was news to me. Guess I fucked up."

"Might not mean anything at all Brock," Dave said. "Don't beat yourself up about it, we've all fucked up now and then. It's getting a bit late. Is there a good hotel nearby? We'll get a couple of rooms and begin fresh in the morning."

"Sure, I'll drive us back, get the reports and then you can follow me to a pretty good Days Inn. Then we can get some dinner and a few beers. I want to hear how Warren went from the NYPD to the FBI."

"You got a deal Brock," Dave said, and we left Chippy's.

As we drove back to the precinct, I wondered if Blake being handicapped had anything to do with his murder. An accident which left a man basically crippled, then laid off, would have some kind of effect on a man. Did it change Blake in a good way, making him thankful he was at least still alive or turn him into a bitter man who hated everyone? And what was up with calling his kid a brat? I didn't know but I felt it was something we were going to have to find out.

Brock drove us to the precinct, got the reports and took us to the hotel. After getting our rooms, he drove us to a nice steak house. We sat and talked until it was getting late. I told a few war stories of my time in the NYPD as a homicide detective, and he had a few of his own. It was a good time and then we went back to the hotel.

When I got in my room, the first thing I did was to call Trace. We spoke a few minutes, and I assured her I would be home late tomorrow. Then I drifted off to sleep with the word brat repeating itself in my mind.

Chapter Nineteen

Billy and Lou had spent the day checking up on the Strauss homicide. The first thing they did was to stop at the headquarters of the Park Rangers. Once there, they had found a park ranger who had then put them in touch with the park ranger who had found Strauss.

His name was Jack Lakewood and had been a Ranger at the park for close to twenty years. A fit man of around fifty, sporting a full, long gray beard, wearing shorts and holding a long walking stick. He had kept up a narrative about the park as the three of them trekked through the park.

He had told them, "It was the worst thing I ever saw in twenty years being a Ranger. He wasn't in a regular area for camping. It was close to Thunder Hole near the water."

As they walked toward the scene of the murder, he had gone on to tell them all about Thunder Hole. It was on the Park Loop Road, and you had to pass it if you were traveling past Sand Beach from the north, or past Otter Cliff from the south. The waves had been battering the tiny inlet for centuries, creating a small cavern below, and an opening on top. When the waves came rushing in, it sounded like a thunderous boom.

Ranger Lockwood told them Strauss had gone into a wooded area near Thunder Hole and pitched his tent. It wasn't actually a restricted area for camping, but it wasn't a regular campsite. He had been alone there with no other campers around.

Before getting to the crime scene, Ranger Lockwood had brought Lou and Billy to Thunder Hole for them to experience it. And for both of them, it truly was amazing. The noise from the waves hitting below was like a sonic boom. They had stood listening, seeing the spray shoot up and looking out on the water for several minutes. Then Ranger Lockwood had guided them into the woods about a half mile to where Strauss had been found.

"This is the spot," Ranger Lockwood said.

"How did you find him, so far into the woods?" Lou asked.

"Part of the job. Always hiking around in the woods and other hidden areas looking for stray campers. He was still in the tent when I found him. God awful sight. All his stuff was thrown around and he had been stabbed a few times. Lots of blood, lots of blood," Ranger Lockwood said, shaking his head.

"And then you contacted the police?"

"Yup, and you guys, the FBI seeing it happened in a National Park."

"Were there any suspects you knew about?"

"Nope. Not a one. We get all kinds coming to the park. Nice folks, families and such. But we also get some thugs and bad people. Motorcycle gangs sometimes and loners too."

"Well you have been a great help Ranger Lockwood. Thank You."

"Well if you both have the time I can take you on a private tour of some spots most folks don't get to see."

"I think we'd love that Ranger."

"Aww, call me Jack."

"And we are Lou and Billy."

They had spent the afternoon hiking around the park with Jack and saw some amazing sights.

When they finally parted, Jack said, "Now where are you two lovebirds spending the night," he said with a twinkle in his eye.

"Oh we're not..." Billy started to say.

"Now, you can't fool a man like me. Don't matter none."

"Ummm, we're staying at the Acadia log cabins," Lou said.

"Renting two...for appearances?"

"Yes Jack, we are."

"Well, you two come back and see me anytime and next time you might have a pair of rings on your fingers."

They had said their goodbyes and over dinner it was Billy who first brought up what Jack had said.

"So Lou, what do you think about what Jack said?" Billy asked with a grin.

"I have no idea what you are talking about," she answered him, looking away.

"C'mon Lou. What do you think about returning here with two rings on our fingers?"

"First of all we have a long way to go before that happens. Second, when I get married I want a honeymoon in Hawaii. And finally, I haven't been asked."

"Okay Lou, I guess we do have a long way to go but..."

"But what?"

"Oh nothing. Just wondering what your answer might be?"

"You will just have to find out when the time is right Billy," she said and leaned over and gave him a kiss.

They had finished dinner, looked over the report Jack had given them and then spent the rest of the night making love. Each of them was thinking about the future and finally they had fallen asleep in each other's arms.

In the morning they awoke and said nothing further about the future, but both of them couldn't help but think about it. Then they went to the jet and left for Strauss' home in New Hampshire.

Chapter Twenty

Dave and I met Brock at the precinct, and then he drove us over to Jimmy's Garage. It had two lifts to raise up cars to be worked on, a small front area with a desk and phone, and another area for storing parts and tires. It didn't look too run down and when we walked in, there was one man under a car.

Brock called out, "Hey Jimmy, come on out."

A man of about thirty-five, covered in grease, wearing a dirty cap rolled out from under the car. He wiped his hands on a dirty rag and then stood there looking from Dave to me and then to Brock.

"What's up Sarge?" Jimmy said. "Don't have time for a chat."

I was impressed that people around here all knew Brock. He must have worked the streets a great deal of the time.

"These two men are from the FBI and want to ask you a few questions about Anthony Blake."

"Wadda you wanna know?" Jimmy asked a bit suspiciously.

Dave replied, "How about you tell us whatever you know about him? His wife, his kid..."

"Don't know nothing about her or the brat. Never met 'em."

"Why did you call his kid a brat?"

"That's the only name Tony ever said. Don't even know if the kid was a boy or girl."

"Was he a good worker? We heard he was crippled."

"Yeah, he was okay. Got around pretty good with those canes and knew how to use them."

"What do you mean, use them?"

"Well, one time two punks came in to rob us when I was out. Tony nearly killed the two punks with his canes. Tony could be a real bad dude when he wanted to be. I think he used to beat his wife a bit too. At least he used to brag about it."

Now that was something we hadn't heard, I thought. I gave Dave a quick look and saw he was as interested in this new information as I was.

"I suppose Tony was pissed at the world after the accident and being laid off from the city," Brock stated.

"Oh yeah. He was always going on about how they had crippled him, how it wasn't fair being laid off. And actually, I think he was right. He knew his way around any kind of motor. They could've kept him on, but I guess that's the city for ya."

I didn't have anything else to ask Jimmy, and neither did Dave. We thanked him for his time and got back in Brock's car.

"How about we take a look at where he lived, Brock?" Dave asked.

"Sure thing," Brock said. "Blake beating his wife is something I haven't heard before. That's two things that got by me."

"Don't sweat it Brock. Probably has nothing to do with his murder."

I sat in the back seat and wasn't too sure about that. I started to feel like we might have just got our first break in the case.

We pulled up in front of Sunshine Manors, Building three, and I understood why it had been known as Shithole Manors. Brock had told us it was made up of ten six story buildings. The brick was a dirty brown, and I saw several windows broken and taped off with cardboard. Must have been pretty cold in the winter.

On the stoop in front of us were ten or twelve young men. They had the same look I had seen all around slums in New York. Desperation, hate and fear all rolled up in their eyes. Looking tough and trying hard to show us they shouldn't be messed with.

When Brock walked up to them, he said, "What's up Little Trip?

"Ain't nothin new Sarge," Little Trip replied. "Same old thing."

"Uh huh. Well keep it cool man."

"Always."

We walked into the building, no locks on the front door, into a hallway which was dirty, and smelled of urine and smoke.

"No elevator," Brock said, "and as you can see, no security. Tony lived in Apartment 402."

"So how did Little Trip get his name?" I asked as we walked up the stairs, trying to avoid stepping in some nasty stains.

"When he was about six or seven, his mother couldn't afford to buy him any clothes. So he wore hand-me-downs from his older brother. Poor kid would trip on the pants every third or fourth step. So, Little Trip. Not really a bad kid but like most of the kids in this part of town, he doesn't have many options. He's too small for sports and quit school after the sixth grade. So he hustles, dealing drugs, doing small burglaries."

"Same story back in New York," I said.

We got to the fourth floor and knocked on the door of Apartment 402. After a minute, a woman opened the door. She was holding one baby resting on her hip and I saw two other young children running around behind her. She turned and screamed at them to settle down. She looked to be at least sixty, but with the baby on her hip, she must have been no older than thirty. Poverty had a way of aging a person beyond their years.

"Yeah, whatta you want?" she said.

"Ummm, we were just wondering if you knew the people who lived here about two to three years ago," Brock asked.

"Are you kidding? I don't remember yesterday," and she closed the door.

As we started to walk away, she reopened the door and said, "Check with old Mrs. Rodriguez down in 103. She's a nosy body and has lived here forever."

As she closed the door before we could thank her, we headed for the stairs. Then we knocked on Apartment 103. The door opened a crack, and I could see one eye and a security chain on the inside of the door.

"Yes?" a woman with a Hispanic accent asked.

Brock didn't want to spook her, so he kept his badge out of sight.

"Are you Mrs. Rodriguez," he asked.

"Yes."

"I'm Detective Sergeant Sommers ma'am, and these two gentlemen are from the FBI. We were wondering if we could ask you a few questions about Anthony Blake, who used to live here."

The door closed and then we heard the chain being removed. As the door opened she said, "It's about time somebody came to ask me about that bastard. Come on in."

Chapter Twenty-One

We wiped our feet on a mat and then walked into a surprisingly clean and well furnished apartment. The living room had a nice sofa along with two wingback chairs. A large screen television was hanging on one wall, and on a few shelves were knick knacks and pictures in frames. The pictures showed a young bride and groom, and several pictures of a good looking young man.

Mrs. Rodriguez grabbed a folding chair from a closet, and we sat down in the chairs.

"Would you gentlemen like some coffee or tea?" she asked. "I have some cookies fresh from the oven too."

Before we could answer, she went into the kitchen and a few minutes later brought out a rolling tray with a coffee pot, some plates and cookies. The aroma filled the air, and suddenly, I wanted the coffee and cookies. Mrs. Rodriguez poured out the coffee, asked if we wanted milk or sugar and handed each of us a cup and a plate with two cookies on it. Then she sat down and smiled.

"I don't get many visitors here," she said.

We all took a sip of coffee and a bite of the fresh baked cookies.

"It seems like maybe you were expecting us," I said

"No, I rarely get visitors, but I bake every day. If no one comes, I give the cookies to Brian...Little Trip."

"I couldn't help but notice some of your pictures. Is that you and your husband, and your son?"

"Yes, my dear departed husband Juan. And my son Stephen. Juan wanted him to have a good Anglo name to not hold him back in life. Now he is a neuro surgeon in California."

"I hope I'm not being out of line, but why do you still live here?"

"Stephen is always begging me to come and live with him. But this has been my home since I married almost forty five years ago. I will die in this home."

"I think I understand. Can we ask you a few questions about Anthony Blake and his wife and child?"

"Ask away," she said and settled back on the sofa.

"First of all, do you know what his wife's name was and his child?"

"Her name was Peggy, and she was a sweet, beautiful girl. Her son was named John. He was only about three when she ran away from that beast."

"She ran away?"

"Yes, and it was the best thing she could have done. Many times I saw her with a black eye or busted lip. But it wasn't like that when they first moved in. Only after he had the accident. Then he started drinking, staying out late at Chippy's. You know, the bar a few blocks away."

"Yes, we know it. Do you know where she moved to?"

"Well, she told me but said not to ever tell anyone. But I suppose..."

"Yes Mrs. Rodriguez. You can tell us. I'm sure she wouldn't mind."

"Mrs. Rodriguez got up and went into her bedroom. She returned with an old address book and opened it. Then she took a pen and paper and wrote down an address. She slowly handed it to me.

"Thank you Mrs. Rodriguez. Is there anything else you can tell us?"

"Well, you might get some more information from Social Services. I know a man from them visited Peggy a few times. They might have more information."

"Do you know his name by chance?"

"No, I'm sorry but I never spoke with him."

We finished our coffee and cookies and before Mrs. Rodriguez could move, Dave carried everything back into the kitchen. Then we stood to leave.

"Thank you for everything Mrs. Rodriguez," I said. Then without much thought, I leaned down and gave her a kiss on her cheek.

We made our way past the boys on the stoop and Brock stopped to say something to Little Trip.

When we got back into the car, Dave asked, "What did you tell Little Trip?"

"I told him he was now responsible for Mrs. Rodriguez," Brock replied. "If anything happens to her , I told him, I would come down on him so hard he wouldn't know which way was up or down."

I smiled and settled back for the ride to the precinct. Brock was going to try and track down the social worker and then let us know. As for Peggy Blake, she had moved to a small town in Florida called Safety Harbor. Seemed like a fitting name to me.

Chapter Twenty-Two

Dave and I had returned to New York late Tuesday night. We both were anxious to get home to our wives. Trace had dinner warming in the oven. We ate and then sat out on the deck with a beer for me and a white wine for her.

I knew she had something on her mind, but I also knew she would tell me when she was ready. After a bit of discussing what Dave and I had found out, she turned to me.

"Warren," she started, "I've been thinking a lot lately about us not having any children."

Uh-oh, I thought to myself.

"Umm, and what exactly have you been thinking about it?" I asked.

"Well, we are both too old to have babies, but not too old to maybe help out an older child."

"I suppose we could adopt a cute seventeen year old girl."

That earned me a quick shot to my arm.

"No really, I think we might be able to adopt a child of five or six. We could give some poor child a good home and life. You know most children past two or three never get adopted. They just get shuttled between foster homes."

"Is this because you are lonely when I go out of town?"

"I suppose that's part of it. But spending time with Melissa has made me realize what we have missed. A baby is out of the question, but what do you think about an older child?"

I sat back and closed my eyes. My plan for our future was retirement one of these days, travelling and spending our golden years doing all the things we never did. Would a child change all of that? Of course it would but I loved Trace with all my heart. There wasn't one thing I wouldn't do for her.

"I think we can look into it."

"Oh Warren! Thank you!"

"I didn't say yes, and we need to figure out some things. But for now, you can find out how we go about it and then we will see. Okay?"

"Yes Warren. And now, if you will follow me upstairs, I will show you just how grateful I am," she said with a wink and a swaying of her backside as she walked away.

I certainly didn't need a second invitation. I cleaned up the deck and then made my way upstairs. We spent the rest of the night like two teenagers. Making love once with wild passion and then later on slow and tenderly. I supposed we weren't too old to adopt.

The next morning Trace made me breakfast and was actually singing. She had a huge smile on her face, and I loved seeing her so happy.

As I was leaving, I turned to her and said, "Now don't go discussing this with anyone until we find out some more about adopting."

"Actually," she said a bit sheepishly, "Melissa and I were going down to Social Services today to get the ball rolling."

"Of course you are," I said, sighing and gave her a kiss. Then shaking my head I had left for work.

When I got to work, the first thing I did was to find Dave.

"Good morning Dave," I said as I sat down in his office.

"Morning Warren," he said, and he could hardly contain the smile on his face.

"So you know!"

"Of course I know. Do you think Melissa wouldn't tell me? You and I will be new fathers at the same time!"

"Uh huh. New fathers. I suppose I lost the war before I even fought one battle."

"Of course you did. Now, let's get to work."

We entered the conference room where everyone was waiting. Of course as usual Aaron had a napkin in front of him with four large donuts.

"Good to see you're cutting down a bit Aaron," Dave said.

With powder falling from his covered lips he said, "Gotta keep this girlish figure boss."

"Okay, let's get to work. Lou, how about you tell us about what you found out about the Strauss homicide?"

Lou looked at some papers and then said, "Billy and I first got in touch with the park ranger who found his body. Ranger Jack Lockwood showed us the site and also a bit of a tour of the park. Fantastic place by the way. Anyway, there wasn't much info we could get there, so the next day we visited his widow in New Hampshire. Not much there either at first, but Billy and I both suspected she was holding something back. We talked for about another hour and then she let something slip."

"And what was that?"

"Seems her husband had a bad gambling problem and owed money to several bookies."

"So you think he was killed for his gambling debts?"

"At first we both thought we would have to look into it. But after trying to get some more details, she finally broke down. She was having an affair with a coworker and together they planned his murder. They made it seem like some crazed lunatic had killed him. But finally the guilt got to her. We made contact with the local police and she and her lover were arrested."

"Great work guys! You both eliminated Strauss as one of our serial killer's victims and solved a homicide. I'd say you earned some brownie points."

Just then ADD Teller walked in. He walked over to Dave and whispered something in his ear. Then he left.

"Well, it seems the police in New Hampshire called ADD Teller this morning and want to send Billy and Lou a special commendation for closing the Strauss murder," Dave said. "Again, excellent work. And of course ADD Teller also said good work to both of you."

We all congratulated them both and I was proud of Billy. He was turning into a good detective and agent.

"We still have a serial killer to catch, and Warren and I may have come up with a new lead," Dave said. "Anthony Blake was an abuser. He beat his wife on a regular basis, and it was new information not found in the original investigation."

"Forgive me for asking, but so what?" Aaron asked.

"So Warren and I are wondering if all of our victims happened to be abusers of their wives and kids, is what."

"You think someone out there is something like an avenging murderer?"

"It is a possibility. So here is what we are going to do. Warren and I will take the jet to find the wife and child of Blake's. Her name is Peggy, and we have a good tip she moved to a place called Safety Harbor in Florida."

"Okay, what do you want the rest of us to do Boss?" Carl asked.

"Billy and Lou will try to locate the social worker who had visited Peggy Blake several times. Get in touch with Detective Sergeant Sommers. He was going to try and run down his name. Once you have it, talk to him on the phone. I don't think you need to take a trip to Newark.

Carl and Aaron will go back over our victims' history. I want to know if their wives and kids were victims of abuse. Contact the local social services. Also contact the wives directly. If necessary, we'll revisit them in person."

"I think we need to find out who their doctors were and see if they treated the wives or kids for any injuries." Billy said.

"Good idea. Carl, you might be able to get some idea through your computer know-how. If you need to, get subpoenas for medical records."

I spoke up and said, "So far this is the only lead we have guys. Let's either confirm or rule it out as fast as possible. We know this killer isn't through and we need to move fast to try and stop the killing."

Dave said, "Okay team, let's get to it."

After everyone filed out, Dave turned to me and said, "Sorry to make you take another trip Warren. I'm going to call Melissa and you better call Trace."

"Yeah," I replied, getting up and grabbing one of the donuts Aaron hadn't got to.

"I'll meet you in ten minutes...Poppa."

I threw the donut at Dave and then smiled. Poppa.

Chapter Twenty-Three

Dr. Winters checked the batteries in his recorder and then left his apartment. He had been there a few days and had visited two shelters, speaking with several women and a few children. It seemed there were more and more cases of abuse happening here in Maine. He wondered if they were finally catching up with the rest of the country. In the past, they were among the lowest of reported abuse cases, but all of that was changing.

Shaking his head, he left the apartment, locking the door behind him. There really wasn't anything for someone to steal in there, but he wasn't going to leave it unlocked. It was just a small one bedroom similar to all his other apartments he kept along the Eastern Seaboard. He never kept any files or information about his patients, and he never decorated any of his apartments. The only thing in there to take was a well-stocked pantry. He carried out a suitcase and a black valise.

He had one more woman to talk to before he left Maine. Her name was Nancy Coleman, and she had been placed in a mental hospital recently, after trying to commit suicide. Normally Dr. Winters didn't speak with the abusers, only their victims. Nancy Coleman had abused her husband as well as two of her children and was an interesting woman.

He originally had seen her after she had taken her two children to a shelter. She had claimed her husband, Steve, had been abusing her and their girls. During the sessions, she had claimed Steve had sexually assaulted her girls, age ten and thirteen. Of course he had contacted the police and Social Services.

After Steve had been brought in on the possibility he was abusing his daughters, Dr. Winters had been contacted by one of the detectives on the case. The detective didn't believe Steve had been the abuser. In fact, he was certain it had been Nancy who had been abusing her husband and the girls.

Changing direction in his sessions with her, he finally got her to admit it had been her all along. The girls had been so terrified of their mother that they had lied, stating their father had been the abuser. After being arrested for her crimes, Steve had divorced her and left Maine with his daughters. Now it seemed, Nancy had tried to commit suicide while in prison.

Dr Winters was not the primary psychiatrist treating Nancy. Nancy was under the care of a Dr. Cosgrove, here at the hospital. Dr. Winters had met with Dr. Cosgrove and had gotten permission to talk with her.

He made his way into the hospital and had been shown into a small room where he waited for Nancy to be brought in. After a few minutes, a large orderly led her in. The orderly stayed in the room, taking a seat in the corner. Dr. Winters was about to say it wasn't necessary, but then changed his mind. Better safe than sorry. The first thing Dr. Winters noticed were the two large bandages covering her wrists.

"Hello Nancy," Dr. Winters said. "Is it okay if I speak with you?"

Nancy looked down avoiding eye contact and only nodded.

"Good Nancy. I would like to find out how you are doing?"

No answer from her.

"Could you tell me why you tried to kill yourself?"

Suddenly, Nancy jumped up and with her hands shaped like claws, attacked Dr. Winters. She managed to scratch his cheek before the orderly grabbed her and got her under control.

"Looks like she got you good, doc," the orderly said. "I'll take her back to her room and then see about getting you fixed up."

"Please, if you could just put her in restraints," Dr. Winters said. "I would still like to talk with her."

The orderly shook his head and then called someone for restraints. After getting Nancy restrained on her hands and legs, Dr. Winters continued.

"You must be very angry with me Nancy," he said. "Can you tell me why?"

"It's all your fault," she said, and spit on the floor.

The orderly got up and said, "Do that again and I put a spit hood on you!"

"Why is it my fault Nancy?" Dr. Winters asked in a soft voice.

With a look of pure evil and rage, Nancy yelled, "You were the one who made my Steve leave! Took my girls! Locked me up! I got nothing to live for and I want you dead! I'm not saying another fucking word to you... *Doctor*!"

Sighing, Dr. Winters told the orderly to take her back to her room. Nancy was a lost cause for him to treat. She blamed him for everything, ignoring her own guilt. Perhaps over time, Dr. Cosgrove would be able to help her.

Dr. Winters spoke with Dr. Cosgrove and then left the hospital. He then grabbed a cab to take him to the small airport where his jet was waiting. He had told the pilot to be ready by noon. His pilot had been with him for many years and was trustworthy.

Dr. Winters knew his pilot would never tell his wife or anyone else about the detour he had made before coming to Maine. Not that his pilot knew what he did on his small detours. He might suspect but there was no way he knew for certain. If his wife ever found out about his taking a small detour from Maine on Monday, she would not have been very happy. In fact she might be angry enough to divorce him. But Dr. Winters had a compulsion he just couldn't control.

As he sat back as the jet took off, he thought about his little side trips he took every once in a while. She would never find out. He smiled and relaxed for the trip home. Soon he would be back in his house with his wonderful wife and son. He was smiling as he drifted off to sleep.

Chapter Twenty-Four

Dave and I got our jet off the ground and headed for Safety Harbor as quickly as we could. There were two airports close to the town and we left it up to our pilot to make the choice. He decided on St. Petersburg – Clearwater International instead of Tampa International, because it was closer to the town and less busy. We called ahead to have a car ready.

Dave and I discussed the case and also the possibility of Trace and I adopting a child. The more I talked about it, the better I liked the idea. Maybe it would turn out to be a great thing for a kid and for Trace and me. In any case, I was getting used to the idea.

We landed at 1:30 and found a local FBI Special Agent waiting with a car for us. He matched the mold of most FBI Agents I had ever met. He was a little over six foot tall, with sandy short hair. He wore a black suit and white shirt with a black tie, even in the heat which assaulted us as we stepped from the jet. I couldn't tell the color of his eyes because he had on dark sunglasses.

He held out his hand and as we shook he said, "Special Agent Kirk at your service sir."

Dave smiled and said, "Call me Dave and this is Warren, and you don't need to be so formal."

"Whew," Kirk said. "I was told two big shots from NY were coming down and I was to treat you with all due respect. Guess you both are just regular guys. I'm Alan."

"Nice to meet you Alan. We're looking for someone who lives on Bay Drive in Safety Harbor," I said. "Can you get us there?"

"Sure can sir, I mean Warren. I was raised in Safety Harbor, and I know all the streets. And I'm at your service as long as you both need me."

We got into the car; Dave took the back this time and Alan drove us out of the airport.

"Is it a long drive?" I asked.

"Only about ten or fifteen minutes," Alan said. "Want me to give you a little information about the town?"

"Sure."

"Okay, let's see. Well, we are on the west shore of Tampa Bay, in Pinellas County. It was settled in the early 1800's and has a population of about 20,000. There have been some artifacts found here, a spearhead for one which dates back about 6000 years."

"How do you know this stuff Alan? I don't even know anything about my town."

"Guess I'm a bit of a history buff. Anyway, where was I? Oh yeah, so the artifact belonged to the Tocobaga people. Safety Harbor is also the home of the Espiritu Santo Springs, or The Springs of the Holy Spirit. They are mineral springs given the name by a Spanish explorer, Hernando de Soto. He had been looking for the Fountain of Youth.

When there were a great many pirates around here, the town was given its name, because it was a 'safe harbor'."

"Any pirate treasure around here now?" Dave asked.

"Well, I never found any, but there are always people digging around, and of course we get scuba divers looking for sunken wrecks. Okay, this is Bay Drive," he said as he turned onto a quiet street lined with coconut trees. The houses were all colorful small bungalows.

"We are looking for number 1710," Dave said.

Alan drove slowly and finally pulled up in front of a neat looking bungalow, painted pink. The lawn was neat and trim and there was a small white picket fence around the front with a gate. Outside were hanging three wind chimes and they were swaying in the breeze, making a soft musical sound. On the side of the front door was a mailbox with the name Walters on it. I thought we might have the wrong place. All in all, it looked like a nice place to live.

We parked and walked up to the door. I knocked a few times, but it appeared as if no one was home. As we slowly made our way back to the car, a man in a wild Hawaiian shirt called out to us.

"Peg won't be home for a few more minutes," the man said. "She picks up little John at his daycare about now. Come on over and get out of the heat while you wait."

Now I figured we did have the right place after hearing the names Peg and John. We made our way over but didn't show our ID's. We didn't want to spread any rumors about Peggy if we could help it. We shouldn't have worried about it.

The man shook our hands and invited us into his home. As he was getting us some iced tea, he called out," Names Fred King. What do Feebs want with Peg?"

As we took the drinks, Dave said, "Umm how did you know we are...Feebs Fred?"

"I was a local cop here for almost thirty years, boys. I know a feeb when I see one. Now why do you need to see Peg?"

"I hope you understand," Dave said, " but I'd rather not say."

"Okay I guess, Peg will tell me."

"How long has Peg been living here?

"Going on almost three years. Nice gal and her son is a real pip! I sure hope she isn't in any trouble."

"No, I can assure you she isn't in any trouble, Fred."

Fred looked out the window and said, "Well here she is now."

We stood and thanked him for the tea and hospitality and then left to meet Peggy Blake. Dave went a bit in front of us and spoke softly to her. Then he nodded to us, and we all went into her home.

We sat down in a small but nicely furnished living room and her son John went into his bedroom to play. Dave introduced all of us and showed her his ID.

"Looks like a nice boy Mrs. Blake," I said.

"I dropped the name Blake a long time ago, Special Agent," she said. "Now I'm Peggy Walters, my maiden name."

"Please Miss Walters, call me Warren, and this is Dave and Alan."

"I'm Peg. Now why did you want to speak with me?"

"Do you know what happened to your husband, Anthony Blake?"

After a small hesitation, she said, "No, and I don't care. After we ran away, I never looked back. Figured I didn't want to know anything more about him."

"I'm sorry to have to tell you he was murdered."

Peggy Walters gasped and fainted dead away slumping to the floor. Then her son John came out of his room, saw his mother, and started crying and screaming. This was turning into quite the situation.

Chapter Twenty-Five

While Alan went into the bathroom to get a cold compress, Dave lifted Peg onto the sofa. I went over to John and picked him up, comforting him. I showed him my badge and soon he was only whimpering a bit and looking on anxiously. I thought in a few months I might be holding a little boy or girl of my own. Then I shook my head and set my mind back to the case.

Peg finally came around and looked at us with wide eyes. She began crying and saying over and over again, "I didn't mean it, I didn't mean it!"

Dave told her to calm down and I brought John over for her to hold.

"What do you mean, Peg, you didn't mean to?" Dave asked her softly.

Peg took a deep breath and then asked if we could take John back to his room, maybe play with him. Alan took his hand and led him back to his bedroom. In a few minutes, we heard the little boy giggling and laughing.

Peg wiped her eyes and said, "I didn't want John to hear. The day we ran away, Tony had come home a little drunk. He saw the suitcase in my hand, and he got really angry. He came over to me, yelling about leaving him again, and then punched me in my face. When I went down, he kicked me. Then he said he was going to teach that brat a lesson too. Can I have a glass of water please?"

I got up and got her some water from the kitchen. After taking a few swallows, she continued.

"Tony turned toward John, and I grabbed a baseball bat he always kept by the door. I meant to hit him in the back, but at the last second he turned. I hit him on his forehead, and he went down. I thought he was just out cold. I didn't mean to kill him!"

Dave put his arm around her and said, "You didn't kill him Peg."

"I...I didn't?"

"No. He was killed in an alley near a bar called Chippy's."

"I don't understand. Who killed Tony? How was he killed?"

"How he was killed doesn't matter. As for who killed him, right now we don't know, but Tony was a victim of a serial killer. We think the killer is going after men who abuse their wives and children. Which is why we are here to speak with you."

"Oh thank God! I mean, thank God it wasn't me."

"I understand Peg. Do you feel up to answering a few questions now?"

"Yes, of course. I can't believe I have been scared of Tony finding us and all this time he was dead."

"Okay, you don't have to worry about him any longer. Did Tony always physically abuse you?"

"We started dating in high school and Tony was always very sweet. He was such a gentleman when we first started dating, and he was still sweet and kind when we were first married. The first three years or so were fine."

"So it started after his accident?"

"Yes, that and John being born. I don't think Tony ever wanted children. Then being crippled, losing his city job and John coming along made Tony angrier and angrier every day. He started cursing all the time and drinking."

"Did he ever hit John?"

"No, and I wasn't going to allow him to. That's why when he went after him, I hit him with the bat. Am I...am I going to be charged with assault?"

"Of course not Peg. Warren, any questions?"

"Peg," I began, "you said he yelled out you were leaving him again. So it wasn't the first time you left?"

"I had left him twice before. Both times I went to a shelter nearby."

"Did Tony know where you had gone?"

"I didn't think so, but he might have. When I was there both times, I spoke to a doctor. I think a psychologist or psychiatrist. I'm not sure which."

"Did you ever speak with a social worker?"

"Yes I did, again at the shelter."

"Do you remember his name?"

"Ummm, I'm sorry, no."

"How about the doctor or the name of the shelter you went to?"

"The shelter was called St. Mary's Shelter for Women. The doctor's name was, ummmm, Wilson, or Weathers. Something like that. I'm sorry but I can't remember."

"No worries, you did just fine. I think that will be all Peg."

Dave stood up and handed her his card.

"If you think of anything else please give me a call Peg," Dave said.

He called Alan out and then we went to leave.

Before we got to the door, Peg asked, "How did you ever find me?"

I said, "Do you remember your downstairs neighbor, Mrs. Rodriguez?"

"Of course," Peg said. "She was the sweetest lady. Always baking cookies and sometimes she would even watch John. I wasn't sure she was still alive."

"She is doing well, and still baking delicious cookies. I think she would really like to hear from you."

"I will definitely give her a call. And thank you. I'm sorry Tony was killed, but I feel as if a weight has been lifted from me. Now John and I can begin to live our lives."

We left Peg holding John and he gave us a little wave as we left. We filled Alan in on what she had told us on the drive back to the airport. Then we got on the jet for the ride back to New York.

As we flew with the clouds below us, I thought about Tony Blake. I wondered if something traumatic ever happened to me if it would turn me into an alcoholic brute. I didn't think so and I hoped I would never find out.

When we got back I was hoping the team had found out some information which might help us solve the murders. Even though the men who had died might have been abusers of women and children, they didn't deserve to die.

Then my mind turned to Trace, and I wondered what she and Melissa had found out about adopting a child. Hell, for all I knew, there might be a boy or girl living in my home by now!

Chapter Twenty-Six

Dr. Winters and his wife Jocelyn were just finishing up a wonderful dinner consisting of roast duck, carrots, potatoes and a very nice wine. Their son Brandon, had eaten quickly, hardly savoring the delicious meal. Ah well, Dr. Winters thought, at his age I never would have savored a meal like this, or even eaten it.

After clearing the dishes, Jocelyn and he went out on their deck with a second bottle of wine. He even allowed himself to have a cigar, which he only did once in a while. He thought to himself, he usually had a cigar after one of his little side trips, but he felt like having one now.

"So Malcolm," Jocelyn asked, "how was your trip to Maine?"

"Unfortunately," he said, "abusing women and children is becoming more prevalent in the State of Maine."

"Really? Why do you think that is?"

"I suppose the people there are just catching up with the rest of the country, and the world."

"Very sad. Did you get to speak with the woman, what's her name, who abused her husband and daughters?"

"Yes I did. It was a very short talk. She apparently refuses to take responsibility for her actions. Blamed me for everything. She even attacked me. See, this scratch over here."

He turned his face to the side so she could see the scratch.

"I didn't notice it before. Did you get it treated?"

"Just a scratch my dear. In any case, she also tried to commit suicide before I got there in the prison. She was transferred to a mental hospital after the attempt. I think she might try again, and this time she may succeed."

"Also very sad. I still find it hard to believe a mother would abuse her own children. And then, terrify them to the point where they would lie and say their father was the abuser. She was abusing her husband as well, right?"

"Yes she was. She had the children and her husband constantly in terror. Hopefully they will be able to live their lives normally, with the help of a good psychiatrist of course. This case is quite rare but maybe not so rare anymore. In any case, I left you the recordings of the session with her and a few more women I spoke with. There is no rush in getting them transcribed ."

"Good, because I have been very busy with a few charities and things at the club. Sometimes I think I'm working a full time job!"

"If it is too much you can always cut back. Or I can have a transcribing company handle my recordings dear."

"No. I enjoy doing it for you. It gives me a sense of helping you and the victims being abused."

"As you wish. Now, I've missed you terribly. How about we retreat to the bedroom?"

"I'm sorry Malcolm but I am very tired. Can I give you a raincheck, my love?"

"Of course. I will read a bit in my study. Why don't you go to bed and get some rest."

"Thank you dear."

Jocelyn gave him a kiss and then left him on the deck. He sat there, smoking his cigar and wondered if something was bothering his wife. Certainly she couldn't have found out about his little side trip. No, if she had found out she wouldn't have prepared him such a splendid dinner. Unless she added some poison. Laughing to himself, he stubbed out the remains of his cigar and headed into his study. He would read a bit and then head upstairs to bed.

Chapter Twenty-Seven

When I got home the night before, Trace had pamphlets and began telling me all about how we could go about adopting a little boy or girl. As I read a few of them, she told me how Melissa and she had gone down to social services. They met with a very nice woman who explained how to get started.

I listened carefully and once in a while my mind wandered between possibly becoming a father and the serial case I was working on. The first thing we would have to do would be to undergo an inspection of our home and an interview of us both. Then if we passed the first hurdle, we would be able to begin looking for a child.

When she had finished talking, she looked at me expectantly. Maybe she thought I had changed my mind or was having doubts. I took her in my arms and reassured her I was on board. I even told her about Peg's son John, and how I enjoyed consoling him.

Trace then broached the next important part of us adopting. How old a child did we want, a boy or a girl, and if it mattered if the child was white or from another race. Honestly I hadn't thought about it at all. Now that she had brought it up, I thought about my answers. I supposed I would love to have a boy who I could play catch with, take to ball games and maybe teach to shoot, of course when he was a lot older. In fact, a boy might even follow in my footsteps and become a Special Agent in the FBI! Or a police officer, maybe becoming a detective in the NYPD.

Then I remembered this wasn't 1950. A girl would be able to do everything a boy could. This was a lot harder than I thought it would be. As far as the age or race, it didn't matter to me. Finally I suggested we should give it some serious thought and see what happens. Trace had agreed with me, and though I asked her what were her choices, she didn't answer. Maybe she needed some time to think it over as well.

Now I was sitting in the conference room trying to get my mind back on the job at hand. Everyone was there and we were just waiting on Dave. Finally he walked in, and it looked as if he had something on his mind.

"Okay everyone, I printed out the information we received from Peggy Walters," Dave began. "She has taken her maiden name. Please take a second to read it and then we can begin to hear what the rest of you found out."

The team took the report and began to read.

When Lou got to the part where Peg had thought she had killed her husband, Lou said, "How horrible for her. To think she had lived with the fear of him coming after her for all those years. And then to believe she had killed him."

"Yeah it was rough for her, but I believe she and her son will now live a peaceful life," I said.

When everyone had finished, Dave said, "Let's hear what you and Billy found out first."

"First, Detective Sergeant Sommers called with the name of the social worker who had seen Peggy Blake, I mean Walters," Billy stated. "His name was Kevin Waxman. Unfortunately, right after Blake was killed, he left Newark. No idea where he is now."

"Okay, Carl can try and track him down, although I don't think we will get much from him. How about you guys?"

Carl spoke up first saying, "I believe our theory of a person killing men who abuse their families is on the nose."

"Were all three of the families of our other three victims abused?"

"I found out Jerry Baxter and Dr. Tomlinson had both been reported to the local police for possible abuse. As far as Robert Heller being an abuser, I couldn't find out. I did have the reports about Baxter and Tomlinson emailed over and I have copies for everyone. But I can tell you they were never charged. Whether or not because their wives refused to press charges or possibly because of their status in the town I can't tell you."

"Ok, then we need to get more information on all of them. I think we will have to pay visits to all of the families again. I want to know how bad these men were in abusing their families. Then we still need to find some connection. Any thoughts?"

"Well," I said, "the first thing which comes to mind would be some kind of support group, possibly online."

"Carl, try and run down any support groups on the web and if possible the names of people who are in them."

"I can find out if there are any groups Dave," Carl said, "but I doubt I can get any names. They probably are anonymous because of their situation. Plus the people who visit the site probably have user names only."

"You're probably right Carl but give it a shot. Any other ideas how these people are connected?"

"It says in your report, Peggy had gone to a shelter," Aaron said. "If these women were being abused for some time, it's possible they had run away a time or two to a shelter as well. Maybe the shelters are connected in some way. Maybe they keep in touch with each other."

"Good idea Aaron, so why don't you try and contact a few of them and see. Start with St. Mary's in Newark where Peggy had run away to."

"You know there are also safe homes where women can go to," Lou said. "I had a friend who went to one of those instead of a shelter. They are more anonymous than shelters. Some of them aren't even listed anywhere. They get women to come to them through recommendations from police, doctors, nurses, EMT's or through other victimized women."

"I never knew that Lou. See if you can find some of them and ask if they keep in touch with each other. Anyone else?"

"I keep thinking about the psychiatrist who Peggy saw at the shelter," I said. "I wonder if there are a group of psychiatrists, psychologists or medical doctors who regularly visit certain shelters or safe homes. I think we need to find out the name of the doctor who saw Peggy at St. Mary's."

"Aaron, when you speak to St. Mary's, see if you can run down the name of the doctor who saw Peggy. Okay, let's figure out who is going to see who."

"I think it might be a good idea to split up the wives of our three victims with different members of our team," I said. "Might throw them off if they are approached by different agents."

"I think that's a good idea. So, Lou and Billy, you will visit Mrs. Baxter in Bolton. Aaron and Carl will take Mrs. Tomlinson in Kent, Connecticut and Warren and I will take Mrs. Heller. This time around we will all have to move a bit quicker. Get to the wives and get them to talk. Explain how each of the murdered men were abusers. If necessary, threaten them with obstruction of justice. No kid gloves this time around. We need to find out if any of them had run away to a shelter or safe home. If they did, we need to know if they spoke to any social workers or possibly a doctor."

"I think we better stay in touch as soon as we learn anything," I said.

"I agree. So let's get started guys. Lou, you and Billy take the jet. Warren and I will drive to Sheffield. Carl, you and Arron drive to Kent and while enroute, make the calls to St. Mary's. Aaron, you drive so Carl can also use his laptop. Warren, come with me to brief Teller please."

We all got started on our assignments. I went with Dave to brief Teller and then we would hit the road. I wasn't thrilled about driving to Sheffield, but it would only be about three to four hours away. It was still early, and I was hoping we wouldn't have to stay overnight again.

After briefing Teller, I called Trace and told her what we were up to. She wasn't too upset, saying she and Melissa were getting together again. Maybe on the drive I would be able to make up my mind on a boy or a girl, or what age. Maybe Dave would be able to help me out.

We grabbed our go bags which we always had on hand, got a pretty good SUV from the car pool, and hit the road. We would be there by the afternoon, and I was excited to be moving the case along. I was getting that old feeling in my gut we were getting close.

Chapter Twenty-Eight

Following the report Carl and Aaron had made about Mrs. Heller's work, we drove directly to the hotel she worked at. When we arrived we contacted the manager. He was a surprisingly young man named Roger Cole. He noticed our surprise and explained his parents had owned the hotel and he had practically grown up in it. After his dad had passed away, he took over managing.

He stated Maria was just finishing up down in the basement. We could wait in a conference room, and he would see to it to bring her to us once she finished. We didn't really want to wait, but we figured it might be easier to talk with her in a closed room. Cole showed us to a conference room set up with coffee, donuts, and some other snacks. There was a long table with several comfortable looking chairs.

Cole said, "We were supposed to have a group of real estate agents here today, but they cancelled at the last minute. Please feel free to have some coffee and eat whatever you want. I'll bring Maria to you in a few minutes."

"Thank you Mr. Cole," Dave said and after he closed the door, he said, "This is working out.

"Yeah," I replied, "I sure can use this coffee and snacks."

We both grabbed two mugs, filling them with steaming coffee. Like most in law enforcement, we took our coffee's black. Less chance for someone to put something into it when ordering on the go. Then we took two seats leaving a chair directly across from us open.

"You want to handle this in any particular way Dave," I asked.

Finishing the donut he was eating, Dave replied, "Judging from what Carl told us, Maria Heller had been scared and nervous. He said he had been gentle and had gotten nowhere. I'll start the interview by being easy on her. Then if we think she is holding back, I'll give you a sign."

"Okay. I'll walk around the room, grumbling. What sign do you want to use?"

"Ummm, I'll stand up and say I'm done with her."

"Works for me."

We waited, finishing the coffee and donuts and clearing the table. Then, the door opened and Cole escorted Mrs. Heller into the room.

Dave stood and escorted her to the chair. As soon as she had sat down, I stood up and began pacing.

Dave shook her hand and said, "Hello Mrs. Heller. My name is Special Agent Dave Anderson. You can call me Dave. And this is..."

I looked at her with a grim expression and said, "I'm Special Agent Warren Temple, and you can call me Special Agent Temple." Then I continued to pace.

"Yes, well, we came back to speak with you because we believe there are some things you might be able to help us with."

Mrs. Heller was nervously wringing her hands and said, "But I spoke with the other agents."

I stopped walking and said, "*Special Agents* Mrs. Heller."

"Sss...sorry," she stammered. "Special Agents."

I grumbled and began pacing again.

"Ummm, yes, well now," Dave said. "We know you spoke with the other Special Agents, but since then, we have gathered some more information about the homicide of your husband. We've discovered there have been four homicides so far. In each of the cases, the men were abusive to their families."

"Oh no!" Mrs. Heller cried out and stood as if she was going to leave. I started to walk over to her, but Dave took her hand and gently had her sit down once again.

"Mrs. Heller," Dave said in a soft voice, "we are sure your husband abused you or your sons or all of you. It is very important you tell us the truth. We are trying to stop another person from being killed. You wouldn't want to see another person brutally killed, would you? Now, did your husband ever abuse you or your sons?"

Mrs. Heller took a deep breath and said in a whisper, "He's dead. I don't want to talk about this anymore. I'm leaving. You have no right to keep me here."

Dave said, "I'm sorry to hear that. Of course we can't force you to talk with us but..." Then he stood up.

"I can make you stay Mrs. Heller," I said loudly, walked up behind her and put my hands on her shoulders, lightly pushing her back in her seat. "Do you think we are idiots? Three men out of four were killed, their throats slit, and they all abused their wives! You think we don't know your husband abused you? Have you ever heard of obstruction of justice? Don't think I won't put you in Federal lockup and your sons can be taken by social services!"

Mrs. Heller began to cry and for a minute I thought I had pushed her too far. Then saying something in Spanish, she looked to Dave. She wasn't going to speak to me.

"Yes, yes, Bobby did hit me," she said softly. "But he never hit our boys, never."

Now that she was telling the truth, I sat down at the far end of the table. It was now up to Dave to find out all he could.

He began by saying, "May I call you Maria? And would you like some water or coffee?"

"Yes, and water please."

"*Agent*, please get Maria some water."

Dave was showing her he was my superior, so I got up, got some water and placed a cup next to her. Then I returned to my seat at the end of the table and turned away. But I was listening carefully.

"I know it is difficult but please tell me what Mr. Heller did to you," Dave said.

Maria took a sip of water and then said, "My Bobby used to be a good man, a good husband. But he changed, and why, I never knew."

"Go on please."

"It started with him losing his temper. For no reason at all, he would fly into a rage, yelling at me and the boys. I figured something must have been happening at work. Then one night, it got much worse."

She stopped, took another sip and continued.

"One night he came home from work, and I could tell he was angry. I had the boys go to their room and then I started to serve dinner. It was arroz con pollo, chicken and rice, and Bobby usually loved it. But this time, he picked up his plate and threw it across the room. He was screaming about always having chicken. Chicken and rice. Why not steak or even lobster. He had never wanted those foods, never. Then he...he slapped me."

"Did it get worse after the first time he slapped you?"

"Yes, yes it did. He began to hit me all the time, but never in front of the boys. He would hit me in my stomach or take a belt to me. He would put me over his lap and beat my rear. Then he went too far. He punched me in the face, knocking out two teeth."

Maria then showed her teeth, pointing out the two front teeth.

"After he died, I had them fixed. After he hit me in the face, I took the boys and ran away to a safe house a coworker had told me about."

I perked up at hearing about a safe house. Dave continued to gently question her.

"Did you stay there or return home?"

"Bobby called me over and over again. He was sorry, it would never happen again he had told me. After a week or so, I went back to him. For a few weeks he had almost been his old self. Then he came to the hotel at lunchtime, surprising me. I had been sitting with several workers, but there was a man right next to me. Bobby flew into a rage, grabbing me by the hair and tried to drag me out of the room. Rodrigo, the man I was sitting next to, got up to stop him. Bobby hit him and then I left with him. He accused me of cheating. I never did, I swear!"

"I believe you Maria. What happened next?"

"He hit me over and over. I was nearly knocked unconscious. I was going to call the police but decided I should just leave again. Rodrigo was going to also call the police, but I talked him out of it. Then, after work the very next day I picked up the boys from school and went back to the safe house again. I then got a small apartment for me and the boys. A few days later, he was killed. I decided I would just put it all in the past and raise my boys."

"Okay Maria, thank you for telling me all of this. I know it wasn't easy. I have only a few more questions please."

"Okay, I will answer you."

"Good. First, what is the name of the safe house and where is it located?"

"It didn't have a name. In fact, if you didn't know it was a safe house, you would never know. It is a large home on the corner of Mason and Connor Streets. A woman by the name of Sister Stephanie Gray runs it."

"Okay. Now, when you were at the safe house, did you speak to a social worker?"

"No, I never did."

"I see."

"But there was a doctor who I spoke with several times. He wasn't from around here. He told me he travels around to safe houses to help abused women and children."

I could feel my heart beating faster. A doctor who traveled around to safe houses? This might be a big break in the case!

"Maria, do you remember the name of this doctor?"

"No, I'm sorry. I have tried to forget everything about all of it. But Sister Gray would know. I'm sure."

"Okay Maria. Thank you for all of your help. You can go now."

Maria stood and went to leave. She turned and said, "If you catch the man who killed my Bobby, please let me know. I still loved him, even after he hurt me."

Then she walked out.

"Some acting there Warren," Dave said.

"Yeah, I feel like a rat but at least she finally opened up," I said. "I suppose our next stop is to the house at Mason and Connor streets?"

"Absolutely. Let's go."

Chapter Twenty-Nine

Thursday, Safe House run by Sister Gray, 3:50 pm

When we got in the car, Dave's cell rang. It was Carl calling, and Dave put the call on speaker.

"Hi Carl," Dave said. "What's up? You're the speaker."

"Hi boss, Warren," I heard Carl say, "We have some good news and bad news."

"Okay, go ahead."

"First, there are some chat rooms for abused women, but they are all very strict on privacy. All the members use phony names and never reveal their locations or the names of their husbands. It would take a long time and a lot of work to try and identify any of them."

"Okay, I wasn't holding out much hope on it being easy. What else?"

"I was able to get in touch with St. Mary's, and spoke to a Joan Abbot there. The social worker was Kevin Waxman, and she thought he had moved up north somewhere. Maybe Rhode Island or Massachusetts. She said he was tired of the area and wanted to try somewhere new."

"Good, now maybe you can track him down. Anything else?"

"Abbot said as far as she knew, shelters and safe houses don't have any contact with each other besides the ones nearby, in the same city. But I did get the name of the doctor who had seen Peggy Walters. He still visits St. Mary's, usually once every two or three months."

"And his name?"

"Dr. Malcolm Waters. I figured when I get the chance I will get some info on him."

"What about Mrs. Tomlinson? Did she admit she was abused?"

"That lady wasn't going to talk. At least not until I took your advice and threatened her with a charge of obstruction of justice in a homicide. Then she told us all about it. She had been abused and she had gone to a shelter. She had spoken to a social worker there, but not any doctor. She did speak to some counselors, and we are going to try and run them down. Then it's back to New York for us."

"Great work guys. We will see you back there tomorrow morning. Oh, please call Lou and Billy and give them everything you found out. Tell them we will see them tomorrow in the office."

"You got it boss."

"Looks like we might be getting somewhere Dave," I said, as he began our drive.

"It does look like it," Dave replied. "But we still need some more info. I'm especially interested in the social worker who left and the doctor who travels around visiting safe houses and shelters."

"I'm disappointed Mrs. Tomlinson never spoke to a doctor. Still, we need to check him out. Maybe Lou and Billy will have some luck with Mrs. Baxter. Between the three of us, we might come up with more of a connection than the wives being abused."

We pulled up in front of the house on the corner of Mason and Connor streets. It was a large Victorian style home. Maria had been right. From just looking at it, it was impossible to know it was a safe home for women and children.

The one thing I did notice was all the windows appeared to have thick drapes covering them. On further inspection, I saw four security cameras. One at the front door, two on the roof, and one more on the second floor of the house. I was sure if we walked around the house, we would see more covered windows and cameras. Dave and I walked up to the front door and rang the bell.

A voice came out of a speaker pretty much hidden from view.

"Yes, can I help you?" a woman's voice said.

"Yes Ma'am," Dave said as he held up his badge and ID card to the camera. "My name is Special Agent Dave Anderson of the FBI. This is Special Agent Warren Temple. We were given this address by Maria Heller and would like to speak with Sister Gray."

We stood waiting for a minute, and then a buzzer sounded, and we opened the door and walked in. We were standing in a small foyer with a solid door in front of us and a thick glass window to our right. Behind the glass was a middle aged woman looking at us.

Then we heard through a speaker, "If you gentlemen would please hold up your identification once again please."

We took out our badges and ID's and held them to the glass. She looked at them carefully, and then pressed a button. We went to the door and opened it. In front of us was a large living room. Several women were sitting around, watching TV, or reading, or playing with a few children. The second we walked in, they all stopped what they were doing, and looked up with frightened eyes. I was saddened by the look in all of their eyes. These women, and even the children were scared at our being there.

The woman behind the glass came out from another door and said, "I'm Sister Gray. Perhaps you gentlemen will follow me into a room where we can have some privacy. It's okay everyone. Go back to what you were doing."

Sister Gray led us down the hallway and then turned into a small office. She looked to be about forty years old, with dark auburn hair. She was dressed in a loose fitting blouse and jeans. Her smile had an immediate calming effect, and I thought to myself this was the perfect woman to run a safe house.

"I assume this has something to do with Maria's husband being killed?" she said.

She was smart too.

"Sister Gray, you are correct in your assumption. Mr. Heller was only one of four victims we know about. All of our victims were killed because they abused their wives and children, at least we are pretty sure it's the reason. Maria told us while she was here, she had spoken to a doctor. She also said she didn't speak with a social worker."

"In my experience, a social worker does no good until a woman has decided to leave her husband. A doctor seems to help a great deal more in convincing them to do so, and to treat them for the abuse they have suffered."

"I see. Do you have several doctors who treat the women here or just one?"

"Usually we have a few who help out here and there, but we do have one in particular who makes regular visits. He has been doing so for many years. All the other doctors leave notes for him. He is well respected in the field of treating abused women and children. In fact, he was here a few weeks ago and will probably return in two or three weeks."

"And his name is...?"

"Dr. Malcolm Waters."

Dave and I looked at each other. Our eyes were open wide, and we both knew the break we were looking for just landed in our laps. There was no way we could hide our surprise.

"Is Dr. Waters in some kind of trouble?"

"I'm not sure Sister Gray, I'm just not sure...yet."

"I do not believe Dr. Waters could be involved in these murders in any way. He is a very kind and gentle person."

"I understand and appreciate your concerns Sister, but in my experience you never really know what goes on in a person's mind. But believe me, we will find out the truth. Thank you for your help."

Sister Gray led us to the door, and we got into the car.

"We're heading back right now?" I asked.

"Absolutely Warren," Dave said and pulled out. "I was a bit tired before, but now I think I will be able to drive straight back. We need to talk to the team."

I had been tired as well but now with the information about Dr. Malcolm Waters, my adrenaline was flowing through my blood. No one in law enforcement believed in coincidences. Even though Mrs. Tomlinson hadn't seen a doctor, it was still too much to think Waters wasn't connected somehow.

Chapter Thirty

Even though Dave and I got back home late the previous night, we were both in the office by 8:00. I didn't sleep well, too excited about the new information we had found out. Mrs. Heller and Peggy Walters had both been seen by Dr. Waters. The fact Mrs. Tomlinson apparently didn't see him was a problem and we would have to look into it further. Still it was a break in the case. I was sure of it.

I had received the profile from the guys in Quantico. It was about what I thought it would be. White male, between 35-50 years of age, probably a white collar worker or professional. Very organized, detail oriented and smart, probably an only child. Might be divorced and more than likely had an abusive father.

I would tell the others about the profile, but I wasn't sure it would help.

Dave and I were in the conference room, awaiting the arrival of the rest of the team. We had both briefed ADD Teller first thing this morning. It was nice having a boss who got to work even before we did.

As we were discussing the new break, Lou and Billy walked in. A few minutes later Carl and Aaron followed, with Aaron carrying a large box of donuts. Even though it was a stereotype, I knew cops did love donuts. Probably because a donut shop was the only place open when working a midnight tour.

Dave began immediately, saying, "Okay everyone.

We might have our first real break. I'm going to let Warren bring everyone up to speed. Warren?"

"First," I began, "I know everyone is a bit tired. We've been hitting this case hard and up until now, we were basically spinning our wheels. But now we may have broken it wide open.

Peggy Blake, now Peggy Walters saw a doctor at St. Mary's, the shelter she went to. It turns out Mrs. Heller went to a safe house as well. There she also met with a doctor. In both cases, the doctor was Dr. Malcolm Waters."

"Wow, that's great!" Billy said. "Too bad we couldn't find out anything at all."

"What do you mean Billy? Mrs. Baxter wasn't forthcoming?"

"She wasn't anything at all Warren. Mrs. Baxter left the country with her three girls right after you and Dave spoke with her."

"She just up and left? Where did she go?"

"Lou and I checked the airlines at three airports in the area and finally found her's and the girls names. They are in Italy."

"Italy! Well damn."

"We will just have to forget about tying her or the doctor to them at this point," Dave said. "Let's concentrate on what we know and where we go from here. Carl, have you got any information on Dr. Waters? Also the social worker, what was his name?"

"Kevin Waxman," Carl said. "Waxman is now working for social services in Boston."

"Boston?" I repeated. "Now that is interesting."

"Yeah, I thought so too. I found out Waxman got his degree from Queens College here in New York. Then went to work at social services in Newark. He worked there for about five years and left shortly after Blake was killed. Then he turned up in Boston a year later. He's not married, and I spoke to a coworker in Newark. Frank Boatman stated he was a quiet guy and strange. Never really interacted with anyone else in the office. He spent his free time travelling around rock climbing. Free hand, which means no ropes. One more thing. Boatman said he was always angry about the men who abused women. More so than most."

"Someone who rock climbs free hand without ropes would have to be very strong," Lou said. "Someone who could easily beat up someone, beat them pretty good."

"It seems we now have two possible suspects," Dave said. "Dr. Malcolm Waters and Kevin Waxman. So let's get everything we can find on Waters Carl. I want to know everything about him. Also, call Boston social services and see if you can find out more on Waxman."

"Should we just bring them in? We probably have enough to question them."

"Not yet Lou, I don't want to tip our hand or for them to lawyer up. Then we'll be dead in the water. Warren, can you give a call to our Boston office and see if they can put Waxman under surveillance. Billy and Lou will track down Waters, wherever he might be. Once you do, let me know and we will keep an eye on him as well. I'm going to give Cory Nash a call. Maybe he can run down some of the safe houses or shelters in his town. He might be able to find out if Dr. Waters ever saw any women there. Maybe even find out if Mrs. Baxter and her girls had ever stayed at one. One more thing Aaron, you guys said Mrs.

Tomlinson never saw Dr. Waters. But she did see some counselors. Find out if any of the counselors have any ties to Dr. Waters."

"That's a great idea Dave," I said. "Until we find out more about our two suspects there isn't too much more..."

Before I had a chance to finish my sentence, Add Teller walked into the room. He looked ashen and angry at the same time.

"What's up Boss," Dave asked.

"I just got a call from the Sheriff down in Greensboro, North Carolina," Teller said. "He had been looking through some of the bulletins I sent out to departments up and down the eastern seaboard. He had been too busy working on his reelection, or he would have called sooner."

"Another victim?"

"I'm afraid so. Here is the report Dave."

I thought Teller not calling Dave by his full title meant he was really upset by this newest victim. He was probably hearing about it from his bosses. Shit always rolled downhill, even in the FBI.

"You and Warren get on this right away. And Dave, we need to stop this bastard, and soon."

"Yes sir," Dave said.

Teller didn't say anything else and just walked away.

"Okay team, it looks as if Warren and I will be heading to North Carolina. You all know what you need to do. If anything comes up, anything at all, I want a call immediately. Now let's get to work and stop this killer."

"Ummm Dave?" Billy said hesitantly.

"Yes Billy?"

"Well, now we know this killer is killing abusive husbands."

"And?"

"And he is killing then in a brutal way. And I just figured we need to name him, for the case."

Dave rubbed his hands over his face and said, "And I suppose you have a name in mind?"

"Well I've been thinking about it. How about, Brutal Abuser?"

"Not bad but not great. But for now we will go with it. So all of you get to work and let's catch this, umm, Brutal Abuser."

Dave gave me a look and I just shook my head. I had to go call Trace right away. Dave and I were on our way out of New York once again. I was starting to miss my days as a simple homicide detective in the NYPD.

Chapter Thirty -One

Dave made the call to get the jet ready once again. How much money this case was costing the government I didn't know, and I was glad I wasn't the one who had to explain it. Teller would be the one explaining it to some congressional committee or possibly his boss. Maybe even the Director. In any case I didn't care.

I had called Trace and once again told her I was going out of town. She wasn't too happy about it, but she understood. There were some wives who made good cop or in this case FBI wives. Some would always complain, and it made it tough. But Trace, and I assumed Melissa were great FBI wives. It wasn't that they didn't mind, they did. But they understood the job and never made a big deal out of it.

Now we were once again in the air heading for Greensboro, to Piedmont International Airport. And once again we would be met by a local FBI Special Agent and a car. Dave gave me the report, too upset to read it himself. I read it over first and then we began to discuss it.

"Victim was a man named Stuart King, African American, age 51 at the time of his death," I said. "Married but his wife had left him several months ago."

"Sounds like he might have been abusive to her as well," Dave replied. "Were the injuries about the same as our last victims?"

"Except for one new added injury. This time The Brutal Abuser, cut off his penis. It was found in his hand."

"That's a bit more aggression. Our killer is becoming angrier. Okay, our killer may get sloppy now. And Warren, we need a new name for this guy," Dave said with a laugh.

"Don't I know it!"

"What else?"

"He worked for the TSA at the airport we are landing at."

"Maybe we will talk to some of his coworkers on the way out of the airport. First I want to speak with whoever caught the murder and visit the crime scene. Do we have the wife's name and location?"

"It's not in the report but the Sheriff might know."

"Anything in the report about him abusing his wife?"

"Nope, nothing."

"Sounds like we will need to find out a lot more about our victim. Hopefully the Greensboro Sheriff's Department will be able to fill in some of the gaps."

"I sure hope so. I'm a bit tired of running all over the place."

"It's the job Warren, it's the job."

We both sat back and waited to arrive at the airport. At least this time we had some new questions to be asked. We needed to speak with our victim's wife. Was she ever abused? Did she run to a shelter or safe house? And if she did, did she ever speak to Dr. Waters or Waxman? If she did, I figured we would be much further along and knew who our killer was. Or maybe not. One thing I had learned over the years is to never think you knew who a killer was until you had a confession or caught them in the act.

We finally landed and found our guy from the local FBI without too much difficulty. He didn't look old enough to shave. Was it him or me just getting older? Besides looking like most FBI Special Agents, he was holding up a large placard with ***Special Agent Anderson*** and ***Special Agent Temple*** written on it in big black letters. Talk about keeping a low profile.

We walked up to him and Dave grabbed the sign, tossing it into a garbage bin, and said, "We're Anderson and Temple. Could you have made our arrival any more apparent to everyone walking by?"

"Ummm," he stammered. "I didn't know it was a secret sir."

"Well, it isn't a secret but it's not a good idea to advertise. Forget it. Your name?"

"I'm Special Agent Lawrence Gold sir."

"Okay, I'm Dave and this is Warren. Do people call you Larry?"

"Yes sir, I mean Dave, they do."

"Great Larry. How about we get in the car, and you take us to the Sheriff's office first."

"Right this way Dave!"

"One other thing Larry," I said. "Do you know either of us?"

"No sir, never had the pleasure."

"Then how do you know we are Anderson and Temple?"

"Uhhh, I guess I don't. Can you guys show me your ID's?"

We took out our ID's and then Dave and I followed Larry to an SUV and then we took off. On the way he asked Dave questions on why we were there, how he could get to a big city like New York, how many years were we with the FBI and a few dozen more. Dave did his best to answer, but I could tell he was getting a bit annoyed. I was glad when we pulled up at the Sheriff's office.

Dave got out and told Larry he should just stay with the car. He was disappointed until Dave said we might have to move quickly, so stay alert! It seemed to have the desired effect. Larry sat up straighter and looked all around, keeping well aware of his surroundings...just in case. I smiled and remembered what it was like to be a rookie.

We walked into a lobby which looked the same as every other one I had ever been in. We showed our ID's and were taken back to the Sheriff's office. We knocked on the door and were told to come on in.

A fit looking light skinned African American man with a big bushy beard came around a desk and shook our hands. He looked to be about forty-five, 6'5" tall, bald with a gleaming head which appeared to be newly waxed, and a hand shake which nearly broke my hand.

"How are you boys doin'" he said in a deep southern drawl. "I'm Sheriff Wilbur O'Doyle."

"O'Doyle?" I asked.

"Dad was Irish, and my mom was black. About the only thing I got from him was his name and a slightly lighter complexion. Sit down, sit down!"

We both laughed and showed the Sheriff our ID's.

Dave said, "So Sheriff, how did you come to get this murder? I would've figured the GPD would have caught it."

"Normally they would have, but the home where our victim lived is in a small, disputed area. Right now, it is part of the county and not the city. The people who deal with that sort of thing have been disputing it for oh, about twenty years now. So, we got the call."

"I see. Well, the first thing we would like to do is speak with the deputy who was the lead. Get the full reports including the Medical Examiner's with photos and then visit the crime scene."

"No problem. Let me take you to the Investigations boys."

The Sheriff led us down the hall and then showed us into the deputy's office.

I was glad we were meeting with someone else. I could hardly understand a single word the Sheriff was saying. His southern accent was so heavy I barely caught a word. Hopefully, the Deputy would actually speak English.

Chapter Thirty -Two

Friday, Deputy Graham Grant's Office, 12;10 PM

Deputy Graham Grant was a thirty something white man with longish blonde hair, a neatly trimmed moustache and bright blue eyes. He was dressed in black slacks, a blue dress shirt and blue tie. His desk was over-flowing with folders and his office was smaller than mine. I saw a few photos on the wall behind his desk and an award for Detective of the Year. He stood as we walked in and put out his hand.

"Graham, this here is Special Agent Dave..." the Sheriff began to say.

"Dave Anderson and this is Warren Temple," Dave said, and we both shook his hand.

"Right. Well they are here about the Stuart King homicide. I'll leave them in your hands."

"Yes sir," Graham said. "Have a seat."

"We're here because this is the fifth victim of a se-rial killer, over the last four or five years." Dave said.

"What's the name you guys gave him? I know the FBI goes in for naming their serial killers."

"Ummm, right now we are using the Brutal Abuser. Not the best but it's what we have so far."

"Well it certainly fits the King murder. You guys up to speed on it yet?"

"Not really. We read the preliminary report. We were hoping you could fill us in and get us the ME's report as well. Plus we would like to see the crime scene."

"No problem, I can drive you over and we can talk on the way."

"Actually we have a vehicle and driver right outside. If you bring the report and photos, we can go over them as he drives."

"Sounds fine to me. Let me get the report and we can go right now."

A few minutes later we were on our way to Stuart King's home on Harley Drive. Dave and Graham sat in the back, and I had turned a bit around to hear everything. As we took off, I told Larry to listen and learn and pay attention to driving. The last thing I wanted was to be involved in a car accident.

Graham was saying, "We got a call for a welfare check on King because he had missed two days of work without calling in. A deputy was dispatched and made entry through a sliding back door which was unlocked. Luckily the dog in the back yard had been friendly."

"We might want to talk to him at some point," I said.

"No problem. He entered and began to clear the home when he went into the master bedroom. King was spread eagle, and he found some rope fibers. He figured the killer took the rope with him. Our deputy checked for vitals and then backed out, calling for a detective and our crime scene guys. All in all, a good job."

"Sounds like he knew what he was doing."

"He's got about ten years on, so he knows how not to destroy a crime scene. I arrived about twenty minutes later. Gotta tell you; I never saw someone so beat up the way King was. And his penis in his hand sure did make my stomach turn. I think the name you gave this killer might just be right."

"What were the full injuries?"

Graham took out the ME's report and said, "Broken jaw, nose, four left ribs, two right ones, left shoulder separation. The ME thinks it might have been from being tied up and stretched to the limit. Also, stomach had ruptured from several hard shots to the abdomen, his testicles had been ruptured as well. The penis cut off and placed in his left hand. The ME said he was alive until the *coup de grace,* his throat being slit. Nearly decapitated him."

"Pretty much the same injuries as our other victims," Dave said. "First time a penis has been cut off. The killer is getting more vicious in the attacks. We read the wife had left a few months ago."

"Yeah, let's see here. Jasmine King, age 49, left her husband about two months ago. That's according to Mark Spencer, a neighbor."

"Was King ever arrested or reported for abusing his wife?"

"No official report, but when I asked Spencer if he knew why she had left, his answer was they used to fight like cats and dogs. We can see if he is home if you'd like to talk with him."

"I think we will."

Larry pulled up in front of a nice looking home. Neat lawn, flowers and some rose bushes. Of course the police tape ruined the idyllic looking scene.

"Ummm, Dave," Larry said as we got out, "would I be able to tag along? Never seen a real crime scene yet."

"Sure, but don't touch anything," Dave said.

I was glad he was letting Larry inside. The only way to learn was through seeing and listening. I just hoped he wouldn't toss his cookies. We all entered and went directly to the master bedroom. I noticed there were no pictures anywhere and no signs of a woman's touch. I supposed after his wife left him he threw out anything which reminded him of her.

On the bed, there was a large blood stain from his penis being cut off. Another on the pillows and on the wall behind the headboard. I looked over to Larry and although he looked a bit pale, he was holding up okay.

"Ropes used were nothing special, could be bought almost anywhere," Graham said. "Our guys found fibers on the posts, and on King's wrists and ankles. They identified them, but they are sold at every hardware store or Wal-Mart."

I said. "Was the dog hurt?"

"No, his dog was out in the yard, and I suppose our killer never got to encounter him. A big Rottweiler."

"Too bad he wasn't in the house when the killer came in."

"Don't think it would have made a difference. We found some raw hamburger in the trash. Just to be on the safe side, we had it analyzed. There was enough barbiturates in it to knock the dog out or possibly kill it."

"Your guys did a great job. Our killer thought of everything. So far at all the scenes we didn't find any prints or DNA at all."

"Funny..."

"What?"

"Usually if a criminal is organized and so thorough in keeping a scene clean, they aren't so overly aggressive with a homicide. I mean all the injuries, the cutting off of the penis and nearly decapitating our victim shows rage. And yet the killer was extremely careful, clean and prepared for the dog. Funny."

"I think we have seen everything here," Dave said. "How about we talk to the neighbor."

Chapter Thirty-Three

We walked across to the neighbor's home to the right of King's home. Again, the lawn was neatly trimmed and so were the bushes on either side of the walk. There was a wooden sign hung up by the front door which read, ***The Spencer's C'mon In!*** Nothing like southern hospitality.

The front door was open, so we knocked on the screen. A voice from inside said just what the sign out front did, C'mon In!.

Graham went first, calling out as we entered, "Mr. Spencer, it's Deputy Grant sir."

A man of about seventy rose from a recliner with a big smile on his face. He was a dark skinned African American, with a big beer belly and smoking a cigar.

"And who might these three white boys be Deputy?" he said with a twinkle in his eye.

"These three white boys be from the F...B...I."

"Uh oh, I guess I put my big foot in my mouth."

"No problem Mr. Spencer," Dave said and held out his hand.

"Glad to hear it!" he said and sat back down after shaking all our hands. "Take a seat boys...ummm, men."

We sat down on a couch and chair and Graham said, "These men would like to ask you a bit about your neighbors, the King's."

"Hah! Neighbors! That man, God rest his soul, wouldn't know how to be a neighbor. Now his wife was a nice woman. She should have left him the day after she married the bum."

Just then a woman of about the same age as her husband walked in from the kitchen. She was a small woman but very pretty. She had on a yellow dress and sandals. In her hands was a tray filled with glasses of iced tea and cookies. She was smiling as she walked in and set it down on the coffee table.

"Mark!" she said. "You shouldn't be talking nasty about the dead!"

"Sorry dear," Mark said. "These men are from…"

"I'm not yet deaf Mark Spencer. I heard the Deputy. How do you think I knew to bring out some refreshments? Nice to meet you gentlemen."

We all said our hellos and then Dave said, "We were hoping you could give us some help Mrs. Spencer with the unfortunate murder of Mr. King."

"Names Naomi, sir. I'll be glad to help anyway I can. Mark! Get rid of that old stogie!"

Mark got up and threw his cigar out the door, grumbling the whole way. I figured Naomi ruled this roost.

Dave said, "We were wondering a few things. First off, do you know if Mr. King physically abused his wife?"

"Oh, lordy, yes. I saw poor Jasmine with a black eye and split lip on more than one occasion. Told her she should leave that animal; God rest his soul."

I exchanged a look with Dave. King did abuse his wife. It looked like he was another of our victims.

Dave continued saying, "Do you know if she ever left him and ran away to a shelter or safe house?"

"She did, a number of times, although I told her she could stay with me. Let me think for a minute. The names on the tip of my tongue. Ummm, yes! I have it! It was the Raleigh Women's Shelter. Over in Raleigh."

"Well where else would the Raleigh Women's Shelter be?" her husband said. "In Asheville?"

"You hush old man, or you'll be sorry!"

I wondered if Naomi might abuse her husband.

"Umm yes, well," Dave said. "Might you know where Naomi is living now?"

Naomi got up and went to a side table. She took out a worn address book and started to look through it. Mark went to say something and then thought better of saying anything more to upset his wife.

"Here it is. She moved to Mount Airy. Nice town. It's where Andy Griffith grew up. Here's the address."

"Well you have been a great help Naomi. Thank you for your hospitality."

We all got up to leave and as we walked out we could hear Mark apologizing to his wife over and over. I couldn't help but laugh. Here was this woman who couldn't have weighed more than 100 pounds keeping her big husband in line.

We got back in the car and Larry said, "Where to, Dave?"

"Let's drop off Graham and then take a trip to Mount Airy," Dave said, "unless you want to take a ride Graham?

"Wish I could," Graham answered. "I love visiting Mayberry."

"I always wanted to visit Mayberry," I said.

"Where?" Larry said. "I thought we were going to Mount Airy."

We all just laughed. Ahh youth, I thought.

We drove back to the Sheriff's office, thanking Graham and then headed toward Mount Airy. While I thought about the case, Dave explained who Andy Griffith was and the town of Mayberry. Then he told him about the show, Barney Fife, Aunt Bea and Opie.

All I could think about was that this case was now speeding up. We were on the killer's trail now and I was sure we would catch him soon. Of course we still didn't know if Dr. Waters had seen Jasmine King, but I was betting he did. Of course there was still Waxman as a possible suspect. But I was placing my money on Dr. Malcom Waters.

Chapter Thirty - Four

Friday, Mount Airy, North Carolina, 3:10 pm

We drove through some beautiful mountains and then entered the town of Mount Airy. As we drove in we saw a big sign saying, ***Welcome to Mount Airy! Home of Andy Griffith***. We then saw a sign announcing the annual Mayberry Days.

"Looks like we might get to see Deputy Fife," I said with a laugh.

As we drove down the main street we saw crowds of people. Along the way we saw a replica of Floyd's Barber Shop and the jail where Andy and Barney would lock up Otis every Saturday night. We found a spot off the main road on a side street, and decided to find Jasmine King's apartment on foot. As we walked along the street, taking in the sights, we saw the marked police car Andy drove on the show. Dave and I were getting a big kick out of it all, while Larry just looked dumbfounded.

Also along the streets were several gift shops with pictures of the show's cast, mugs and other similar knick knacks.

"I'm going to have to find something for Trace before we leave," I said.

"Me too," Dave replied.

Jasmine king lived on Blue Mountain Avenue and after asking someone impersonating Ernest T. Bass, we found it a few blocks ahead. Now we just had to hope she was home.

We walked up to a small apartment building and

found her name next to a set of buzzers. We rang hers and a second later the front door buzzed, and we walked in. Jasmine King lived in Apartment 202, so we walked up the stairs. As we got to the second floor, we saw a middle- aged African American woman standing near the open door to 202. She was a thin woman, with gray hair. She had on glasses and a tee shirt with a picture of Barney Fife on it.

"You must be from the FBI," she said. "Naomi gave me a call the second you left her. You're lucky she called me. I was going to go and enjoy the crowds. Might as well come on in."

We stepped into a neat looking apartment and were escorted to the living room. There was an upright piano against one wall, several comfortable looking chairs, a sofa and two end tables. On the walls were some pictures, but nothing of family.

We showed her our ID's and sat down.

"Would you all like some tea?" she asked.

"No thank you Ma'am," Dave answered for us all. "Nice piano."

"Well, it's not as nice as the grand I had back in Greensboro, but it does the job. Now, what do you want to ask me?"

"You are aware your ex-husband was killed?" Dave asked.

"Yes, I heard it from Naomi. I guess the law didn't know where I had moved to officially notify me."

"How do you feel about it?"

"Don't feel much at all. I loved Stuart when we were younger, and when we got married. But when he started hitting me, my love for him just dried up like a peach on a hot August day. So I suppose I don't feel anything."

"Your husband abused you. Naomi said you left him a few times and went to a shelter in Raleigh."

"Yes I did. Should never have gone back to him any of the times I left. But finally, the Doc convinced me I would be better off leaving him. Have my life back and be happier. I finally took his advice and left Stuart. Just sorry I couldn't take my grand piano with me. I wonder if it is still in the house."

"We were in the house and I'm afraid there was no piano inside. I'm sorry but I think your husband must have gotten rid of it."

"Figures. He always was a mean spiteful man. Oh well, what's done is done."

"You mentioned a doctor?"

"Yes, Dr. Waters. I saw him once or twice for a few sessions. He wasn't there one time I ran away. He used to travel around to other shelters. He was a nice man, very compassionate and smart too. I finally took his advice and left."

"Did you ever meet a man named Kevin Waxman?"

"Hmmm, I don't seem to recollect the name, but I suppose I could have. Was he a doctor too?"

"Actually he is a social services worker."

"Then no. Never had any need for one of them."

"Well, I think we have everything we need . Any other questions guys?"

"I have just one Mrs. King," I said. "Do you want to know how your husband was killed or maybe why?"

"Well, I figure the sins of my husband finally caught up with him. Don't matter how or why. He's gonna be judged by a higher power than me."

"Thank you for your time ma'am," Dave said.

We left her and made our way back into town. There were too many people walking around to discuss the new information. We walked into a few of the souvenir shops and Dave bought Melissa a signed picture of Andy Griffith and a mug with Barney Fife on it. I got a picture of Deputy Fife and an Aunt Bea cookbook for Trace.

Then we passed the statue of Andy and Opie in bronze outside the library. The statue showed them just like in the beginning of the show. Walking along with fishing poles on their shoulders. We had Larry take a picture of Dave and I in front of it. Then Larry asked if he could get one with Dave and then me.

We finally got back to the car and decided we didn't need to stop back at the Sheriff's office. Dave called Graham and thanked him for his help. We informed him of what Jasmine King had told us. Dave asked him to check with the Spencer's to find out if they knew what had happened with Jasmine's grand piano. I thought it was nice of him to ask.

Dave called our pilot to tell him we were heading back to the airport. We decided there was no point in talking to any of the TSA workers Stuart had worked with.

Larry dropped us off and we thanked him for all his help. He asked Dave to keep him in mind if we ever needed another agent to join our team.

When we were settled on the jet and winging our way home, we finally had a chance to talk.

"Well," I said, "that makes three who definitely spoke with Dr. Malcolm Waters."

"I'd say he is our number one suspect Warren," Dave replied.

"Still, I don't like the coincidence of Kevin Waxman seeing Peggy Walters and then moving to Boston."

"I don't like it either. Maybe the guys who were watching him will be able to give us some new info. We also have to find out if the counselors who saw Mrs. Tomlinson had any connections to Waxman or Waters.

"Let's hope Cory Nash found out something about Mrs. Baxter. And maybe we can get Detective Stone to run down the name of the counselors Mrs. Tomlinson saw."

We both sat back, each of us thinking about the case. I also was thinking about Trace and the possibility of us adopting. I had a lot on my mind but somehow I fell asleep, lulled by the sound of the engines.

Chapter Thirty - Five

Malcolm and Jocelyn Waters had just finished a round of golf at their club. They played with another couple and were just going over their scores. Unfortunately, Malcolm had double bogeyed the last two holes, letting the other couple win by two strokes.

"I thought you had us Malcolm," Will Harper said with a big grin.

"Yeah, Yeah, and we would have if I didn't screw up the last two holes!" Malcolm replied.

"It's okay Malcolm, we'll take them next week," Jocelyn said laughing.

"Don't you count on it," Carla Harper replied. "You up for a game with just the ladies this week Jocelyn?"

"I'll give you a call, I have a lot to do this week."

"You should cut down on all the charity work and doing things for the club."

"I keep telling her that," Malcolm said with a laugh.

"Are you guys staying for lunch?" Will asked.

"Not today," Jocelyn said. "Brandon has his last swim meet this afternoon and Malcolm is definitely not missing it!"

"Okay guys, see you next week."

Malcolm and Jocelyn rode their golf cart out to the parking lot and placed their clubs and shoes into the trunk of their car. Then Malcolm returned the cart and got into the driver's seat.

As he pulled out of the lot he said, "I hope we have time to take a shower before taking Brandon for his meet."

"Plenty of time Malcolm, and if you play your cards right, I might just join you," Jocelyn said with a smile, although feeling a shudder run through her.

"Well then, I might just risk a ticket for speeding!"

Laughing, Jocelyn said, "Take it easy tiger. Although, for double bogeying the last two holes, I'm not sure you deserve to take a shower with me."

They drove on and arrived home twenty minutes later. Malcolm went up to the bedroom while Jocelyn went in search of her son. She finally found him outside in their pool, swimming laps. She stood there watching him glide through the water effortlessly, his long arms moving in a smooth rhythm. When he took a break, she walked over with a towel as he lifted himself out of the water.

"Don't wear yourself out before the meet son," she said.

"Nah, just keeping loose mom," he replied. Then hesitantly he asked, "Is dad coming this time?"

"Yes he is. Said he wouldn't miss it for anything!"

"That's great!"

"You know Brandon, your Dad works very hard and what he does is very important."

"I know mom, but he's always so busy and you are too."

Ruffling his long wet hair, Jocelyn said, "I know we are. Now go get ready. Dad and I will be downstairs, ready to go in about an hour."

Brandon took off lightly running and then stopped.

"Hey," he said. "Did you guys beat the Harper's?"

"Not this time, but we'll get them next week."

Jocelyn then made her way upstairs. She really didn't want to join Malcolm in the shower, but It had been some time since they had sex. Although she never really enjoyed it, she knew it was still something she would endure for his sake. His travelling and sessions always seemed to work him up, winding him tighter and tighter at home. This was the only way to get him to relax.

She went into the bedroom and heard the shower running. Taking a deep breath, she undressed, catching a look of her naked self in the mirror. She knew she wasn't what most people considered beautiful. Her face was pretty enough, and she had a dazzling smile. But she was too broad in the shoulders and had thick legs and arms. But her breasts were not too small or big, and they were still firm. She knew her breasts were her best feature judging by the way her husband loved to fondle and suck on her nipples. Still, she had a certain look, one which obviously still turned on her husband. Not bad for nineteen years of marriage.

Taking another deep breath, she prepared for the shower. They would soap each other up, hug and kiss a bit. Then she would get down on her knees and she would take his penis in her mouth. She wouldn't bring him to orgasm, that was never going to happen. Then they would get into bed, and he would make love to her. It was an ordeal but one she had come to accept. At least once in a while.

She knew she wouldn't have to deal with him for another two weeks. This next week he was leaving for two weeks. He was going to make several stops in a few different states. She really didn't mind too much. After all, she was a very busy woman.

Of course when he finally returned home, he would be very tense and expecting her to have sex at least once. Oh, well she thought as she opened the glass door and stepped into the shower. She did love her husband and the life he had given her. Putting up with him making love to her was just her personal cross to bear. It was one of many she endured.

Chapter Thirty - Six

After returning to New York late Saturday, Dave and I had stopped at the office. We briefed ADD Teller and he had told us both to take the weekend to unwind. We had been going at it hard and needed a break. Dave and I didn't argue.

After writing up some notes, we split the calls to the rest of the team telling them to relax and enjoy their weekend. We would meet to confirm at the office on Monday morning, bright and early, and ready to go. As we were leaving, Dave asked me if Trace and I would like to come over Saturday night for a barbecue. I told him it sounded great, and I would give him a call to confirm after speaking with Trace.

Trace and I had arrived at their home in Mill Basin, Brooklyn. It was a nice looking ranch home with a double garage. In the driveway was a basketball hoop and I was surprised because I never knew Dave did any type of sports activity. There was a large picture window in the front, with a nice flower garden underneath it.

We knocked and Melissa opened the door, saying Dave was out back getting the steaks ready. We both hugged her, and it was now obvious she was pregnant. Then she showed us around the home.

There were three bedrooms and one of them was decorated for the new baby with toys and wallpaper in pastel colors, but no furniture. Melissa said they were waiting to buy a crib and changer once they knew if they were having a boy or girl. I supposed they were playing it safe.

Then there was a guest bedroom which looked like it was used as an office for Dave. The master was large and had a great bathroom with a huge shower and free standing tub. We ended the tour up some stairs to a converted attic. Here Melissa had an art studio and there were several paintings around the room.

I saw one in particular leaning against a wall. It was a scene of Central Park, near Bethesda Fountain. The time of year was autumn, with the trees bare and the sky gray. In it a lone man was sitting on the fountain, throwing feed to a single squirrel. Something about it made me both sad and happy.

Melissa saw me looking at it and said, "You like that one?"

"Very much," I replied. "Something about it."

"Well then it's yours."

"No way, I couldn't accept this!"

"Of course you can, and I insist. I'd rather it was with someone who liked it instead of stuck up in this dusty attic."

"Well I don't like it, I love it! Thank you Melissa."

We went downstairs with me carrying the painting out to the car, and then out to the back. Dave was standing over a grill and he was wearing an apron with *Kiss the Cook!* on it. I started laughing and walked over to him.

"I've got to get a picture of this for the team," I said.

"You do and I'll have to shoot you Warren!" he replied.

We both laughed and he told me to get a beer for myself and one for him out of a cooler sitting nearby. Melissa and Trace were in the house getting the table set. After taking a drink of my beer, I sat down on a deck chair.

"Nice place Dave," I said. "I can't believe this is the first time I have been here."

"Well it's about time," he said as he turned the steaks. "How do you guys like your steaks?"

"I like mine medium rare, but Trace won't take a bite unless it is well, well, done."

"I hate to ruin a good steak like that, but she will get what she wants."

We soon were inside eating a great meal. The steaks were perfect and there was corn on the cob, potato salad, Cole slaw, and mashed potatoes. He had opened a nice wine as well. Of course, Melissa stuck with water.

The talk was nice as well, covering a bunch of subjects, none of them about work or the possible adoption.

When we finished the meal, the women went outside to enjoy the night air and Dave, and I cleaned up.

As he was putting some dishes into the dishwasher Dave said, "So any thoughts on our Brutal Abuser?"

I carried over the glasses and replied, "I actually think we need to get a look at Dr. Waters, his home and his background. We need to find out everything we can."

"Yeah, Carl got some info, but I agree. We need to know everything we can. Billy and Lou drove out to his house but that's about it. What about Waxman?"

"We can probably either rule him in or out just by trying to track down his movements. If we can prove he wasn't anywhere near where any of our victims were killed , we can forget about him as a suspect."

"Okay, but how do we do that without tipping him off?

"Good question. Let's think about it and see if any of the others have a good idea. For now, I think we should join our gorgeous wives out on the deck."

We went outside, grabbed two beers and sat down with our wives.

"Has Tracy told you anything about the adoption process yet Warren?" Melissa asked me.

"Actually, we haven't had too much time to talk about it," I said. "But I know you two have probably got everything worked out by now."

"Not everything, but a lot," Trace said. "The first thing we have to do is get a room ready for a child. Then a social worker will come out to inspect it after we make an application. We can go about it two ways."

"Two ways? What two ways?"

"The first would be an adoption and the second would be to foster a child with an adoption down the road."

"I'm not sure what you guys think," Dave said, "but I kinda think if you want a child to raise as your own, why go through fostering first? I mean it seems like that would be like taking a car for a test drive, when you already know you are there to buy."

"What do you think, War?" Trace asked me.

I took a minute to think about it and said, "I think if we are going to get a child, let's try to go straight to adopting one."

"Great! I was thinking the same thing. Now, all we have to do is find a child."

"Uh huh. And just how do we go about doing that?"

"Oh War, don't you give it another thought. Melissa and I will take care of everything."

We spent the rest of the night laughing and joking, telling each other war stories about work. I found out Dave had played basketball in college and considered going pro. But the Destroyer killing his family when he was a kid put an end to any thought of it happening.

I told him some screw ups I did when I was a rookie and then Melissa and Trace told us some stories as well of their growing up. We all got to know each other a bit more and it was just what I needed after pushing so hard on our serial killer case.

Before we left, Dave and Melissa sat us both down in the living room.

Melissa said, "I know we haven't been friends too long, but Dave and I have decided the two of you should be the godparents of our new baby."

Trace was shocked and said, "Us? Me and Warren?"

"I don't see anyone else in the room."

Trace actually began to cry, and I stood and shook Dave's hand. Trace hugged Melissa and then Dave.

"Of course we will!" Trace said.

It turned out to be the perfect ending to a great night. On the drive home all Trace could talk about was being godparents, the new baby and our adopting a child of our own. I had never seen her so happy, and it made me smile.

When we got home the first thing I did was to hang up the picture in my study. Then I went upstairs to my wife and made love to her. I was also never happier in my life.

Chapter Thirty - Seven

I was sitting in the conference room, going over some notes when the rest of the team came in. As usual, Aaron had a box of donuts and took out three for himself. The others grabbed a donut, got some coffee and sat down. We were waiting for Dave, and he finally came in twenty minutes later. In his hand were a bunch of papers.

"Good morning everyone," Dave said. "I hope everyone had a great weekend and you all are relaxed and ready to get going. I have received some news from Cory Nash and Detective Terry Stone. Let me tell you what they have found out and then we can discuss our next moves."

We all settled down and gave Dave our full attention.

"Okay then. Cory Nash said he tracked down three shelters and one safe house. None of them were too willing to give out information concerning Mrs. Baxter having been there or not."

"Damn, too bad they wouldn't talk," Billy said.

"If you will let me continue Billy," Dave said, "they wouldn't confirm Mrs. Baxter had been to any of them, but the safe home confirmed Dr. Malcolm Waters is a regular visitor and has been treating women there for a number of years."

"I guess Dr. Waters is our killer then," Billy said.

"Not so fast Billy," I said. "You should know better by now. He is looking like our best suspect at the moment but what did I teach you?"

Hanging his head he said, "We only have a confirmed killer when we catch them in the act, we have indisputable evidence and or a confession."

"Right, so let's not jump the gun. Anything else Dave?"

"I have a report from Detective Terry Stone as well," he said. "She tracked down two counselors Mrs. Tomlinson spoke with. One of them said he had never heard of Dr. Waters. But the other one said he does consult with him. He goes over all of his sessions with the abused women he meets with. Then he sends Dr. Waters his notes. The counselor consults at several shelters, including the shelter where Mrs. Tomlinson had gone to. So although it is not a direct connection, it does connect Waters to her. One more thing. Terry Stone said to say hi to, now let me get this right, that cute, sexy FBI Agent Billy."

"Wow, I can't believe she thought of me," Billy said with a big smile.

I kicked him under the table.

"Ummm, I mean, that was nice of her."

"What's our next step?" Carl asked.

"Obviously we have to find out everything we can on Dr. Waters. And I mean everything going back to where he was raised, who his parents were, what school he got his degree from, if he is married and has any kids etc."

"Carl and I can handle it Dave," Aaron said.

"Okay. Next we need eyes on him to see where he goes. We know he travels around to different shelters and safe houses, but we don't know exactly where. For that matter, we don't know how he gets around."

"Do you think we can get a wiretap on his home and cell?" Lou asked.

"I think we could, but I want some more information on him first Lou. Once we know more we can do more to find out if he is our killer."

"What about Kevin Waxman?" I asked. "Does anyone have any ideas how we can find out if he has been in the same areas at the time of the murders. Also if he has any connection to Dr. Waters."

"Do you think it is possible for Dr. Waters and Waxman to be working together?"

"It crossed my mind. What if Waters picks out the target through his sessions with abused women, and then Waxman carries out the killing?"

"I suppose it is a possibility. Now how do we find out about Waxman?"

"I have an idea, but I don't think any of you will like it," Billy said.

"Well you won't know till you tell us Billy," Dave said.

"Waxman likes to rock climb. Guys like him climb every weekend if possible, especially in the summer months. I used to do some climbing myself. What if we keep an eye on him and when he goes somewhere to climb, I happen to be there too. I can talk with him and maybe find out where he has been climbing. It might get us the information we need."

Dave looked at me and I just shook my head. It might work but what if Waxman was involved and he suspected Billy. If they were on the side of a mountain, with no ropes or safety gear, it wouldn't take too much to possibly injure or even kill Billy. I didn't think it was worth the risk.

"Are there any other suggestions on how to figure out if Waxman is involved one way or another?" Dave asked.

"Ummm, maybe I could get close to him," Lou said, looking Billy in the eye as she said it. "I'm sure we can get his supervisor to let me work there as well, and then I could try to draw him out. I could try to seduce him."

"I like that idea much better," I said, "except for the seducing part."

I figured Lou was sending a message to Billy after what Dave had said about Detective Stone.

Dave was thinking and then finally said, "I like both ideas. Lou, we will get you a position working where Waxman is working. I'll ask Teller to arrange it. Billy, you will be Lou's brother. The two of you will go to Boston and get close to Waxman. Lou, you will introduce him to Billy once he brings up rock climbing. You will have to get him to tell you he climbs. If you find out something first, then Billy will not go climbing. If you don't, then Billy it will be up to you."

"I know it's up to you Dave, but I'm not sure I really like this idea," I said.

"I'm going to get Billy some protection, Warren. I'll find two agents who climb to be in the area and keep a close eye on him. I really don't see any other way."

"Okay boss. The two of you just be very careful."

"We will," Billy said, and he looked like he had just won the lottery.

We finished up working things out and then Dave went to Teller to get Lou working with Kevin Waxman. Carl and Aaron got to working on finding out everything possible on Waters.

I went into my office and thought about our plans. I wasn't thrilled with Billy going rock climbing with a possible murderer, but he was an adult and a Special Agent with the FBI. I supposed I couldn't coddle him or watch over him anymore.

I couldn't just sit and wait for more information to be found out, so I found Dave and said I was going out. I wanted to talk with someone. He didn't ask me what it was and just nodded. I knew we had the best behavioral pro-filers anywhere, and they had given me a profile, but there was someone who I trusted more. I headed out to see if the walk over to One Police Plaza would be worth it.

Chapter Thirty - Eight

One Police Plaza, known to cops as 1PP, is a large, ugly, red-brown square edifice located in lower Manhattan, not too far from FBI headquarters. Going east on Chambers Street, it is diagonally behind City Hall, no pun intended. The walkway leading up to the front entrance is made of cobblestone, roughly the same color as the building.

There are a few sculptures located in front—large metal shapes welded together that must have some meaning, although I have no idea what that might be. A large Bronze Plaque in the main lobby hangs on a wall in full view when you walk in. On it are the names of officers killed in the line of duty. There were way too many names on it. I knew Tom Delaney's name should be on it.

I went through two checkpoints to get into the building using my FBI ID and badge. Then I spoke to a female officer, telling her I wanted to see Deputy Inspector Ellen Vance. She made a call, checked my ID again, and told me to take the first elevator up to the eighth floor.

I thanked her and as I passed by the plaque with the names of dead officers, I said a silent prayer. I got on the elevator and when I stepped off on the eighth floor, Ellen was standing right there.

Ellen Vance and I had worked a few cases when I was in Midtown North. Back then she was a beautiful young woman with long black hair, green eyes and a figure any man would drool over. As I looked at her now, more than twelve years later, I saw she had some gray in her hair, now wore glasses but was still a beautiful woman. I was sure she hadn't lost any of her smarts as well.

"Well, well, well," she said with her hands on her hips. "Mr. Bigshot, Special Agent of the FBI, has come to visit!"

"Awww cut it out Ellen," I said, "and give me a hug."

"I'll give you more than a hug Warren," and she gave me a light kiss and a hug. "Come on down to my office."

We walked down a tiled hall with pictures of police uniforms through the years. There were also pictures of vehicles through the years and patches from police departments around the country. Finally we arrived at a large corner office with a uniformed officer sitting out front.

Ellen said to him, "This is Special Agent Warren Temple of the FBI, formerly First Grade Homicide Detective of the NYPD, Harry."

Harry stood and shook my hand and said, "I've heard of you sir. Nice to meet you."

"Just call me Warren," I said.

We walked into her office, and I let a low whistle escape my lips. Her office looked to be about ten times the size of any office I ever had. There were large glass windows at the corner of it, giving a great view of lower Manhattan and Wall street. To the south I could see the new Freedom Tower, where the Twin Towers used to stand.

There was a nice oak desk filled with paperwork, a computer and two phones. Then there was an area with a comfortable looking couch, several chairs and a glass coffee table. Finally an area with coffee, fruits, snacks and a few bottles of high end bottles of scotch.

"Wow, Ellen," I said. "I guess being a Deputy Inspector has its perks."

"It does but as you can see I still have a ton of paperwork," she replied. "I'm in charge of the K-9 unit, Mounted and Emergency Services. Keeps me hopping, but I love it. Let's sit down and you can tell me why you are here. I also want to hear how you became a friggin' Feeb!"

We spent the next half hour catching up. Going over our careers, talking about old friends and laughing a great deal.

Ellen said, "I was very sad to hear about Tom dying. Unfortunately I was out of town for the funeral."

"Yeah, I miss Tom," I said. "Ellen, I'm here to pick your brain a bit. You worked in the SUV, special victims unit, for a few years, right?"

"Yes I did. It was both the most rewarding work and the hardest to deal with. All those children and women were sexually assaulted and abused. But putting away their monsters made it all worthwhile. And believe me, they were monsters. What did you want to know?"

"Did you ever work with any psychiatrists or psychologists?"

"Some, but not too many. Once we had statements from the victims, they were cared for by social workers and doctors. But unless there was new information told to them, we really didn't have too much contact."

"I'm working a case now where the abusers of women and children are being murdered. In each case there is a psychiatrist named Dr. Malcolm Waters connected to each of the women. He apparently goes around to numerous shelters and safe homes to treat women. For free I might add."

"It's unusual but not unheard of. I've known of several doctors who volunteer their time. Where have the murders taken place?"

"Two in Massachusetts, one in Connecticut, one in Newark and the most recent in Greensboro, North Carolina."

"Wow, so he gets around. Over what period of time?"

""We think back about four years or more, and the most recent was last week. What I want to know is, do you think a doctor who volunteers his time would really then go after the husbands of these women victims?"

"Tough question Warren. Doesn't the mighty FBI have their own behavioral profilers? I'm sure they could give you an answer."

"Yeah they could and they did, but I trust you more. So what do you think?"

Ellen got up and paced, something she always did while thinking.

She stopped and said, "I think it is a very good possibility. Hearing about abuse over and over and not really being able to do anything about it would start to make anyone angry. Helping the women might not be enough after a number of years. Plus he would have the men's names, locations and habits direct from the victims. But, I would think it would take more than just hearing from the women and children."

"What more?"

"I think he would have been abused by either his father or mother in the past. There would probably need to be a personal act which happened to him. At least that's my thoughts on it."

"Sounds about right to me Ellen. As usual, you are smarter than me."

"Oh, cut it out Warren. You were the most intuitive detective I have ever known." Looking at her watch she said, "But I have a meeting with the Chief in five minutes. Don't be a stranger!"

I gave her a kiss and hug and left the office. On the way down in the elevator, I saw a few guys I knew, and we each promised to get in touch. Unfortunately I knew we probably wouldn't.

Back on the street, I thought about what Ellen had said. We would need to find out if Dr. Malcolm Waters had ever been abused in the past. Of course if he had been and it was reported to the police, there was a good chance the records would be sealed because he would have been a juvenile. If he hadn't been abused, it didn't mean he wasn't our killer, but it would be a better sign if he was. I would have to go over this with Dave as soon as I got back to HQ.

Chapter Thirty - Nine

Dr. Waters was sipping on some tea, looking out at the bright blue sky and clouds below him. He had left Jocelyn early this morning. He told her he might be gone for a week or two, depending on the victims of abuse he would see. He was going to go back to Maine, and then start working his way south, ending up in Tampa Florida before coming back home. Once or twice a year he made this big trip visiting at least ten shelters and safe homes.

Of course he didn't tell her about the two side trips he would make. He was looking forward to them more than he could say. He knew if Jocelyn ever found out about his little side trips she would be so angry she might even divorce him. He loved her and never wanted to lose her, but he felt a compulsion he couldn't resist.

He knew what he was doing was wrong, so wrong in fact that if any law enforcement officers found out, he might spend some of his life in prison. Still, what he was doing was something he couldn't resist. Sometimes he thought he would be able to stop, but he never could. Besides, they all deserved what they got. And he deserved what he would get too.

Between leaving Maine and then going to New Hampshire, he would make a detour. He was smiling and looking forward to it and knew he would be able to do it. He was always well prepared and never had been caught. This time would be no different.

Chapter Forty

Tuesday, 307 Charles Street, Boston MA, 10:40 am

ADD Teller had come through getting Lou a job at the same place where Kevin Waxman worked. They had gotten to their hotel late the night before, two rooms of course. They were pretty sure Teller knew they were together, but they still had to get two rooms so there would be no questions. If Teller's boss ever found out, it would be bad for him, them and probably Dave as well.

They spent some of the night eating from room service, discussing their plan and then making love. Lou had gotten up early to get to her new job, and Billy had slept in. He was planning on going to a rock climbing gym where he could get some time training. If he did go rock climbing with Waxman this weekend, he didn't want to look too rusty. He also didn't want to fall and get injured or die.

Teller had arranged for two other agents with rock climbing experience to be in the area. If Billy did go to climb, he would call them, and they would be there as well. It wouldn't be suspicious because many times there were a lot of enthusiasts climbing in the same area. How they would be able to prevent any injuries or possible death to Billy was something both Lou and Billy had discussed. Unfortunately, Lou was very worried, and Billy acted like there was no problem with him climbing. Lou figured it was dumb macho attitude.

Lou had shown up for work and was given a desk right near Waxman. Her new supervisor introduced her to several people including Waxman. He appeared to Lou to be a quiet, introspective person. He hardly looked up when she was introduced. Getting to know him was not going to be so easy.

Lou spent the morning on the phone and was given a few cases to work on. She did her best to actually do some work. One file described an eleven year old girl with a brother who was only five. The kids were found living in a burnt out building, scrounging for food. They were discovered by the police; the kids had been abandoned by their mother who was a crack addict. Their father was unknown. Now they were waiting to be placed in foster care. The hard part would be keeping them together.

Another file dealt with a man who was abusing his girlfriend and her two kids. Lou figured this would be the perfect case to ask for help from Waxman.

"Excuse me Mr. Waxman," she said. "I'm sorry to bother you but I think I need some advice on this case. Could you give me a hand?"

Waxman looked up and mumbled, "Ummm, I guess you should call me Kevin since we will bc working together."

"Great! Please call me Lou, everyone does."

"Okay Lou, let me see the case."

Lou handed over the file and stood close to him as he read. The more he read, the redder his face turned, and his hands actually started shaking.

"This bastard!" he finally said. "Every one of them needs to be locked up or put down like dogs!"

"Whoa Kevin," Lou said. "I agree they need to be locked up, but put down, like dogs? Isn't that a bit strong?"

"How long have you worked in Social Services?"

"Going on one year right now. I transferred here because my brother Billy wanted to move to Boston for work and his hobby."

"Well once you have been doing this for a bit longer, your mind might change about putting these men down."

"I suppose you are right Kevin. What do you think my first move should be?"

"Go talk to them at the safe house. It says here they are staying at the Women and Children's home on Bently and Main street. Talk with them and see if they are getting any treatment from a counselor or doctor."

"A doctor? Do doctors treat abused women and children at shelters and safe homes?"

"Not at all of them, but I know of a few psychiatrists who make regular visits."

"Oh, okay. Well, could you maybe go with me to the safe house. I don't have a car because my brother is using it. He dropped me off today. I wouldn't know how to get there by bus, and I don't want to take a cab."

"Well, I suppose I can take you. We can leave in ten minutes."

"Great! I'll just go to the ladies room first."

Lou went into the restroom and after checking no one was there, she called Billy.

"Hey Lou, what's up?" Billy asked. "I was just about to start climbing."

"I was introduced to Waxman, and I even have a desk right next to him. He looks a bit nerdy, but I saw his arms. He definitely works out and is strong."

"Did you find out anything about him?"

"I showed him a file I'm supposed to work on. It's about a woman and her two children who had been abused by her boyfriend. They are at a safe house. Waxman almost went ballistic when I showed him the file and he read about the man abusing his girlfriend and kids. He even said men like that should be put down like dogs!"

"Wow! I guess he might be angry enough to do the killings. What are you doing next?"

"I told him I didn't have a car; you dropped me off. So he is taking me to the safe house."

"Okay, but be careful. I'll catch a cab and pick up your car while you are out. Then I'll pick you up later. What time would work?"

"Be outside a little before five. I want to introduce you to him if I can."

"See you then and be careful. We don't know how much of a nut he might be."

Lou hung up and saw Kevin waiting near the exit. She walked up to him and together they walked out. He had a beige sedan, just the kind of car nobody notices. He didn't open the door for her. Instead he got in on the driver's side and waited for her to get in. Then without another word, he pulled out of the lot.

Chapter Forty - One

Lou had tried to engage Kevin in conversation on the ride to the safe house, but he said he didn't talk while driving. It wasn't safe to take your mind off the road. So Lou had kept quiet, not wanting to irritate him in any way. The ride only took twenty minutes, and they arrived in front of a plain looking three story home in a relatively nice neighborhood.

They got out and Lou looked the house over. If you didn't know it was a safe house, you would never know. The grass was freshly mowed and there were flowers planted on either side of the walk. The house was painted a neutral brown, and she was able to see a fence surrounding the back area. All of the windows were covered with drapes. Lou took a closer look as they walked up to the door and counted three security cameras. She was sure there were more around the sides and out back.

Kevin hit a buzzer and a few seconds later, a voice came through a speaker.

"Yes, can I help you?" the voice said.

"Kevin Waxman and Louise Carmichael from Social Services," he said. Then he held up his ID and a buzzer sounded. He opened the door, and they walked in.

They walked into a foyer and there was a middle aged woman standing in front of them. She was dressed in a plain dress with no makeup on her face, giving her a stern look.

"Hello Mr. Waxman," she said. "Please let me see your ID's again."

"Of course Mrs Kahn," Kevin said, even though Mrs. Kahn knew him well.

They held up their ID's and then they were escorted into an office. Mrs. Kahn sat down behind a desk, folded her hands in front of her and just looked Lou over.

"I don't believe I have ever seen you Miss..."

"Carmichael," Lou said. "Louise Carmichael, Mrs Kahn. I just transferred here from New York City."

Dave had told her to say she had transferred from New York figuring it would be harder for Waxman to check up on her, if he was suspicious or just wanted to.

"Mr. Waxman, you know you need to make an appointment to visit our women or children," Mrs. Kahn said. "You aren't setting a good example for Ms. Carmichael, being new to Boston."

"I know Mrs. Kahn, but seeing how Miss Carmichael is new, I figured I would bring her the first time she comes here," Kevin said. "She has been put in charge of the Tanya Washington case."

"Well I suppose it will be all right this time. Come with me and I will take you to the room where interviews are done. Then I will get Tanya. Do you want to speak to the children now as well?"

"Ummm, no," Lou said. "I think we will talk with Mrs. Washington first."

"It's not Mrs. Washington. She isn't married."

Kevin gave her a look. She screwed up by saying Mrs. Washington. He obviously was a stickler for knowing the facts. She would have to be more diligent.

Mrs. Kahn got up and led them to the interview room. Lou began to ask Kevin something, but he held his finger up to his mouth, shushing her. She looked around and saw there was a camera in the corner. It probably had a microphone in it as well. Lou wasn't sure if it was legal for recordings to be made while interviews were conducted. She would have to ask Kevin later.

A minute later, Mrs. Kahn escorted a frail looking African American woman into the room. She was looking down as she entered. She had on a worn sundress and slippers on her feet. Mrs. Kahn introduced them to her and was about to leave when Kevin spoke up.

"Please turn off the camera Mrs. Kahn," he said.

Mrs. Kahn nodded and left.

Lou would have to ask Kevin about the camera later. Maybe when others used this room they needed the camera to make a record.

Lou waited a second for Kevin to say something and then realized this was her case, and he was letting her do the interview. Lou had done hundreds of interviews with criminals and sometimes victims of crimes. She figured she could get through this one without tipping Kevin off.

"Ms. Washington, my name is Louise Carmichael but please call me Lou," she began. "May I call you Tanya?"

Tanya just nodded.

"Great Tanya. I read your file, but I would prefer hearing from you. Would you mind telling me a bit about yourself, your children and your boyfriend?"

Tanya took a deep breath and said, "Tommy ain't no boyfriend of mine no more. He tried to make me work the streets. I did that years ago, before my babies were born and I ain't going to do it again. When I refused he began beating me. Not where you could see, but he punched me, kicked me and put out cigarettes on my arms and legs."

Tanya lifted her dress and showed them the burns and bruises. Lou glanced at Kevin and saw he was getting very angry.

"Please continue Tanya," Lou said.

"I could take most of what he was doing to me, but then he hit my son, Vince," Tanya said. "He's only 13 and thinks he's a man. He was trying to protect me and his sister Nedra. She's eight. Anyways, that was the last straw. It was his apartment, and I had nowhere else to go. Now I don't know what we are gonna do. Can't stay here forever."

"First off, we have a lot of things we can do to help you," Lou said. "There are many programs and funds to help you get your life started again. For the moment, staying here is the best thing for you. I will get started to find you a place to live and a job. Would you like that?"

"You gonna do all that for me?"

"I'm certainly going to try Tanya. Can I ask you one more thing?"

"Yes...Lou."

"Was your boyfriend arrested?"

"I don't know. When I first got here Mrs. Kahn called the police and I told them what he had done. But I don't know if they did anything to him. I sure hope so."

Lou was about to say something when Kevin finally spoke.

"Tanya, I need you to agree to talk with a counselor or doctor while you are here. I know there is a good doctor who visits here. His name is Dr. Waters."

Lou thought she might jump out of her chair when Kevin mentioned Dr. Waters! He confirmed he had a connection with him.

Kevin continued, "And don't worry about your ex-boyfriend Tanya. He will get what is coming to him."

"I think we should go now, but I will be back in touch, Tanya," Lou said.

We stood and said goodbye to her. Then Kevin asked Mrs. Kahn when Dr. Waters was scheduled to return.

Mrs. Kahn said he was making a visit in the next few weeks. She assured us Tanya was not going anywhere, and she would be well taken care of. We said our goodbyes and exited the house.

As they left, Lou checked her watch. Seeing it was now close to one, she stopped walking to talk with Kevin. Once they were back in the car he wouldn't want to talk.

"Wow," she said. "That was intense."

"Yes, seeing these women and children who have been abused takes a great deal out of you," Kevin said. "It gets me very angry."

"Well how about we go to lunch. My treat since you were nice enough to take me here. Plus I still could use your opinion on my next move."

Kevin checked his watch and then nodded and said, "I know a good diner near here. But you don't have to treat me Louise, we can go Dutch."

They got into the car and Kevin pulled out. Lou kept on thinking how in one morning she had found out so much. She couldn't wait to tell Billy and then call Dave with the new information.

Chapter Forty - Two

I was sitting in Dave's office going over some of the information Carl and Aaron had run down concerning Dr. Malcolm Waters. They had gathered a lot of information, but going over it didn't seem to give us much insight into the man.

"It says here, our Dr. Waters grew up in a very wealthy home," I said. "His parents both worked in finance for a major bank, as well as having many real estate investments. They made their fortunes at a young age, plus it appears they inherited a great deal from each of their parents. They lived in a big home located in Westchester. When Waters was twenty, both his parents were killed in a car accident. He inherited somewhere in the neighborhood of fifty million dollars."

"Holy cow!" Dave replied.

"Dr. Waters has a mansion In Great Neck, and he lives there with his wife Jocelyn and son Brandon. Billy and Lou saw it, but they weren't able to do much else. He's been married about 19 years now and his son just turned 15. Carl found out he has several apartments in several states, along with multiple vehicles. He also has a private jet and a full-time pilot. Oh, and he has a pilot license too."

"That's a problem Warren. If he has his own jet and several apartments, it's going to be very hard to keep track of him. Or to find out where he was when all of the killings took place."

"I was thinking the same thing. But at least Carl was able to get us all the apartment locations. Unfortunately, Waters could file a flight plan, and then he could deviate from it at any time. Maybe we could get some information from his pilot. Carl found out his name is Dennis Trask. Former Air Force colonel, retired. He started working for Waters about twelve years ago. He's single and is on call but usually has a lot of free time."

"What about Waters possibly being abused as a child?"

"Carl couldn't find out anything at all."

"Where did he go to school?"

"He started at Yale, did a few years at Cornell. Then he did his residency at Johns Hopkins Hospital in Baltimore, where he met his wife, and here in New York at Bellevue. He originally had an office in Manhattan but then decided to travel, visiting safe houses and shelters up and down the east coast. Carl did find out he doesn't charge the shelters or safe houses most of the time."

"How did he find out that?"

"Through his income tax filings. His income is mostly from some properties left to him by his parents, investments and he has written a half dozen books. All on the treatment of abused women and children. Plus interest on his money alone increases his wealth by millions a year. He really doesn't need an income with the money he inherited."

"So let's sum it up. He has a way to get around anywhere he wants to go. He also has no lack of funds. He has a pilot's license but employs a full time pilot."

"I think he is probably our killer Dave. Unless Lou and Billy find out something about Waxman to keep him as a suspect, or some connection with Waters of course. By the way, have we heard from Lou and Billy yet?"

"Not yet but I do know she began work as a social services worker this morning. Teller explained everything to the supervisor in Boston and was assured of their cooperation. He also has two agents with climbing experience, ready to be there to keep an eye on Billy if he does any climbing with Waxman. What do you think we need to do next Warren?"

I sat there giving it some thought. It would be extremely hard to keep track of Waters. Maybe we could get something out of his wife? Would it be possible to put a tracker on his plane?

"Let's get all we can on Mrs. Waters," I said. "Maybe we can get someone close to her and find out where her husband is traveling. She must have his agenda, and we could also get some idea about her life with him. What about putting a tracker on his plane?"

"Good idea," Dave said, "but we would need a warrant. We probably could get one if we laid it all out to a federal judge. Why don't you look into it. Get Carl to help you with it. Maybe get some info on their son Brandon as well. I'll brief Teller on where we stand. I can tell you this, Teller is starting to breathe down my neck. I suppose his boss is doing the same to him."

"Shit always rolls downhill Dave, so if you need to breathe down my neck, go for it."

"Nah, I can handle the heat. By the way, what have the two musketeers been up to?"

"They have been making calls and writing down all kinds of information. They went shopping today to put a bed in our unused room. Then some dressers, wallpaper or paint and who knows what else. They are going to turn it into a nice bedroom for our adopted child, whoever it may be."

"Have you guys thought about whether you want a boy or a girl?"

"I'm sorta leaning toward a boy and Trace is of course leaning toward a girl. But I think I would be better off letting her decide. What about you? Any preferences?"

"I suppose every man wants a son, but I really don't care. As to leaving the decision up to Trace, I think it is a wise decision Warren. When are you going to actually start the process?"

"I told Trace I would like to wait till this case is closed. She told me I have two weeks to close it and then we would get started. So, I better go get Carl started on the wife and son and have him help me with a warrant. I just hope Lou and Billy are able to find out something one way or another about Waxman. I hope they can connect him to Waters or clear him completely."

"Lou will get the info herself, and if not, then Billy might be able to. I know he is still young and a bit raw, but he is turning into a good agent."

"Yeah, he is. I just wish he would sometimes think twice before speaking. I'll see you later, I'm gonna go get Carl on the hunt."

"See you later Warren, I'm off to see Teller."

"Good luck."

I went in search of Carl and Aaron. I knew within a day or so he would have found out almost everything about Jocelyn Waters and her son. We had better get moving in a positive way soon. Getting a warrant would only be half the battle. Somehow we would have to find Waters' jet and place a tracker.

Soon I wanted to devote my time and mind to adopting a child. I knew if this case was still going on, I wouldn't be able to. And I didn't want to do that to Trace, seeing how excited she was. Who knows, maybe I'll be a daddy soon. Me a daddy. It made me smile.

Chapter Forty - Three

Lou had spent the rest of the day working on finding some help for Ms. Washington. Kevin gave her some programs she could use to track down inexpensive apartments. They were funded by the city and were available to victims of abuse. She was also looking for jobs where Ms. Washington might be able to work. There was the problem of child care for her two children while she was working. Finally was the issue of finding a school for the children, but Lou would have to wait to see where an apartment could be had. All in all it was a ton of work. Lou was glad this was only a temporary assignment. She liked working for the FBI.

Billy had picked her up at five, but Waxman had stayed behind, so she wasn't able to introduce them. But she had brought up rock climbing with Waxman over lunch. At first he wasn't very interested but finally had told Lou he climbed as well. Lou had suggested he might show her brother some good places to climb. He had said maybe. At least it was a start.

Now Lou and Billy were back in their room after eating at a diner across the street from the hotel. Lou was giving Billy a run down on her day before calling Dave. She was waiting to find out if Billy had anything to add to her report.

"Do you think he could be involved in the murders, Lou?" Billy asked.

"I'm not sure one way or the other, but he does get

very angry about men abusing women," Lou replied. "And he does know Waters."

"Yeah, you must have been ready to shout when he mentioned him."

"It definitely took me by surprise. But I still don't know if he knows him just because Waters visits the safe house, or they are working together. Tomorrow I will try to draw him out some."

"Just don't appear too nosy, we don't want to spook him. I had an idea about tomorrow."

"What?"

"How about I come by to take you to lunch and then you can introduce me to Waxman?"

"That's not a bad idea Billy. If we can get him to come to lunch with us, you could bring up rock climbing. Then we might be able to get him to tell you where he climbs."

"By Saturday I will be ready to climb. I worked out at the rock climbing gym today. I'm a bit rusty but I intend to work out every day this week. I'll be ready."

"You better be, I don't want to bring you back to New York in pieces."

"It's getting late. You better call Dave and tell him what we have found out. Are you going to call Warren or do you want me to?"

"I'll call Dave and ask him if he wants us to call Warren first."

"Okay, you call and I'm going to get into a hot shower. My muscles are a bit sore from my workout."

Billy went into the bathroom and Lou called Dave on his cell. At this hour, he was probably at home. The phone rang a few times and then Dave answered.

"Hello," he said.

"Hi Dave, it's Lou," she replied.

"How's it going Lou? Any news yet?"

"Actually I have a few interesting things to tell you. First, Waxman knows Dr. Waters."

"How did you find that out so soon? And did he say how he knows him?"

"He was helping me with a case. We went to a safe house and while interviewing an abused woman, he told her he wanted her to see a counselor or doctor. Then he asked the woman who runs the house if Dr. Waters would be visiting soon."

"Now all we need to do is figure out if he just knows him, is working with him, or killing people on his own."

"Yeah I know and that's the tough part, but I'll work on it."

"Has Billy met him yet?"

"Not yet but he is meeting me for lunch tomorrow. Hopefully I can get Waxman to join us and then Billy will bring up rock climbing. I did manage to tell Waxman we moved from New York so Billy could pursue some rock climbing in the area."

"Sounds like you are doing well. Keep up the good work and be safe."

"One more thing Dave. Do you want Billy to call Warren to report what we found out?"

"No, I'll take care of it. Call me tomorrow at about the same time, unless you need to call with something important."

"Okay Dave, Goodnight."

"Goodnight Lou."

Lou wanted to tell Billy what Dave said and figured

why wait. She slipped out of her clothes and into the shower with Billy.

"Did you talk with Dave?" he asked.

"I did, but I think we could do better things than stand here and talk about work," she said as she ran her hands over his body.

"I do believe you are right as always."

Chapter Forty - Four

Max Gardner was a man in his mid-forties with long brown scraggly hair. He always needed a shave and a shower but most of the time he did neither. People would naturally walk on the other side of the street from him because he always had an angry face with dark eyes. He was also overly muscled, due to the last twenty years working out for hours a day in prison.

He was just finishing mopping the floor outside of the ICU. He was in his second week of working in the hospital. It was a lousy job he had gotten through his parole officer, a jerk named John Lincoln. Max hated him and one day he swore he would teach him a lesson. Working at this hospital was ironic and he was still surprised he had been placed here. Sometimes he would laugh out loud thinking about it.

As he continued mopping he thought back to twenty years ago. Back then Max had been a young, strong, good looking man and newly married. He had been working for a cable company, installing cable hookups in apartments and homes all over Baltimore. His new wife, Brandy, had been a nurse working at the famous Johns Hopkins. Brandy had been a blonde, blue eyed gorgeous woman, smart and in love with Max.

Things had been going well for them, they were making enough money to begin saving up for a house. Until then they had a nice apartment on the fourth floor of a decent building. No elevator but hey, they were both young.

Things were going just fine until he started to suspect she was having an affair with a doctor. Why he had begun to suspect her, he didn't know, but it was always on his mind. Even when he tried to shake thoughts of her in the arms of a doctor, he couldn't do it. He knew how sexy Brandy looked in her nurses uniform, and he was sure the doctors thought so too. He didn't know which doctor she was having an affair with; in fact he had no proof at all. But in his mind he kept on picturing her sneaking into supply rooms or empty patient rooms and making love to another man.

At first he would question her more and more as to what she had been doing during the day. Then he had started leaving his work without authorization and showing up at the hospital. He would try and sneak around looking for her, trying to catch her in the act. One time he saw her with another nurse and a young handsome doctor. They were laughing and he saw her put her hand on his arm. Then they had looked at each other and Max was now sure. The look in her eyes used to be the way she looked at him. She was fucking a doctor behind his back!

He had gone back to work, angry and thinking of what to do. He was so angry he couldn't get his hands to do anything properly. When his customer had asked him how much longer he was going to be he had snapped at her. He had told her he would be there as long as it fucking took! She had called his company, and before he had finished, his supervisor had shown up. He was fired on the spot.

Max had gone to a bar and began drinking. He was putting shots down, one after the other, grumbling to himself about his job, the bitch who got him fired, his wife and any other thing which he hated. He had ordered another drink, but the bartender had refused, saying he had had enough. When he went to hit the bartender, the guy had brought out a Louisville slugger from under the bar. Max knew he could take him, but he left grumbling and angry.

Making his way home, his anger grew and grew. Then his wife came home an hour later than usual.

"Where have you been," he'd yelled at her.

Brandy had replied something about some patient coding or some nonsense. He knew in his heart where she had been. Fucking that young doctor! When she then asked if he had been drinking, he had slapped her. Then he didn't stop slapping, punching and kicking her. She dragged herself to the door, barely got it open and crawled out the door. When she tried to leave, Max had caught her at the top of the apartment's staircase, lifted her in his arms and threw her down.

Brandy had died immediately when her neck broke. He had been arrested, tried and sentenced to twenty-five years. Due to the large amount of alcohol in his system at the time of his wife's death, he had received twenty-five years instead of life. Now he was out on parole for good behavior after twenty years of his life had been taken from him. His parole officer had gotten him a room in a halfway house and a job as a janitor at the same hospital Brandy had worked at.

Now he was a damn janitor where she had been a nurse, fucking a doctor behind his back. Every single day he had worked there, he kept looking for the doctor she had been fucking. He had only seen him that one time, but he would never forget his face. The fact the man would have aged or even gone somewhere else never occurred to Max.

Max finished mopping and made his way down to the basement to stow his mop and get out the waxer. The only good thing about the job was the hours he worked. He never had to see any visitors and there were less doctors and nurses during the late hours.

He got off the elevator and made his way to the janitor's room he always used, one of many throughout the hospital. He opened the door and switched on the light. He had begun to make this room his own. He had gotten a small coffee maker, a hot plate and an old comfortable chair they were throwing out. He also had a few pictures of naked women hanging up. Maybe one day he would get a nurse down here to fuck him or at least give him a quick blowjob.

He started making a cup of coffee for himself. He would need to get a small fridge down here somehow; he thought to himself. He was just pouring the coffee into a stained mug he had stolen from one of the offices when he heard something. It sounded like someone was calling his name.

He put the mug down and opened the janitor's room door. He looked out but saw no one. Must be my imagination, he thought. He got his mug again, sat down in his chair and took a sip. Then he heard his name once more. Now he was angry. He stepped out and took a few steps down one hallway, and then he turned and started walking down the other. Still he saw no one and returned to his room.

Unfortunately for Max, he never saw the person standing behind the door as he entered. He never saw the taser, but he certainly felt it. He didn't go down right away, but a second jolt from the taser had him hit the floor with a thud.

When he finally came to, he was sitting in his chair. He tried to get up, but discovered he was thoroughly tied to it. He had a stinking rag in his mouth with tape over it. He could hardly breathe, and he was shaking with anger and fear.

Then the person softly said, "Hello Max."

Max tried to say something and the person in front of him just laughed.

"Did you think you were now going to go about your happy little way," the person said. "Tsk, tsk Max. Serving twenty years in prison is not enough. You need to suffer some more, and I am going to be the one to do it."

Max then saw the person put on some thick black gloves. His eyes grew wide and then he felt the first blow across his nose. It felt as if he had been hit with a brick! The blood began to flow, and he almost couldn't take in a breath. Then the blows fell on his eyes, his ribs, his arms and finally his groin. He was going to pass out from the pain and lack of air.

Then Max saw something which truly scared him. Through swollen eyes and blood, Max saw the person take out a wicked looking blade and hold it in front of him.

"Now Max, you won't have to worry about mopping any more floors," the person said.

The last thing Max felt was the blade slicing into his neck. Then he finally felt nothing more.

Chapter Forty - Five

I was sitting in the conference room with Dave and Aaron, talking about the case. While we talked we drank coffee and ate a donut. Well, Dave and I ate one while Aaron managed to put away four. We were waiting for Carl to show up. He had left word he was finishing up some information on Dr. Waters, his wife and son.

Finally Carl walked in with a few folders in his hand. He got some coffee and went to get a donut, but they were all gone.

"Jeez Aaron, could you have left one for me?" Carl said

"You snooze, you lose, brother," Aaron answered.

"Okay you two, let's settle down and get to work," Dave said. "Before you give us a report Carl, Warren will fill you in on what Lou and Billy have found out so far."

I cleared my throat and said, "Lou is working side by side with Kevin Waxman. He's a tough guy to get close to, but she is managing to crack him open a bit. He is helping her on a social services case, and they have been to lunch together. This afternoon, Billy, acting as her brother, is going to meet her for lunch. Lou will try to get him to go to lunch with them."

"Has she gotten anything from him?" Aaron asked.

"Yes she has and it's something big. Dr. Waters visits the same shelter where Lou's case is. And Kevin Waxman knows Dr. Waters. He was the one to bring up his name. Now, if he knows the doctor only through work or his relationship is more than that, we don't know. It's one of the things Lou is going to try and find out."

"And Billy is going to get close to him through the rock climbing?" Carl asked.

"Yes, but I'm hoping he won't have to go climbing with Waxman. But if he does, Dave has two agents familiar with rock climbing who will show up wherever Billy and Waxman go."

"We should hear from Lou late this afternoon or this evening," Dave said. "Now Carl, let's hear what you have found out."

"First, I'll just remind you all of the info we have on Dr. Waters. He inherited in excess of fifty million dollars when his parents died. He was twenty years old at the time. He went to several high end schools and did his residency at Johns Hopkins in Baltimore. There he met his wife, Jocelyn, who was working as a nurse. They married and had a son named Brandon. They have been married for nineteen years and Brandon just turned fifteen.

Dr. Waters owns a very nice fast jet and even though he has a pilot's license, he employs a retired Air Force Colonel by the name of Dennis Trask. He has apartments in several cities and garages a car in each city for him to get around."

"Damn, this guy can go anywhere at a moment's notice," Aaron said.

"Which is why Warren visited a federal judge and obtained a warrant to put a GPS tracker on his jet, when we find it. Which may be a bit of a problem. When he isn't travelling he keeps the jet at a small airport out on Long Island. We know where but we don't know when. Right now he and his jet are gone, and we don't know exactly where. Trask filed a flight plan taking them to Maine. But after that, we have no clue."

"I have an idea," Aaron said. "When he leaves Maine he will have to file a flight plan, right?"

"Yes, at least he is supposed to."

"Okay, so let's say he goes to Vermont or New Hampshire for example. We can have one of our local agents get to the jet and put a tracker on it. If he misses him for some reason, we find out his next stop the same way."

"Does anyone know what would happen if he either doesn't file a flight plan or deviates from it?" I asked

Carl said, "I checked on that very scenario Warren. A pilot is required to file a flight plan. If he doesn't he could be fined. Of course, with Waters' money, he wouldn't care about paying some fines. There is another way, he could still file a flight plan and just deviate from where he is scheduled to land. If the pilot radios with some type of engine trouble for example, he would be able to land anywhere nearby. Which means, if Waters wants to, he could land just about anywhere without us knowing. One other thing. We could get a ping off his cell phone unless he turns it off."

"Which is why we need the tracker on his jet asap," I said.

"Aaron," Dave said, "I'm leaving it up to you to get a tracker on his jet. It's your number one priority starting right now."

Aaron got up and asked, "Which airport does the Doc keep his jet at Carl?"

"MacArthur Airport located in Ronkonkoma, Long Island" Carl replied.

"See you later guys."

Aaron headed out and Dave asked Carl, "Anything on Dr. Waters' wife and son Carl?"

"His wife's name is Jocelyn, and she is two years younger than her husband. Her maiden name was Mason, and she grew up in Philadelphia. After the usual high school years and graduation, she went to nursing school and then she got a job as a nurse at Johns Hopkins, a little over twenty years ago."

"So basically nothing in her history is unusual?" I asked.

"Nothing Warren but I want to be thorough. I'm not done yet. I'll keep working on it. As for the son there really isn't anything there. He is a decent student, is the school treasurer, is on the swim team and writes for the school newspaper."

"What about where they live and other activities?" Dave asked.

"As we know, they have a very large home, actually a mansion in Great Neck. I have the address, ummm let me see...here it is. 73 Manor Road. Not too many other homes on the road, only a few other mansions. As to other activities, they both play golf at the Great Neck Golf and Tennis Club. I found out by speaking to the guy who runs the pro shop, they usually play together during the spring and summer every weekend, if Waters is in town."

"I hope the guy at the pro shop isn't going to say anything to them."

"Nah, he won't. He is a retired Nassau County detective. He told me Waters and his wife usually play with the same couple every weekend. A William and Carla Harper. I don't know what they do or where they live yet, but I can find out. Jocelyn waters is a very busy woman. She is on the board of several local charities and volunteers some time, doing different things. She is active in the PTA, golfs with Carla Harper during the week when she has the time. She is also on the board of the Golf and Tennis club. That's about all for now but I will keep digging Dave."

"Good job Carl," Dave said. "You keep digging. Warren and I are going to go over everything we have and see if we missed anything. Until we hear more from Lou and Billy, or Aaron and you, we will be here."

"Okay Dave, I'll let you and Warren know if anything else pops," Carl said and went back to his office.

When they were alone, Dave said, "So Warren, shall we get started?"

"I suppose we might as well Dave," I answered, and dug into the files.

As I began looking through what we had compiled so far, I thought without either Billy, Lou, Aaron or Carl coming up with new information, we were basically dead in the water. I knew cases sometimes went cold, but the problem with them going cold was sometimes thcy never defrosted. I didn't want this case to become a dead cold case. Plus I was sure whoever our killer was , he wasn't stopping anytime soon.

Chapter Forty - Six

Billy drove Lou to work in the morning, and then showed up to take Lou to lunch and to try to meet with Kevin Waxman. When Billy had arrived and called Lou saying he was there, Lou looked for Waxman at his desk. Unfortunately, he had walked away from his desk minutes earlier. Lou met Billy in the lot, and she and Billy decided to wait there for a bit, to see if he would come out to go to lunch. And right now, their waiting had paid off. Lou saw Waxman coming out of the back of the building and walking toward his car. While they were waiting, Lou had Billy move their car to a spot right next to his car.

Lou called out to him, "Hi Kevin. I'd like you to meet my brother Billy."

Waxman slowly held out his hand and shook Billy's outstretched   hand.

"Nice to meet you, can I call you Kevin?" Billy said, with a big smile on his face.

"Ummm sure, I suppose," Waxman said. "Well, I'm going to lunch."

"Hey. So are we! Why don't you join us? I'd really like to pick your brain about some good places to go climb Kevin. My treat!"

"Well I ..."

Lou put her hand onto Waxman's arm and said, "C'mon Kevin, I owe you for all your help, and Billy really could use some good places to climb. He wants to go this weekend."

"Okay, I suppose I can give him some good places."

"Great. Where should we go?"

"Well I was heading to JM Curly, it's a nice pub nearby. It's still early so we should be able to get some seats. It's on Temple Place. I'll direct you."

They all got into Lou's car, and she sat in the back, hoping Kevin would talk with Billy. But as he did the day before, he said driving should be done without conversation. The only words he spoke was to direct Billy where to drive. It only took them ten minutes and then they pulled up to the restaurant. Even at this hour, there was an attendant who parked their car.

Lou looked over the place as they entered. There was a nice dining room and bar. Lou saw a sign which read, *Bogies Place*, pointing downstairs. Being a Humphrey Bogart fan, she asked the Maître d, what it was. He told her it was a Speakeasy Steakhouse. It sounded great and expensive. But what the hell, she and Billy weren't going to be paying for it, Uncle Sam would get the bill.

Lou asked if it was open, and the Maître d said yes, but cell phones were not allowed to be used or turned on.

Lou said, "C'mon men! Let's get some good steaks."

The Maître d summoned someone on a house phone, and a man came up the steps to escort them down into the steakhouse. They were seated at a large table, given menus and they settled in. They also turned off their phones.

Lou looked around and saw several booths, some which could probably seat ten people. There were small intimate tables for two, as well as larger ones. The pictures on the walls were all of Bogart films. There was one of *The Maltese Falcon, Casablanca, The Treasure of Sierra Madre* and others. Lou loved the place.

A few minutes later a waiter came to their table. Lou asked about this room, and the waiter told her normally it was used for private parties, or with reservations, but during the weekday, they allowed people to just walk in. They looked over the menu, and all three of them ordered a 12 oz. ribeye, with vegetables and baked potato. Billy got a Boston Lager, but Waxman and Lou stuck with water, since they were returning to work. When Lou asked for her steak to be well done, the waiter simply said no, the chef would not allow his meat to be ruined. Lou shrugged, smiled and just said okay, and the waiter left.

"Do you believe that?" Lou asked. "The chef will not allow his meat to be ruined."

"Well, I think he is right," Billy said. "Anything more than medium rare is a sin."

Their food was brought to them shortly, and Lou hated to admit it, but her steak was delicious. They were also served hot buns with a delicious butter on the side. As they ate, Billy tried to get Waxman to open up a bit.

"So Kevin, do you climb a lot?" Billy asked.

"Usually every weekend during the warm months," he answered. "Sometimes if it's not too cold and there hasn't been any snow. I usually travel around a lot."

"Great! Do you have any recommendations but not too far away?"

"Well, as I'm sure you know, the best rocks are out west, but we still have several nearby. There's Middlesex Falls, but it's mostly for beginners and intermediate skills. Have you been climbing for a long time?"

"Since I was ten. I used to climb with my dad. We even took a trip to Devil's Tower in Wyoming when I was fifteen. Now that was a climb!"

"Yes, I've been there too. So you are better than intermediate I would say."

"Sure am," Billy said and looked at Lou who was not smiling.

"I was planning on hitting Quincey Quarries this Saturday. It is usually called the Q. It is a giant slab of granite standing 85 feet high with several great trails to climb. I was going to climb the C wall. It is rated at 5.6 to 5.9. I've climbed a few that have been mapped out but this weekend I was going to tackle one of the hardest ones. Do you think you are up for it?"

"Ummm, absolutely Kevin. What time shall we meet?"

"How about 6:00 am. You can meet me at the social services building, since where I live would be in the opposite direction."

"Sounds great Kevin. I'm looking forward to it."

They finished their meal, which was awesome and returned to the social services building. Waxman thanked them for the meal and went into work. Lou said she had a few things to discuss with her brother and would be right in.

As soon as Waxman was out of sight, Lou turned to Billy and shouted, "Are you out of your friggin mind?!"

"Take it easy Lou," Billy said. "This is why I am here. And I can handle it, I think."

"You think? What if you can't. What if you get injured or even..."

"I'm not going to fall or get hurt Lou. I've been doing well at the rock climbing gym. I'm almost ready for some intermediate climbs."

"Almost? Now I know you are nuts. I'm calling Dave to get you out of here. We can make some excuse."

"No way Lou. When I said I had climbed up Devils' Tower, it wasn't a lie. I did climb it with my dad when I was fifteen. I can do this Lou. Please don't stop me."

Lou was standing there, thinking. It was their job to do this, and Billy wasn't a kid. He was a Special Agent of the FBI. On top of that, she trusted him and his judgement.

"Okay Billy, but I'm going to make sure you have those two agents climbing right there with you," Lou said.

"Thank you Lou," Billy replied. "Now how about a kiss?"

Lou pushed him away and said, "Are you nuts! What if Waxman saw us Billy. Go home, or better yet, you better get to the gym and train. You only have three more days till Saturday. Now go."

"You owe me a kiss Lou, and a whole lot more. I'll pick you up at five."

Billy waved and drove away. Lou still wasn't sure this was a good idea. She knew Billy would be upset, but she needed to discuss this with Dave and Warren. As soon as she could get away from Waxman, she would call them. Plus, Dave would have to get in touch with the two agents who were supposed to climb near Billy. Maybe she could get enough information out of Waxman before Saturday, and then Billy wouldn't have to do the climb.

She slowly walked back into work, thinking of ways to draw Waxman out. So far he had been a bit aloof. Maybe if she came on to him, he might tell her something she could use to either clear him of the murders or make him a prime suspect. She stopped at the restroom before returning to her desk. She combed out her hair, put on a little eye shadow and some fresh lipstick. She decided he wouldn't know what hit him.

Chapter Forty - Seven

Aaron had been on the phone with an airport supervisor at MacArthur Airport. It had taken almost an hour to be connected to the person who knows the flight plans which are filed by small planes and private jets leaving the airport. He was finally connected to a Mr. Tom Winslett, a snobby sounding man who was trying to act very self-important.

"Okay Mr. Winslett, you have told me Dr. Waters' jet left your airport early Monday morning," Aaron said for the third time. "But what I need to know is where they were going?"

"And I told you for the third time, *Agent*, I cannot release that information," Winslett answered.

Aaron had had enough of this snooty fellow.

He took a deep breath and then said, "Mr. Winslett, I am a Special Agent of the FBI. If you do not cooperate with me, I will have ten Special Agents at your door in one hour. Besides going through every log of every plane or jet at your dinky little airport, they will inspect every single hanger. It will take some time, and your airport will be shut down for as long as it takes. But that's not all Mr. Winslett. Then they will begin to look into you. I will ask the IRS to look into your personal taxes, your home, your family, everything about you. Have you ever had a colostomy Mr. Winslett?"

"Ummm...yes?"

"Well this will be ten times worse when my Special

Agents crawl up your ass! Now, where did Dr. Waters' flight plan say he was going to!"

Aaron heard some papers being shuffled and then Winslett said slightly sobbing, "They, they are going to Bangor International Airport. Is that all?"

"Yes Mr. Winslett, that will be all. You have yourself a pleasant and blessed day."

Aaron shook his head and then looked up the number for Bangor International Airport. He really didn't like to get tough, well, actually he did, sometimes. There were times when you needed to put the fear of not God, but the might of the FBI into people to get them to talk. He hoped he wouldn't have to do it again.

He dialed the number, and after being rerouted three times, finally found himself speaking to a woman with a very sultry voice.

"This is Miss King," she said. "How may I help you?"

Aaron found himself sitting up straighter and fixing his tie, even though Miss King obviously couldn't see him.

"Umm, Miss King, my name is Aaron, I mean, I am Special Agent Aaron Devlin of the FBI."

"Oooo, the F...B...I... Now what can I do for you, Special Agent Devlin?"

"Ummm, call me Aaron, Miss King."

"Well then you can call me Cassandra, Special Agent Aaron."

Aaron gulped some air and then said, "Well Cassandra, I am investigating a homicide. One of our key witnesses is a Dr. Malcolm Waters. He should have landed at your airport on Monday. I need to know if he did, and if he has left yet."

"Well Special Agent Aaron, I would need the tail number to tell you."

"Right. Of course. The tail number is NDOC/5647T."

"Okay, give me a second and I can look it up." After a few minutes Cassandra said, "Okay, you were right, he landed Monday morning. But he left just an hour ago."

"Damn! I mean, darn. Would you be able to tell me where his pilot filed his flight plan to?"

"Well, I could but first, you will need to give me some more information, of a personal nature. Are you married, Special Agent Aaron?"

"Ummm, no, I'm not Cassandra."

"I see. And what do you look like, Special Agent Aaron?"

"Well, I'm black, I mean, ummm, African American, I'm about six foot six, 260 lbs., umm..."

"Mmmmmm, well now. Do you ever get up to Bangor Special Agent Aaron?"

"I will now. But if I do, how will I know you?"

"Well let me see. I am five foot twelve, which sounds better than six foot tall, 125 lbs. with bright long red hair, green eyes and ...do you want my measurements?"

"No, I'll wait to see for myself. Of course it might be a while till I can get up to you. Unless you want to come down to the Big Apple?"

"Hmmm, I will give it some thought. I do get discounts on flights after all. Now, you wanted to know where he went?"

"Yes, it would be a great help Cassandra."

"It says he filed a flight plan to Burlington International Airport in Montpelier, Vermont. Does that help?"

"Very much so Cassandra. Thank you and keep your eyes open for a big black man visiting you."

"I can't wait. Unless I beat you to it and fly down to New York. Bye now."

Aaron said goodbye and then wiped the sweat from his forehead. He must be crazy to tell some woman he had never met he would go all the way to Maine to see her. But she sounded so sexy, and she was a redhead. He loved red haired women. Maybe she would come to see him.

He stopped himself from thinking about Cassandra and found the number for Burlington International Airport in Montpelier, Vermont. Again he was rerouted, and finally was speaking to the right man. He was glad this time it wasn't a sexy sounding woman.

After identifying himself and giving the man the information, he waited while he checked to see where the jet was now.

"I'm sorry Special Agent, but that jet has not landed here," the man said. "Of course he could be late or changed his flight plan. Could have had some trouble and landed somewhere else. Sorry."

"That's okay, thank you for your help," Aaron said and hung up.

Now where was Dr. Waters? Could he have had some trouble or was he off the grid so he could kill someone else? Aaron didn't know but somehow he was going to find him if it took all day and night.

The first thing he did was try and get a cell phone ping. He called the cell phone carrier, gave them his name and FBI identification. He waited for almost an hour for them to call back and when they did, it wasn't good news. They informed him the cell must be turned off.

Now what was he going to do?

Chapter Forty - Eight

Wednesday, On Dr. Waters' Jet, 5:15 am

Dennis Trask had been in the Air Force as a pilot for over twenty years. He had risen to the rank of Colonel and had learned one of the most important lessons in life. When a superior officer or boss, as in the case of Malcolm Waters gives you a direct order, you follow it. Unless it is against the law or military standards. Trask had worked for Waters for going on twelve years. All he had to do was be ready to fly him from Florida to Maine and everywhere in between.

He was to be ready to fly, usually during the week at a moment's notice. He knew Dr. Waters was a psychiatrist who treated abused women and children, in shelters and safe houses, and that was all he knew. Trask liked his job, was well paid and got to fly an Embraer Phenom 300 light jet. It was a beauty, could go around 2000 nautical miles on a full tank and handled almost as good as the fighter jets he had flown in combat. It could hold five to ten people and was very luxurious inside.

The only time Trask had a bit of concern was when Dr. Waters would ask him to deviate from the filed flight plan. He knew he would be fined sometimes, which Dr. Waters would pay. Still, he hated to do anything which was improper, even though it was only bending the rules, not really breaking them.

Like yesterday, Dr. Waters had him file a flight plan saying they were going to Burlington International Airport in Montpelier Vermont. They had stayed in Maine until almost ten pm at night, and after takeoff, Dr. Waters asked him to land at a small private airport near Washington, D.C. Trask had changed course and when he got closer, Trask had called the small tower at a private airfield and stated he was having an issue with his instruments. He had been granted emergency landing.

They had landed in the dead of night and then Dr. Waters had exited the jet with a black valise. Whether Dr. Waters was taking something off the jet, or bringing something back on, Trask had no idea. Dr. Waters had done this several times over the years. He never told Trask the reason why and Trask never asked. He figured it was none of his business.

The only thing Trask noticed was when the doctor returned, usually after four or five hours, he was always very excited. Normally Dr. Waters was a very calm person. But when he returned after his little ventures, his face was usually flush, his hands would be shaking, and he was always in a great hurry to take off and return to the filed flight plan.

Now, while waiting for the doctor to return, Trask had refueled the jet, even though it had plenty of fuel left. Dr. Waters liked to have the jet fully fueled after every flight, no matter how short a trip it was. Trask was reading a new James Patterson novel, waiting on the doctor. Just as he got to an important part of the book, Dr. Waters returned. He appeared the same as always. Excited, hands shaking and in a hurry to take off.

"Did you refuel the jet Dennis?" Dr. Waters asked.

"Yes sir and refiled the flight plan to take us to Vermont," Trask answered.

"Excellent!. Well let's get going then."

Trask radioed the small control tower and was given permission to use runway 17a. Trask began to taxi out of the hanger, got to the correct runway and then took the jet into the sky with ease. They were cruising within minutes. The flight would only take a bit over two hours, so Trask didn't bother with the automatic pilot function. He enjoyed being in control, soaring through the skies. As he flew above the clouds, he remembered doing the same thing over the Middle East during the war. He was much happier now, not having to avoid ground fire and enemy jets.

Meanwhile in the seating area, Dr. Waters was sitting in a very comfortable chair. He was sipping on some 18 year old scotch. He felt his heartbeat slowly returning to normal. But he noticed his hands were still shaking.

He thought back to what he had done and was smiling ear to ear. Of course if Jocelyn ever found out, she would divorce him or even worse, club him over the head with an iron from her golf club set. That would still be preferable to the law finding out what he did on his little side trips. If they found out, he would be highly embarrassed, lose his license and probably be put in prison for a very long time.

Oh well, he thought. It was worth the risk. Besides, it was a compulsion he couldn't resist. Now he needed to calm down and return to his normal demeanor. They would be landing soon. Then he would go to a hotel he usually stayed at while visiting the three shelters and two safe homes in the area. He was thinking of getting another apartment, but the hotel he stayed at was fine. He would be in Vermont for two to three days, and then it was on to Boston.

He made a mental note to call Jocelyn as soon as he arrived at the hotel. She would never guess he had Trask deviate from his original flight plan. But he had to call her as soon as possible so she had no suspicions. He sat back, smiling, sipping on his scotch and awaited the landing.

Chapter Forty - Nine

Lou and Billy had returned to their hotel room after having a nice dinner at the diner nearby. Over dinner, they had both avoided discussing Billy's upcoming climb with Kevin Waxman. Lou was worried about him and Billy wouldn't admit he was scared, so they both avoided the subject. They had eaten and talked about everything but the case. Now they were back in their room and Lou was going to call Dave. Billy had gone down to the lobby to get some drinks and snacks.

"Hello Dave," Lou said, "it's me, Lou."

Dave put down the file he had been looking at and replied, "Hello Lou. How are things going for you and Billy?"

"Well, I am getting closer to Waxman, but I have a feeling he has little or no interest in women."

"Why?"

"I gave him my best seductress moves, and he completely ignored me. I was hoping I could get some more information from him if I got a bit closer."

"I don't want you getting too personal with a suspected serial killer Lou."

"You don't have to worry about it Dave. He's not interested in the slightest. Which brings me to Billy."

"What is the boy wonder up to now?"

"This Saturday, he and Waxman are going to climb a place called the Quincey Quarries. It is also called the Q. It's a giant slab of granite standing 85 feet high with several trails to climb. They are planning on climbing a trail called the C wall. I don't know what it means but Waxman said it is rated at 5.6 to 5.9."

"I'm not sure what that means either, but I will find out. What time are they meeting up?"

"Billy is picking him up at the social services parking lot at 6:00 am."

"Okay Lou. I will have our two agents there to keep an eye on Billy and Waxman. We have arranged for both of them to be wearing red helmets with a yellow stripe. You and Billy should be able to recognize them. They already know what Billy looks like."

"Great."

"You seem to be upset about this. Isn't it what we planned to do if you couldn't get the info?"

"Yeah but, I'm not sure it is a good idea anymore. I mean Billy has been training every day at the rock climbing gym, but he hasn't climbed in years."

"I understand your concerns Lou, but Billy knows his limitations. Are you going to be there?"

"We figured it would look strange for me to accompany him, but I'm going no matter what. I'll just tell Waxman I like to watch Billy climb."

"Maybe you can find out something tomorrow or Friday. Keep at it and you might save Billy the climb."

"Oh, I'll be trying. You can count on it. Anything new on your end?"

"Aaron is working on getting a tracker on Dr. Waters' private jet. Unfortunately, he isn't having too much luck getting a fix on where he is now. Waters flew to Maine on Monday and then was supposed to go to Vermont. But he never landed there, so we figured he deviated from the flight plan. But Aaron is still working on it. Also Carl has been getting more info on the doc, his wife and son. Still nothing there though."

Just then, Billy walked back into the room.

"Is that Dave on the phone?" he asked Lou.

"Yes Billy, but I am hanging up now," Lou replied.

Before she could hang up, Billy called out, "Hey Dave! Things are super here!"

Lou gave him a look and disconnected the call.

"I'm sure Dave is pretty sure we only use one room Billy, but we don't have to confirm it," Lou said.

"Sorry Lou," Billy said. "What did Dave have to say about my climb Saturday?" he asked as he put some drinks into the mini fridge.

"He said you know your limitations and you shouldn't do anything risky," Lou replied. "Also, the two agents who will be watching you and Waxman will be wearing red helmets with a yellow stripe."

"That reminds me. I have to get some equipment for the climb. I'll go tomorrow while you are at work. Boy, this climb is going to be fun!"

"Uh huh. Just remember why you are doing it. We need to figure out if Waxman is working with Waters, or if he is doing the killings alone. Or whether or not he has anything at all to do with the killings."

"Don't worry Lou. If there is a way to get Waxman to talk, I'll find a way. Now, how are we going to spend the rest of the night?"

"You have a one track mind."

"Yes I do when it comes to you Lou. I'm going to say something, and I don't want you to be upset. Okay?"

Oh no, Lou thought. If he asks me to marry him right now, I don't know what I am going to say!

"Umm, ok Billy," Lou said hesitantly. "What do you want to say?"

"They only had one three musketeers candy bar so, it is mine," Billy said with a big smile and then pulled Lou down on the bed.

Lou hit him with a pillow a few times and then he got on top of her. He leaned down and kissed her gently.

"Lou, I think I am in love with you," Billy said.

Lou looked him in the eyes and said, "God help me William Groat, I think I am in love with you too."

Soon they had nothing else to say.

Chapter Fifty

We were back in the conference room, trying to come up with what to do next. We had thrown around a few ideas, including getting a female agent to try and get close to Jocelyn Waters. That idea was shot down as taking too much time with little chance of working. The son Brandon was out of bounds because he was still a minor.

We were going over it all for the tenth time when an agent came in and stated Aaron had a call. He left to take it and was back in the room in a few minutes, with a big smile on his face.

"I just got off the phone with the guy I spoke with at the airport in Vermont," Aaron said. "Seems Dr. Waters returned to his flight plan a few hours late. His jet is now sitting in a hangar at Burlington International Airport in Montpelier, Vermont."

"Great news Aaron," Dave said. "Can you get a couple of agents out there to put a tracker on his jet?"

"I'm going to make the call right now Dave. But before I do, I was thinking I might take the jet and fly out there. I might be able to keep an eye on him."

"Let me run it by ADD Teller first Aaron. In the meantime, get those agents to put that tracker in place."

"Yes sir," Aaron said and left to make the call.

"At least we have some good news," I said.

ADD Teller walked in just then and said, "I'm afraid I don't have any good news for you both."

"Please don't tell me we have another victim."

"I'm afraid you are going to be disappointed, Special Agent Temple. We have a victim found at Johns Hopkins Hospital in Baltimore. He was just discovered, and the local police have been informed not to move him. A sharp detective saw the beating he took and his slit throat and remembered the bulletins we sent out. So Special Agent Anderson, you and Special Agent Temple better get moving."

"There goes Aaron flying out to Vermont. I think maybe we should take him and Carl with us, Dave."

"I think so too Warren," Dave replied. "You go tell them and I'll get the jet ready. You better give Trace a heads up. I'm going to call Melissa as soon as I get the jet ready. Maybe this time we can find something."

"Yeah, this time we will be able to see the victim and the crime scene. Be ready in ten minutes Dave."

I went to tell Carl and Aaron to get ready for a trip to Baltimore. Then I went to my office and called Trace.

"Hi Honey," I said, "I'm off gallivanting to Baltimore."

"Oh no," she replied. "Don't tell me there has been another murder!"

"I'm afraid so. We're hoping we can find something to help us catch this animal. The body was just found, and it is the first crime scene we will be able to see before the body is moved. Maybe we will find something. I really hope this bastard has messed up this time."

"Just be careful War, remember you are going to be a father one of these days. Melissa and I were going to spend the day figuring our next step in the adoption process. And keep an eye on Dave too. He is going to be a father soon too."

"Yes dear, I will stay safe and make sure Dave is safe as well. I love you baby."

"And I love you."

I hung up and double checked my go bag. I didn't think we would be spending more than one day there, but better to be prepared. I walked out of the office, and we all met at the elevator. Then we went to the garage where a black SUV was waiting for us.

Dave got behind the wheel and started the drive to JFK airport.

"How much do we know about our vic?" Carl asked.

"I don't know anything yet Carl," Dave answered. "All ADD Teller was told was there was a victim who fit the other victims killed. I do know the victim was a janitor and was found in the basement. But that's all."

"He was found in Johns Hopkins hospital," I added.

"Now that is interesting," Carl said. "Remember, Dr. Waters did his residency there. He also met his wife there as well."

"Yeah but it was over twenty years ago. How do you think it could be related?"

"I don't know Warren, but it is something to keep in mind."

We arrived at the airport and within fifteen minutes we were on board. Then we taxied down a runway and took off. I was sure each of us were thinking about many things. I thought about what Carl had said. It was strange a victim should be killed at the same hospital Waters had done his residency in and met his wife. Then again, it might just be a coincidence. The only problem was, I didn't believe in coincidences.

Chapter Fifty-One

We arrived at Johns Hopkins Hospital and were met by a detective from the Baltimore PD. His name was Don Harrington, and we all shook hands, made introductions and then went to the crime scene.

The door to the room had been taped off with police tape and there were two uniformed officers standing on either side of the door. One of them had a clipboard, and entered our names and affiliations to it, along with the time. Don, Dave and I put on suits to protect contaminating the scene, along with head and foot protection. We pulled down the tape and then we entered the room.

The first thing I did was to take a look around the entire room, trying to take it all in. I saw the victim in the middle of the room, sitting on a beat up chair, obviously deceased. A few posters of naked women, a hot plate, and a coffee maker. A mug which probably held coffee was lying on the floor with a stain spread out from it. There was an assortment of cleaning supplies, a mop and bucket and a waxing machine.

"We haven't moved a thing," Don said. "We did have the Medical Examiner come in to declare the victim dead, even though it was pretty obvious. We also had one of our guys take pictures of the entire room. One of our CSI guys did find rope fibers around his body. We figured the killer had removed the rope after he was dead."

"We really appreciate you treating this scene and keeping it pristine Don," Dave said. "I'm glad you saw the vic and knew it was related to our serial killer."

"I had read your bulletin only two hours before I got the call. Once I saw him, I knew it had to be your guy. What was the name you guys gave him again?"

"Ummm, the Brutal Abuser."

"Yeah, that was it. I guess you can't argue your killer is brutal."

"Do you have his name and any information on the vic yet?" I asked.

Don pulled out a notepad and began to read.

"Victim was Max Gardner, age forty-six. He was working here after being paroled. His parole officer, John Lincoln, was called and he informed us he would send over Gardner's file, when he got around to it. He did tell me Gardner had murdered his wife, twenty years ago. He had been sentenced to twenty five years but got parole for good behavior. He's been out about two weeks."

Dave leaned out the door and repeated the info to Carl, asking him to get what he could on Max Gardner. Then he came back in.

Taking a closer look, I said, "Looks like our guy for sure Dave. He has a busted nose, a couple of teeth knocked loose, probably his jaw is broken as well. I can't tell about the ribs or groin, but I'm sure there will be injuries. Again the throat was cut almost from ear to ear."

"Is there anything else here Warren?"

"I don't think so. Do we have an approximate time of death?"

"He was seen mopping outside the ICU by a nurse around 1:15 am Wednesday," Don replied. "He was discovered this morning at 7:00 am by another janitor. So we figure between 1:30 and about 6:00. Once the ME gets him on the table we will have a better idea."

"I don't suppose we would be lucky to have any security cameras in this area?"

"Afraid not. They have them at the front and rear doors, the loading dock and near the pharmacy where the drugs are kept. But that's about all."

"Still, I think we need to get all the footage from say ten on Tuesday night till six the following morning from all the cameras."

"Okay, I'll get them sent to you, along with the ME's report once he has finished it. Anything else in here?"

"No, I think we have all we can get here," Dave said.

We exited the room, and I took a look along the hallways. I didn't see a damn thing which could help us. It seemed as if this killer was either extremely careful or was a ghost. And I didn't believe in ghosts.

"I think we would like to visit the parole officer now," Dave said. Turning to Aaron and Carl, he said, "Carl, you stay here and run down everything you can on our victim. Aaron, I want you to interview some of the staff. Get a feel for our victim. Then tonight, you can come back and interview the staff who were on duty as of midnight last night. Maybe someone saw someone suspicious, although I seriously doubt it. Still we need to cover all the bases."

Carl and Aaron nodded and then Don, Dave and I left to speak with the parole officer. We got into Don's unmarked car, and he took us to the parole offices. It only took about ten minutes, so we didn't have much time to talk.

We all showed our ID's and then we were directed to a small office on the third floor. We found what we thought was John Lincoln's office and saw a small man, smoking a cigar, sitting behind a pile of paperwork on his desk.

"Excuse me, but are you John Lincoln?" Don asked.

"Yeah, yeah, what the hell do you want?" he replied, not even looking up.

Dave decided we didn't have time for Lincoln's attitude and went into the room, pushing aside some of the paperwork.

"I'm Special Agent Anderson from the FBI, Officer Lincoln," he said. "I'm investigating the sixth victim of a serial killer, and I don't have time for your attitude."

"Geez, okay, don't get all federal on me. What can I do for you?"

"Is there somewhere a bit less crowded we can talk?"

"Sure, sure, right down the hall."

"Great, let's go down there and bring the file on Max Gardner with you."

Dave turned and walked down the hall, finding a small conference room. We all sat down and waited for Lincoln to bring the file.

"Hey guys," Lincoln said, "I'm sorry about all that. But as you saw, I'm swamped with work and this job can get to you. I'll help any way I can."

Lincoln then sat down and put out a slightly dirty hand toward Dave. Dave shook his hand and then said," Okay Officer Lincoln..."

"Please, call me John."

"Okay John, do you have the file on Max Gardner?"

"Right here. What do you want to know?"

"Just run down what you have and then I will need a full copy of this file."

"Sure, I can do that. Let's see now. Max Gardner, age forty six, sentenced to a twenty five year sentence. Seems he was a good boy, never getting into any trouble in prison. Ummm, paroled two weeks ago. I got him a room at a halfway house, and a job as a janitor at Johns Hopkins."

"Does it say anything in there about who his victim was and the circumstances of the murder?"

"Ummm, no, nothing like that."

"Okay, I'll need a copy now please."

Lincoln nearly jumped out of his chair to get Dave his copy. We stood, waiting at the door and within two minutes, Lincoln returned with the copy.

As we were walking away, Lincoln called out, "Anything else I can do just say the word!"

We got on the elevator and returned to Johns Hopkins. We found Carl set up in a small office the hospital allowed him to use. Don was going to head back to his precinct to get all the information on Max Gardner's arrest, who he killed and any other pertinent information. We sat down, watching Carl work his magic on his laptop. After about ten minutes, he stopped, looked up and said, "You guys are never going to believe this."

Chapter Fifty - Two

"Okay Carl, you have our attention," Dave said.

"When I heard our victim was working at this hospital, I knew it couldn't be a coincidence. So I kinda hacked into the Baltimore PD's computers..."

"You hacked into their what!"

"I just figured you wouldn't want to wait...sir."

"Okay, what's done is done, but don't tell anyone else."

"Anyway, I found out who Max Gardner's victim was and all the circumstances," Carl said and sat back with a big smile on his face.

"Go on Carl."

"Oh right. His victim was Brandy Gardner, Max Gardner's wife. He apparently beat the hell out of her in a drunken stupor and then threw her down a set of stairs. Broke her neck on the way down and she died immediately."

"Okay, so he not only killed his wife but abused her. Anything else?"

"I figured there had to be a connection to this place, considering Waters and his wife both worked here around the time she died. So I hacked into the hospital records..."

"You hacked into the..." Dave said as he ran his hands over his face.

"Ummm yeah, it wasn't hard. I mean they had this firewall from like ten years ago and..."

"Never mind Carl. Just tell me what you found out please."

"Right. Brandy happened to be a nurse at Johns Hopkins during the same time Dr. Malcolm Waters and his wife Jocelyn worked here."

"Now that is very interesting Carl," I said. "Did you work your magic and find out if they knew each other?"

"What do you think. Of course I did. Both Jocelyn and Brandy Gardner had worked in the psych ward. They would have known each other and worked together. How's that for a coincidence!"

"Yeah well, I don't believe in coincidences. So let's see now. Brandy Gardner and Jocelyn both worked here with Dr. Waters. Brandy gets murdered by Max Gardner. Waters marries Jocelyn. And twenty years later, right after Max Gardner gets released, Max is killed here at Johns Hopkins. I don't suppose you found anyone else who was working here at the same time who might still work here?"

"Warren, this is why they pay me the big bucks. There was another nurse who worked here then. Her name is Margaret Timmons, and she just so happens to be in charge of nursing. She is also on duty today and her office is on the fifth floor."

"Carl, if I wasn't married and you weren't so ugly, I'd kiss you!" Dave said.

"Awww you don't have to kiss...hey, what do you mean I'm ugly!"

"You keep looking into Brandy Gardner Carl. I want to know everything about her. Also find Aaron and tell him what you found out. Warren and I will go and visit Head of Nursing Margaret Timmons."

We stood up and were about to leave when Dave turned back.

"Great work, although a bit unorthodox Carl," Dave said. "And you really aren't ugly."

Dave and I made our way to the elevators and went up to the fifth floor. There we were directed to the office of Miss Timmons.

Dave knocked on the door and we were told to enter. We walked into a nice office, decorated with some comfortable furniture and pictures of the hospital through the years. Sitting behind an uncluttered neat desk, was a woman who was approximately fifty years old. She had her brown hair tied up in a bun, with an old fashioned nurses cap on her head. She wore glasses with a chain holding them around her neck, and no makeup. She was dressed in a white nurses outfit and looked to be a stern no non-sense woman.

"Excuse me Miss Timmons..."Dave began.

"Head Nurse Timmons," she said.

"Ummm, Head Nurse Timmons. My name is Special Agent Dave Anderson, and this is Special Agent Warren Temple. We are from the FBI and would like to ask you a few questions."

"Then you best come in and take a seat gentlemen. Would you care for any coffee?"

I guess she wasn't as stern as I thought she would be. Dave and I sat, declined the coffee and then Dave began.

"Head Nurse Timmons..."

"Please call me Maggie." She said with a smile. "I only use my full title to scare young nurses and to people who I don't know. Please continue."

"Thank you Maggie. We are here because a man was found murdered in the basement early this morning, a Max Gardner."

"Really? I hadn't heard about it yet."

"I understand. Max Gardner killed his wife, Brandy Gardner twenty years ago."

Maggie's face lost all color, and I thought she might pass out. I grabbed some water from a pitcher on her desk, poured a glass and handed it to her. A few minutes later she was composed again.

"Oh, I'm terribly sorry, gentlemen. I haven't heard her name or thought about her in almost twenty years. And you said Max Gardner, the man who killed her, was working here, in this hospital?"

"Yes he was. He was given parole and his parole officer got him a job as a janitor. Can you tell us about her?"

"How ironic for him to be working here. But of course I can tell you about Brandy. Back then I had only been a nurse for a few years. I was assigned to the psych ward along with a few other nurses. Brandy, Jocelyn and I..."

"You knew Jocelyn Waters?"

"Back then it was Jocelyn Mason. But I knew right from the start Dr. Waters was smitten with her. I knew they were destined to be married. So, there was Brandy, Jocelyn and me working the psych ward. We were like the three musketeers. We got along so well, and I think we grew to love each other."

"Then Brandy was murdered."

"Yes, I remember the day Jocelyn and I heard about it. We were working with Dr. Waters, and we were concerned because Brandy had not shown up for work. It wasn't like her, and I was worried. Then a police officer informed us of her death and her husband had been arrested. I never did like him, seemed so jealous. He was caught several times spying on Brandy. Not in the psych ward because it is a locked off floor, but in other places around the hospital. It was ridiculous! Brandy truly loved him, but I suppose he just didn't believe her."

"How did Dr. Waters react when he heard about Brandy being killed?"

"Let me think. He was upset of course. But Jocelyn and I were devastated. It was only a few weeks later Dr. Waters proposed and then he and Jocelyn left the hospital. I kept in touch with her for a few years but then we drifted apart."

"Is there anything else you think we need to know?" I asked.

"I can't think of anything else but…"

Yes?"

"Now that I think about it, I remember Dr. Waters saying men like that who would hurt and kill their wives should be put down like dogs. Yes, that's what he said, like dogs."

"Thank you very much Maggie," Dave said. "I think that will be all."

Dave and I stood, and he handed her his card.

"If you think of anything else, please don't hesitate to give us a call."

As we turned to leave Maggie said, "Max's death can't have anything to do with what he did twenty years ago…can it?"

"That's what we are going to find out."

As we rode the elevator down to find Carl and Aaron, I asked Dave what he thought about what Maggie had said.

"What I think Warren, is we need to stop pussy footing around with Dr. Waters," Dave said. "I think it's about time we have a talk with him."

"I couldn't agree with you more Dave," I said.

We went to find Carl and Aaron and in the pit of my stomach I felt an old ache like I used to feel back in the NYPD. We were hot on the trail of a killer now and it wouldn't be long till we had him behind bars. But something was bothering me. It was like an itch I couldn't reach. I'd had an itch just like it many times in the past and usually whatever was bothering me would come to the surface, sooner or later. I would just have to wait on it.

Chapter Fifty - Three

We had stayed over in Baltimore so Aaron could interview the personnel who had been working on the midnight tour when Max Gardner had been murdered. He spoke to some doctors, nurses, and other janitors, but not one of them had seen anyone suspicious.

Carl had tried to find out any and everything he could on Brandy Gardner, and he continued digging into Dr. Waters and his wife Jocelyn's background. Unfortunately, he hadn't come up with anything new. But Carl was like a dog with a bone. He wasn't going to stop searching just because he couldn't find anything new...yet.

Meanwhile, Aaron had contacted the agents who were supposed to put a tracker on Dr. Waters' jet. It hadn't been easy, but one of them posed as an airport worker and managed to get close enough to put the tracker inside the wheel housing on the jet. Hopefully it wouldn't come loose and fall off. The tracker was now being monitored on Carl's laptop. As of a few hours ago it showed Dr. Waters' jet sitting at the airport in Montpelier, Vermont.

We had been going over plans all day, trying to figure out the best way to confront Dr. Waters. We still were waiting on an answer from Lou and Billy concerning Kevin Waxman. It would now be up to Billy on his climb to try and get Waxman to open up. We needed to either connect him to the killings or eliminate him, and I was beginning to think we could.

As for Dr. Waters, he had deviated from his flight plan on Tuesday night. He could have flown into an airport near Baltimore, maybe a small private one. Then he could have killed Max Gardner, gotten back on his jet, and flown to Vermont. The timing worked but it would have been tight.

I kept on thinking back to Waters, Jocelyn and Brandy all working at Johns Hopkins. What were the odds for Brandy's husband Max, to be killed twenty years later in the same hospital they had all worked at? And seeing how Waters was connected to all the other killings by having had sessions with all the victims' wives, seemed to defy the odds. Well, not all the victims' wives. One of them had been seen by a counselor but that counselor had been in contact with Waters. So he still fit as our killer.

Then why was I still trying to scratch the itch in the back of my mind? Something didn't fit but for the life of me, I couldn't figure out what.

We were getting ready to leave, having decided we would have to wait for Dr. Waters to return to New York before we finally questioned him. Carl was checking on the tracker one more time before we called it a night. He would keep an eye on it over the weekend.

"Ummm, guys," Carl said.

"What is it Carl?" Dave asked.

"Waters' jet left the Vermont airport and now he appears to be close to New York. I had checked about four hours ago, and it was still in Vermont. But it looks like he is coming home."

"Do you think we should head out to the airport and grab him tonight?" I asked.

"I don't think so, I've been rethinking talking to Waters just yet," Dave said. "I really want to give Billy a chance to get some info on Waxman. He is climbing with him early tomorrow morning. Carl, you keep an eye on

Waters' jet and call me as soon as he lands. Then I want to know if he takes off again."

"What about speaking to his pilot, ummm Trask."

"Carl, in between everything else you are doing, can you get us Trask's home address? Maybe we will speak to him after we find out about Waxman."

"You mean if we find out about Waxman. I have faith in Billy, but he might not be able to eliminate or connect Waxman on one climb."

"Very true Warren. Here's what we will do. If Billy doesn't come through, I will have them pull him into the FBI offices in Baltimore Saturday after the climb. There, they will interrogate him and find out what we need to know. Then on Sunday, you and I will talk with Trask first thing in the morning. After him, we will confront Dr. Waters. We can't let this go on too much longer. What do you think?"

"I guess it's as good a plan as any. We will just have to hope our good doctor isn't planning on taking off to somewhere else. Maybe we should put eyes on him at his home."

"I think you are right Warren. I will call Teller and ask him to get 24 hour surveillance on Waters at his home. Carl, you keep an eye on the tracker. Aaron, you can head home but be ready to move if we need you. Warren, I will call you on Saturday after I get a call from Lou and Billy."

We all agreed to do what Dave had laid out. I left the building heading for home. Maybe all of this would finally come to its conclusion. Maybe even by Sunday.

I got to my house, and I decided I would try not to let the case bother me. I wanted to hear all about the adoption. I also wanted to spend some quality time with Trace.

I walked in the back door, seeing the watering can in its usual spot, sitting on a small stool near the door. Seeing it always made me smile and be thankful for having Trace in my life.

"Trace," I called out. "Trace," I called out louder and I began to get nervous.

I looked around downstairs, getting more nervous, but then I found her in the bedroom, and she was crying. I went to her, sat down on the bed next to her and wrapped my arms around her.

"Oh Warren," she said while sobbing.

"What's wrong baby?" I said.

"Melissa and I were talking to some adoption agencies...and...and every one of them told me it would be almost impossible to adopt a child at our age!"

"It's okay baby. Someone saying it's almost impossible means it is also possible. A little thing like our age isn't going to stop us now. I promise you, as soon as this case is done, I will give it my full attention. Soon you are going to be a momma. I promise."

"Really? Do you really think we can do it?"

"No matter what it takes."

"Oh Warren! I love you so much!"

"Okay now, stop crying. It's a beautiful night. How about we get some wine, put on some soft music and go count the stars in the sky?"

Her answer was to kiss me deeply, and then she went into the bathroom to splash some cold water on her face. I had just made her a promise, and I wasn't sure how to keep it. But whatever it took, I would make sure I didn't break it.

Chapter Fifty - Four

Dr. Waters had planned on leaving Vermont on Saturday morning to go to his next stop, which was Rhode Island. Then he had received a call from Jocelyn. She was nearly hysterical. She had finally calmed down enough to tell him Brandon had been involved in a car accident. He was in surgery as they spoke at North Shore University Hospital. He assured her he was on the way and then called Trask. He explained the situation, and they had taken off within an hour after the call from his wife.

Now they were close to landing at MacArthur Airport. He knew Dennis had pushed the jet to its limits, flying toward home as quickly as possible. He moved into the cockpit and sat down in the second seat up front.

"How much longer Dennis?" Waters asked.

"We will be landing in ten minutes," Trask answered. "I radioed ahead and there will be a Nassau County police officer there to meet us to take you to the hospital."

"I guess it pays to contribute to our local police a few hundred thousand dollars every few years."

"Yes sir, it surly does. Buckle up now."

"Dennis, I don't want to take my valise with me. Would you please take it home with you. Just do me a favor and keep it closed. Can you do that?"

"Of course sir. No problem. Now go buckle up, we are almost on the ground."

Waters hurried to the back of the jet and belted himself in at his seat. He didn't want to give his valise to

Dennis, but he didn't want to take it into the hospital either. Leaving it unsecured on the jet was unacceptable as well. He trusted Dennis would never open it.

He felt a small jolt as the jet's wheels hit the runway. Dennis taxied to the hanger. As he did, Waters undid his belt and brought his valise up to Dennis. A few minutes later they were in the hangar,

Waters hurried off the jet and waiting there was an officer standing next to a marked car.

"Dr. Waters?" the officer asked.

"Yes, I am Dr. Waters. Thank you Officer..."

"Sgt. Atwell sir. At your service. Please sit up front sir. I don't think you would be very comfortable in back. I'll have you at North Shore as quickly as I can."

"Thank you Sergeant Atwell."

Waters got into the car and with lights and sirens blaring, Sgt. Atwell headed for the hospital. Waters was so concerned for his son; he didn't even think about how fast Atwell was driving. It took much shorter time than he thought possible, but soon Sgt. Atwell pulled up to the front entrance.

"Thank you Sergeant Atwell, I can't thank you enough," Waters said.

"No problem sir and I will pray for your son," Sgt. Atwell replied.

Waters ran into the hospital and after finding the correct elevator up to the surgical ward, he found his wife crying in the surgical waiting room. As he approached, she stood, and he wrapped his arms around her. She finally stopped crying and together they sat down.

"Tell me what happened," Waters said.

"He was out with his friend Jake," Jocelyn answered. "They were going to a movie. I don't know exactly what happened, but I think the officer who came to the house said they were hit by a drunk. The bastard ran a red light and hit the driver's side. His friend Jake was killed!"

"Oh God! And Brandon?"

"Brandon had been in the passenger seat. He was thrown hard against the passenger window. He hit his head! I'm not even sure how badly he was hurt or why he is in surgery!"

"Okay Jocelyn, calm down. I am here now. I will find out exactly what is going on, but you must calm down. Now wait here for a second and I will go see what is going on with our boy."

Dr. Waters left Jocelyn and went in search of someone he could speak with. He finally found a nurse and identified himself.

"Please wait in the waiting room Doctor and I will get in touch with the doctor in surgery," she said.

Reluctantly, Dr. Waters returned to his wife to await word. Another twenty minutes passed, and just as Dr. Waters was about to go looking for someone else to find out his son's condition, a surgeon approached them both.

"Is he..." Jocelyn began to say.

"He is out of danger Mrs. Waters," he said. "I am Dr. Patel. Your son had a few serious injuries, with the most serious being a concussion and fractured skull. He had an intracranial hematoma, a bleed on the brain. Blood was building up on his brain, so we had to put in a shunt and relieve the pressure. But I believe he will pull through with no permanent damage."

"Thank God!" Jocelyn said.

"I am Dr. Waters, Brandon's father," Waters said. "First, thank you Dr. Patel. You said there were other injuries?"

"Yes, he broke his right humerus from the impact and also he hit his knee very hard. We will have to get an MRI for his knee once he has recovered from the surgery. We did set his arm, and luckily it was a clean break. I'm afraid he is in for a few months of recovery and some physical therapy. But he will make a full recovery. He is in post op right now. I will have a nurse let you know when you can see him."

"Thank you doctor once again."

Dr. Waters and Jocelyn held hands and waited for a nurse to come and get them. They didn't say anything else, both of them lost in deep thoughts.

Chapter Fifty - Five

Saturday, At the base of C wall, 7:10 am

Billy and Lou picked up Waxman at 6:30 am just as planned. Waxman was smiling as he put his equipment into the trunk. But then when he saw Lou he seemed to be annoyed. A few minutes into the ride with Billy talking a mile a minute about the climb changed his attitude. He was even speaking while Billy drove.

"Great weather for a climb," Billy said. "I can't wait!"

"Hopefully the good weather hasn't brought out a ton of climbers," Waxman replied. "If there are too many of them we will just go somewhere else."

Lou wasn't too happy to hear him say they might change locations. How would she be able to tell the two agents who were going to be at C wall to look after Billy? Lou figured the only thing she could do would be to call Teller after they arrived somewhere else. Hopefully he could get in touch with them and have them go wherever they would be. They would be late but maybe they would still arrive in time for Billy.

Soon they pulled into a small parking lot and Waxman clapped his hands because the lot was pretty empty. Only three other cars were parked there. Lou couldn't tell which one belonged to the two agents, and she hoped one of them did. Billy parked and he and Waxman got out their equipment. They put on different shoes made for climbing, gloves with the finger tips cut off, two small pouches which contained powder and helmets. Lou grabbed a pair of binoculars she had asked Billy to get while he was buying his equipment.

Waxman was smiling ear to ear as they began to walk toward a tower of granite ahead. They followed a small trail marked with signs with the names of different trails and their difficulty. Lou wasn't happy when they came to a turnoff showing the way to C wall. It stated it was for high intermediate climbers or experts.

Waxman turned into the trail and Lou pulled Billy back a little.

"Are you sure you can climb this?" Lou whispered.

"Don't worry Lou, I got this," he answered and hurried to catch up to Waxman.

Lou was upset but there wasn't a thing she could do. Maybe she should fake being sick? She could even fake passing out and then they wouldn't be able to climb. But Billy would never forgive her. Besides, they had a job to do. Shaking her head, she moved quicker to catch up to them. A few minutes later they were both standing at the base of a wall of granite.

"What do you think Billy?" Waxman asked.

Billy looked up, walked around a bit and said, "I can't wait to attack this baby!"

Waxman began pointing out different spots on the wall, and Billy was paying rapt attention. Lou was looking for the two agents and finally spotted one about a quarter of the way up the wall. Then she saw the other one approaching up the trail. Lou figured one would be looking down as Waxman and Billy made the climb, and the other would be under them. As she looked at the one coming up the trail, he gave a small nod to her. Seeing both men made her feel a bit better. They both looked to be strong men, and she hoped they wouldn't be needed to do anything.

Billy came over to Lou and gave her a kiss on the cheek.

"Don't worry Lou, this doesn't look too bad," Billy said.

Waxman said, "Okay Billy. It looks like we will have two others climbing but I don't think it will be any trouble. I'll go first and you come up about ten feet behind me. Ready?"

"Absolutely!"

Lou was too nervous to sit so she paced watching Waxman start to climb up the wall. He looked at ease and soon he was at least fifteen feet off the ground. Billy began to climb right below him, and he too looked amazingly at ease. She watched as he climbed using his feet, hands, and fingertips. She knew he was strong, but didn't realize just how strong he really was. At one point he seemed to pull his whole body up by his fingertips alone.

Looking up, Lou saw Waxman move into a crevice in the face of the wall. He began moving up by placing his back against the wall, his feet against the opposite side, and then inching up. Lou watched as he slowly made progress higher. After about fifteen minutes, he emerged out of the crevice and sat on a small ledge, about six feet long, waiting for Billy.

Billy reached the crevice and seemed to be deciding what to do.

Waxman called down to him.

"Billy," he said, "Just use your back and feet to inch up! It's a snap."

"Right," Billy yelled up.

Lou watched as Billy moved into the crevice. His back and feet tightly pushed in opposite directions. Billy began to inch his way up. Lou was watching with the binoculars she had brought along. She saw the one agent about ten feet above Waxman and the other steadily catching up from below.

Billy was about halfway up the crevice, and it looked as if he was going to be fine.

"Hey Lou," he yelled down. "See, I told you, nothing to worry about."

Lou waved to him and then she saw one of Billy's feet slip! He began to slide down the crevice, small pebbles becoming dislodged and tumbling down. He was trying to gain purchase somehow but to Lou it looked as if he was going to tumble out of the crevice and fall!

"Open yourself up!" Waxman called out. "Like a cork in a bottle Billy!"

Billy must have heard him. He stopped trying to get a handhold and pushed his feet out and pressed his back against the opposite side. He slowed and finally stopped, just a few feet from the bottom of the crevice.

Lou took a few deep breaths and saw Billy was okay but shaken. Even from her position she could tell he had been scared of falling from the expression on his face.

"Maybe you should come down!" Lou yelled up to him.

Billy didn't answer at first, but then yelled down, "No way Lou! I'm going up!"

Lou knew there was nothing she could do but watch and pray.

Billy got into a better position and then began the crawl back up the crevice. Fifteen long minutes later he emerged and sat side by side next to Waxman on the small ledge. Lou let out a breath she didn't realize she had been holding. The agent below Billy gave her an ok with his fingers. Then he reached the crevice and waited.

Lou couldn't hear what Waxman and Billy were saying, but they seemed to be conversing.

"Close one," Billy said.

"I had faith you would figure it out Billy," Waxman said.

"Where else have you been climbing Kevin? I've done some in New Jersey, New York and Connecticut. How about you?'

"I've done some in Jersey. I used to work in Newark."

"Were you a social worker there too?"

"Yeah, but I left after my supervisor turned into a real ass."

"I know how that is. Where else have you been?"

"I've done some climbing in upstate New York, some out west. Never been to Connecticut. How was the climbing there?"

"It was okay. I'm looking forward to doing more in Mass."

Billy thought about Waxman stating he had never been to Connecticut. If he believed him, he couldn't be the killer. Or maybe Waters and he had split the killing? Nah, he somehow doubted it. It would be rare for two serial killers to work together. It had happened in the past, but Billy doubted he and Waters were a team.

"Okay, you rested for the next bit?" Waxman asked.

"Ready when you are Kevin," Billy replied.

"Okay, we climb out to the side about ten feet and then we have to make a jump."

Billy had done some jumps from one hold to another over the years, but he hadn't done any in a long time. He was a bit nervous but what else could he do?

"I'll watch you Kevin and then I'll follow behind, okay?"

"Sure, just watch me. When I do the jump, be sure to notice where I make the grab."

Kevin began to move to his right, holding on with his feet and hands. About ten feet out, he came to a spot where there was a deep crack in the granite. It looked to be about three to four feet wide. The crack continued down, staying about four feet wide for about fifteen feet and then narrowed till it closed up again. Billy watched as Kevin rocked a bit and then with a smooth move, released himself from the granite face and leaped across the opening. He grabbed hold of a small outcropping of stone with his hands and dug his feet into the granite below him. He made it look easy. He maneuvered a few feet up to watch Billy.

Lou watching from below was suddenly scared to death. Billy wasn't going to do that crazy jump, was he? She watched from below, her heart beating fast as she watched Billy begin to move off the ledge. From above, Waxman had wedged himself in, able to stay where he was, keeping an eye on Billy.

Billy got to the spot where Waxman had jumped from. Billy reached the crack in the wall and stopped. He was looking across the opening and began to rock back and forth as Waxman had done. Then he stopped rocking, taking another look at the jump. Maybe he wasn't going to jump, Lou thought. Maybe he had come to his senses and was going to work his way down.

Lou had never been more scared in her life watching Billy above.

Billy took a few deep breaths, rocked back and forth a few more times, and then leapt off across the opening.

Lou watched in horror as Billy tried to grab the outcropping Waxman had grabbed, slipped and then began to fall!

Chapter Fifty - Six

Saturday At Home, 12:35 pm

I was sitting on the patio eating a terrific club sandwich Trace had made for me. We had discussed our next move in the adoption process into the night. In the morning when we woke up, Trace had seemed more positive and had stopped being worried. She knew we would do whatever we needed to do to adopt a child. Perhaps we would have a better chance if we changed the age of the child she originally wanted. Instead of a child of five or six, maybe we should consider an older child of ten or twelve. Neither of us knew for sure if we would have a better chance with an older child. I had made a suggestion to contact an attorney to help us. Up to now, Trace and Melissa had been asking questions and trying to do everything themselves. Trace had agreed on an attorney, and I told her I would get in touch with a guy I knew in the NYPD who had adopted a year ago.

Trace had been excited again and we had made love after taking a morning shower together. Then she had made the sandwiches, and we were sitting out on the deck. I had a beer, and she had an iced tea. We had some oldies music playing, and I was singing an old song by Sam the Sham and the Pharoahs.

"Wooly bully, wooly bully," I was belting out when the phone rang. I turned down the music and answered.

"Warren, it's Dave," I heard Dave say.

I was feeling good and without really thinking I said," What's up my brother!"

"I'm afraid Billy had an accident."

My mood changed immediately.

"What happened?"

"From what Lou was able to tell me, he was climbing with Waxman. They had gotten about halfway up this granite wall. She said Waxman had made this jump over a large crack and landed okay. Then Billy had tried to do the same thing but missed the handhold."

"Holy shit! He tried to jump across a crack and missed! Is he ...dead Dave?"

"Thank God no. But he was lucky because he fell back into the crack. It was about four feet wide for ten feet or so, and then closed up a bit lower. He was sliding feet first down it. It was lucky he fell back into it at all. The fall straight down probably would have killed him. Unfortunately, he landed very hard on his left foot. His femur broke and the shaft punctured through the skin, a compound fracture. I'm not sure if he was lucky, but the pain must have been terrible because he passed out. He was sort of wedged in, so he wasn't going to fall out."

"But they got him down and to a hospital?"

"Yeah, our two guys reached him quickly. Lou called for an ambulance right away. Our guys got some ropes from another climber nearby, and they were able to slip it around him. He was still unconscious and lowered him down to the ground. Good thing we had those two agents in place. Lou and he were taken to a hospital nearby. They had to do surgery and put a bar in his thigh to support the break. But he is going to be okay."

"How is Lou?"

"She didn't sound great, but she was able to tell me she didn't think Waxman was a suspect any longer."

"Huh? Why?"

"While they waited for the ambulance, Waxman climbed down and when he got to the ground he took one look at Billy's leg, and all the blood and promptly fainted. When he came to, he told Lou he couldn't stand the sight of blood. If he saw even a few drops he would get nauseous and pass out."

I laughed but then said, "I suppose you are right. I doubt he would be able to slice someone's neck from ear to ear. So what's next for Lou and Billy? Will he be able to come home soon?"

"Lou wasn't sure yet, she figured it would be five to seven days at the least. She told Waxman she was resigning and taking her brother back home to New York."

"Quick thinking on her part. Okay, where do we go from here?"

"I got a call from the guys keeping an eye on Waters' home. Waters and his wife left the house early this morning and went directly to North Shore University Hospital. One of our guys followed them in. He found out their son Brandon had been in a bad car accident last night."

"Damn, was the kid hurt badly?"

"He had a concussion, a fractured skull with a brain bleed and a broken arm. Possibly an injured knee, but he is going to make a full recovery. But the kid driving was killed instantly. The guy who broadsided them was drunk and has been arrested. He ran a red light."

"When the fuck are people going to stop driving drunk! How old was the other kid?"

"Not sure but he couldn't have been too old if he was Brandon's friend. Brandon is only 15."

"Right. Okay so Waters and his wife will be occupied with their kid for at least a week I suppose. Gives us more time to work out what we are going to do."

"Yeah I figure we can wait till Monday to go to his pilot's home. I asked Teller to assign a couple of guys to keep an eye on him till we talk with him. So take the rest of the weekend and I'll see you in the office early Monday morning."

"Do you need me to call Carl or Aaron?"

"No, I'll call them as soon as I hang up. See you Monday...my brother!"

"Yeah, sorry about that," I laughed and then said goodbye.

I hung up from Dave and gave Trace the rundown on everything which had happened.

"Do you want to take a ride up to Boston to see Billy and Lou?" she asked.

"How did I ever get so lucky to find a woman like you," I said. "No, I doubt he will be up for visitors, and I have a feeling Lou will be taking excellent care of him. But now we do have the whole weekend to ourselves. How about we take a little trip?"

"Where would you like to go?"

"I was thinking we head into the city, get an outrageously expensive hotel room, maybe catch a Broadway show, eat only expensive food and then screw the night away!"

"I'll go pack a few things, Tiger!"

Trace went upstairs to pack, and I sat back for a second, finishing my beer. It was strange how things happened. If Billy hadn't fallen and nearly bled to death, we wouldn't know Waxman couldn't stand the sight of blood.

And if Waters' son hadn't been in a car accident, Waters wouldn't have flown home. Then we might not get to speak with him for who knows how long. Now we wouldn't have to worry about another murder, at least for a week or so. Crazy how fate seemed to work sometimes.

Oh well. I finished my beer and went upstairs to pack. I was going to forget all about the case for another day and a half. I was going to spend some wonderful time with the love of my life. It was going to be fantastic, at least until Monday morning. And then the hunt will begin anew. But this time I felt better about closing this case and stopping the murders. Dr. Waters was in our sights and somehow we would get him.

Chapter Fifty - Seven

Dr. Waters and Jocelyn were sitting by the side of their son's bed. They had spent most of Saturday at his bedside and were there again. He was still unconscious, and Jocelyn had been upset he still hadn't woken up. She kept on saying he may never wake up. She was nearly hysterical until Waters had gotten in touch with Dr. Patel. He had come to the room and assured her he was fine; it was just his body's way of dealing with the trauma. Many times when a body needed to heal, it put itself into a temporary coma.

Now the two of them sat silently, each in their own thoughts. Dr. Waters had made a ton of calls to all the shelters and safe houses he was scheduled to visit. Then he called several fellow doctors in the different states he always kept in contact with. In case he couldn't make it to a patient in need, he would call one of them to see a victim. Then they would send him a full report. Of course he would pay them, but he didn't care about the money. He had more than he would ever spend.

What was on his mind besides his son's condition, was his valise. He knew it was safe with Dennis, but he still wanted to get it back in his possession. He trusted Dennis, but he knew better than most what temptation was. He doubted Dennis would be tempted to take just a little peek, but then again, maybe he would. How would he ever be able to explain what was inside to him? He couldn't.

He had called Dennis to tell him they wouldn't be flying anywhere anytime soon. He told him to enjoy a week or so off. Then he asked if he would perhaps meet him at the hospital with the valise. Then he thought better of it, telling him to never mind. Just keep it at home, safe and sound. The next time they flew somewhere he could bring it with him. He was glad he thought better of having Dennis bring it to the hospital. What if Jocelyn saw it and asked what was inside? And why did he need it now? No, he couldn't risk it.

"What are you thinking about Malcolm?" Jocelyn asked. "You seem to be in such deep thought."

"Nothing really love, just about how lucky we are to have our son alive and healing," he replied.

"I really don't know what I would have done if he had been killed. I spoke with Jake's mother this morning. They are absolutely devastated. They said there will be a funeral on Thursday at the church in town, the Catholic one. I think we should be there."

"Yes, I think so too. Of course they may have a little anger toward us."

"Why would they be angry with us?"

"Because they lost their son, and we still have ours. It isn't logical but it does happen all the time in situations like this. But we will go. Just be prepared if they are angry at us."

Brandon let out a low moan and Jocelyn jumped up to hold his hand.

"Do you think he is waking up Malcolm?" she asked in a tense voice.

"No dear, he is probably dreaming, or he is in some pain," Malcolm replied. "I will get a nurse to give him some more pain meds."

"Yes, please do. I don't think there is any reason for him to be in pain right now."

He watched Jocelyn holding her son's hand and thought to himself how this was only the beginning of pain for their son. He would probably need surgery for his knee. And then it might be weeks or months of physical therapy. How the concussion affected his son only time would tell. And Brandon might not be able to compete in swimming or any other sports. Perhaps he could bring in someone full time to live at the house to take care of Brandon. He knew Jocelyn would like it if he did.

He went in search of a nurse and couldn't help but think of his valise again. He had to get it back soon or it would drive him crazy. He found a nurse and went back to be with his wife.

"A nurse will be right in Jocelyn," he said. "I suggest we go to the cafeteria and get some food and coffee. We have to keep up our strength and stay healthy to take care of Brandon. She said it was time to empty his urine bag and change his bedding."

He watched as she bent down and gave him a soft kiss. Then they left to go to the cafeteria together, arm in arm. While waiting for the elevator, the thought of his valise again broke into his thoughts. He really must get it back soon.

Chapter Fifty - Eight

Monday, FBI HQ Conference Room, 8:35 am

We met early Monday morning, and I had a huge grin on my face.

"What have you been up to Warren?" Aaron said as he finished eating his third donut. "You look like, as my mother used to say, the cat who ate the canary."

"I just had the greatest weekend with my beautiful wife," I answered.

"Somehow I think it was better than mine. I spent it working on the deck in back of my house. So what did you do?"

"First we booked a room at the Plaza."

"The Plaza? Hey Dave, you better check to see if Warren is selling drugs on the side."

"It wasn't that expensive, and we decided we would go all out. If we get to..."

"Get to what?"

I almost had said if we get to adopt. I promised Trace only Dave would know what we were trying to do.

"Nothing. We just went all out. Ate out and had room service. Went to a Broadway show, *Hamilton*, and it was great. Then we took a horse drawn carriage ride around Central Park."

"Sounds like a weekend to end all weekends," Carl said.

"And what did you do Carl? I asked.

"I'm sort of ashamed to tell you guys."

"Well now you are going to have to spill the beans."

"I got together with some old Marine friends, and we went upstate to do some paint ball wars. We do it a few times a year and it was fantastic. We all should do it one weekend!"

"Before you ask," Dave said, "Melissa and I spent the weekend looking at baby furniture, clothes, toys and anything else she could think of. Then we went maternity shopping for her. She is really starting to show now. Then she allowed me to watch some sports on Sunday. But now, I think we need to get to work."

"Okay Dave, where are we with our next move?"

"I spoke with the two agents keeping an eye on Trask. He went for a run this morning, early, and then went back home. Since Waters probably isn't going to go flying anywhere this week, he probably has the week off."

"I guess we should get a move on and try to interview him first thing then, before he disappears," I said.

"My thoughts exactly, Warren, and the agents will call me if he goes out. You and I will head out to his house. He lives in Lake Success. Meanwhile, Aaron, I want you to head out to the hospital. See if you can get a look and a feel for Dr. Waters and his wife. But you have to be a bit sneaky. I don't want to tip our hand."

"No problem Dave," Aaron said.

"Carl, I guess you can keep trying to find out anything more on Waters, his wife and Brandy Gardner. I have a feeling everything started with Waters when Brandy was murdered."

"I'm on it Dave," Carl said. "I was going to try attacking their past at another angle. I'll let you know if I catch a break."

"Any word on how Billy is doing?" I asked.

"I heard from Lou Sunday night," Dave replied. "He will be laid up for more than a month, and then he will probably be on crutches. At some point down the road, he will have the bar in his leg removed."

"Will he be able to come back to work?"

"I asked Teller about it this morning. He can work here in the office until he can take and pass a physical test. The good news is, Lou said she will be driving him back to New York in a day or two. She is going to rent a small RV so he can be comfortable on the ride home. She said a plane ride would be too uncomfortable for him. Now I can tell you guys she might be taking some time off to take care of him...at her apartment. I don't want Teller to know."

We all nodded and said we would keep it under our hats. I was just happy Billy was returning home. I couldn't wait to see him.

"Okay then, Warren and I will hit the road and head out in a few minutes," Dave said.

"I have a few calls to make Dave and then I will be ready to go," I said.

I went into my office and looked up the number for an old friend of mine from the NYPD. He had been on the same team with me back when I worked at Midtown North. He was a few years younger than me, and I knew he and his wife had adopted a child a few years ago. I was hoping he could give me some insight into what I needed to know, and maybe which attorney he had used.

I dialed the number and after a few rings, it was picked up.

"Lieutenant Cooper," I heard.

"Hey there L.T." I said, "do you have some time for your old partner?"

"Is that you Temple? Damn, I figured since you are now a big bad FBI Agent, you would have forgotten about your old friends!"

Roger Cooper was a great detective back in the day and now was a lieutenant in Robbery/Homicide at Midtown North. Because of his name we always called him Coppa. He always called me Temple.

"That's Special Agent to you Coppa. How have you been?"

"Same shit, different day Temple. What about you?"

"Busy but I'm loving it. On the trail of a serial killer right now. But I called for a different reason."

"Ask and you shall receive."

"Trace and I were thinking about adopting a kid, I mean child. I knew you and Debbie adopted a few years ago and I figured you might put me on the right road."

"Wow, that's a great Temple. I sure can help but right now I have to get to a meeting with the P.C."

"The Police Commissioner? You must be a very important person, Coppa."

"Cut it out. Look, I will put together some info and then I can bring it all out to you at the mighty FBI headquarters."

"I have a better idea, Coppa. How about you, Debbie and your kid..."

"Brian and he is nine years old."

"Right, Brian. Why don't you all come out to dinner, say this week any night."

"Sounds great. I'll check with my boss and let you know. You better check with your boss too!" he said with a laugh.

"Terrific," I said. "Just text me what night and I will confirm. Let's say about seven."

"Absolutely Temple. I mean...Special Agent Temple."

We both hung up and I called Trace right away. I told her about the dinner, and she was excited to see Debbie and Coppa. And of course, Brian. She was also excited about all the information about adopting Coppa would be bringing. I told her as soon as Coppa texted me with what night, I would let her know. Then I told her I loved her, hung up, and went to find Dave.

I found Dave in his office, and I went in and sat down.

"I'll be ready in a minute Warren," he said. "Just finishing up a quick report for Teller. Why is there so much damn paperwork in our jobs!"

"Tell me about it," I answered. "I figure over the last twenty five years I could have written a hundred novels! That is if I knew how to write one."

Dave finished typing up the report and then asked me, "How do you think we should handle Trask?"

"The problem is, we don't have any idea if Trask is a loyal employee who would never say anything bad about his boss. Then again, seeing how he is a retired Colonel, if we approach him with it being his duty to help us catch a serial killer, he might be cooperative."

"I think you're right. We need to make him see it as his duty to help us. You take the lead when we talk with him. I think he might respond better to someone closer to his age. Okay then, let me drop this report off and then we can hit the road."

We left in Dave's car, and it was going to take some time to get out of Manhattan. Dave figured the best way was through the Midtown Tunnel, then the Long Island Expressway out to Lake Success. Most of the traffic was heading westbound toward the city, but nowadays, it seemed it was always rush hour going both ways. Luckily, Lake Success wasn't too far out on the island. It was right on the border of Queens.

As he drove, I told him about my old friend Coppa. I told him a few war stories and how Coppa was coming out for dinner and to help Trace and I with the adoption. As we drove, Dave asked for one more.

I thought for a second and then began, "One day Coppa and I had seen two kids painting graffiti on the side of a neighborhood store in Bedford Sty. We hadn't had much to do so we figured we would give chase. The kids ran up an elevated train station. One went down another staircase, and the other went up toward the mezzanine. Well, the kid who went up was followed by Coppa, and I went for the other. My kid got away, so I went to find Coppa. He was standing by a window halfway up to the station. I had asked him where his kid was, did he get away? He just pointed out the window. I looked, and there was the kid lying in the street. 'You threw him out the window!' I said. He said, 'no, the kid jumped.' While we were trying to decide what to do, seeing we were two white cops, the kid was black and we were in Bed Sty, the kid got up and limped away. We hightailed it out of there as quickly as we could."

"Great story Warren," Dave said. "I'll have to think about a good war story to tell you on the drive back to the city."

Before I knew it, we were pulling up in front of some nice condo's, on a tree lined street. The place looked like a nice place to live, and I noticed some expensive cars parked in some driveways. Must be a bit on the expensive side I thought. Trask was living in number 1220.

Dave pulled up and made a call to the guys who had been keeping an eye on him. First he checked that Trask was still home. He nodded to me that he was. Dave then advised them to stay in position until we finished talking to Trask. Maybe after we had talked with him, they would be able to leave. Then we walked up to his door and knocked.

Chapter Fifty - Nine

We were standing in front of Trask's door, waiting for him to open the door. After a minute the door opened. We saw a tall, well-muscled looking man in his early fifties, clean shaven with some gray in his black short hair, wearing shorts and a tank top. He was sweating and had a towel wrapped around his neck.

"Hello, can I help you?" he asked in a friendly tone with a big smile.

"Dennis Trask?" Dave asked.

"Yes, and you are?"

Dave and I took out our ID's and Dave said, "I am Special Agent Dave Anderson, and this is Special Agent Warren Temple, sir. We would like to talk with you about some serious matters."

"Please come in. Would you mind if I take a quick shower? I've been exercising. I like to try and keep in shape."

"No problem, go right ahead."

Trask directed us to a nicely furnished comfortable living room. He asked if we wanted coffee or anything else, and then went down a hallway to grab a quick shower. Dave and I didn't want to snoop, but we did look around a little.

We saw Trask had a large record collection, what are now called vinyl's. Flipping through them I saw he had quite an eclectic taste in music. There were a lot of old jazz records, along with some old fifties and sixties groups.

Then some more modern ones and some from Sinatra, Tony Bennet and Dean Martin.

Right above them was an expensive player with a radio tuner and Bluetooth receiver. I looked around and saw speakers in every corner of the room.

While I was looking through his records, Dave was looking at some framed photos. I got up to look and saw there were several of Trask in uniform and two with him flying in some military jets. Over his fireplace were several pictures of him with a very beautiful woman. I was surprised because Carl hadn't said anything about him being married.

We stopped looking around, sat down in two chairs, just as Trask reappeared. He was now wearing a tee shirt, slacks and loafers on his feet.

"Are you sure you men wouldn't care for some coffee?" he asked. "I'm going to have a cup, and I have some great bagels from a place here in town. I have the works, cream cheese and lox."

I looked at Dave and then I said, "I use butter on my bagels. Do you have an everything bagel?"

"Sure do."

"Okay then, how about you call us Dave and Warren and we can call you Dennis, okay?" Dave said.

"Sure, let's go into the kitchen. I have a table in there."

Trask set out about a dozen bagels, cream cheese, butter and some fresh sliced lox, also known as salmon, and then brought over some mugs filled with coffee. He had some sugar and milk, and we all made ourselves some of the best tasting bagels I had in a while. Trace said they were too fattening but right now I was enjoying one. We ate and drank for a few minutes.

Then Trask sat back and said, "What can I do for you guys?"

Dave gave me a nod, so I said, "First I'd like you to give us a bit of your background."

"Okay, but I'm sure you must know most of it," Trask said. "Right out of High School I enlisted in the Air Force. I found out I had an aptitude in flying jets. I flew almost every kind of plane and jet we had. Flew in the war, Desert Storm. Then I retired and kicked around a bit. Then I got a job flying Dr. Malcolm Waters around. That's about it."

"Ever been married?"

"I came close once but before we could get hitched, she died in a traffic accident."

That explained the picture on the mantel and why Carl had missed it.

"This may come as a shock to you Dennis, so I want you to just listen to me for a few minutes," I began. "Okay?"

"Sure, but I don't know how I can help you with anything. But, go ahead."

"In the past four or five years there have been several homicides. In each case, a man has been murdered who had been abusive to his wife and in some cases his children. They have been spread out up and down the east coast, in several states.

The places of the murders so far have been in Bolton, Massachusetts, Sheffield, Massachusetts, Kent, Connecticut, Newark, New Jersey, Greensboro, North Carolina, and most recently, at Johns Hopkins Hospital in Baltimore, Maryland."

Trask rubbed his hand through his hair and said, "Obviously terrible, although I can't shed a tear about men who had abused women and children. But what do these murders have to do with me?"

"We don't believe they have anything to do with you, personally Dennis. Not specifically but..."

"But what?"

"You fly Dr. Malcolm Waters to several states up and down the east coast, correct?"

"Yes, I have been flying Dr. Waters for going on twelve years now. But you can't seriously think Dr. Waters would have anything to do with committing murders. He is one of the kindest men I have ever known. Do you know he treats women and children who have been abused almost always for free? He travels to safe houses and shelters at a moment's notice. He is a very dedicated psychiatrist, husband and father."

"I'm sure what you believe is true as far as you know. Let me ask you a couple of questions, okay?"

"Sure, I want to cooperate even though I think you've made a terrible mistake."

"Right. Have you ever flown into airports near or in the places I told you the murders have occurred?"

"Let me think for a minute. We do go to Boston, and Raleigh, North Carolina at times. It's about an hour by car from Greensboro. But we also go to Vermont, Rhode Island, Washington and Tampa Bay in Florida. Have there been any murders there?"

"As of now, we don't know of any. Maybe we can get this settled. This past week, you had filed a flight plan for Vermont coming from Maine, right?"

"How did you... doesn't matter how. Yes, we did file a flight plan, but ummm we had some engine trouble and had to deviate."

"And where did you deviate to?"

"A small airstrip we have used in the past on the outskirts of Washington, D.C. Belongs to a friend of Dr. Waters."

"But flying from Maine to Vermont, if you had engine trouble, why would you go out of the way to Washington?"

Dennis just looked down and didn't say anything.

"Look Dennis, I understand you are an upstanding man, a retired Colonel. So I know you believe in loyalty. I get it. But I'm also sure you believe in right and wrong. I don't think it would be an act of loyalty if it meant protecting a possible serial killer, no matter who his victims are. Why did you deviate to Washington?"

Dennis got up and paced around the room. Then he finally sat back down.

"There have been a few times when Dr. Waters has told me to deviate from a filed flight plan. He tells me where he wants to land, and I comply."

"And when you land, where does he go?"

"I have no idea where he goes but we are never on the ground for more than four to six hours."

"This last time, when you landed in Washington, did he have access to a vehicle?"

"Yes, the guy who owns the airstrip keeps a car there, and Dr. Waters can use it."

"And when he comes back how is he? Does he seem nervous or anything you have picked up on?"

"I guess each time he has been a bit excited. His hands are shaking, and his face is flush."

"Okay. What time did you land in Washington?"

"We left Maine around ten pm and landed in Washington by a little after eleven. Then we took off at about 4:30 am and landed back in Vermont."

Dave was thinking about Max Gardner's TOD, his time of death. Would Waters have the time to get to Johns Hopkins, kill Gardner and get back to the airport? Dave was sure he could.

"Dennis, Dr. Waters would have been able to kill Max Gardner at Johns Hopkins and get back to the jet," Dave said. "It would be tight but not impossible."

"I still can't believe it!" Dennis said. "But maybe..."

"Maybe what Dennis?" I asked.

"Every time he leaves the jet when we do these detours, he carries a black valise. I've never seen inside it, and I have no idea what is inside. This last time when we flew back because his son was in a car accident... ummm, he had me hold onto it."

"This black valise is here, in your home right now?"

"It is, but I really am not sure I should give it to you."

"Dennis, I'm sure we could get a search warrant, and we still will, but I don't think you want us to go through all of that without knowing for yourself. I tell you what. You look inside and if there is anything within which looks like stuff used in a murder, you let us know. Then we will get a search warrant for it. If there is absolutely nothing within which points to killing someone, you let us know that too. Is that a deal?"

"I still think you guys are wrong but, I'll go look."

Dennis walked back down the hallway into what was probably his bedroom. We sat waiting for him, and my heart rate was definitely up. Within a few minutes, we might have everything we would need to close this case and put Malcolm Waters behind bars and stop the killings.

Dennis came back into the kitchen with the bag still closed. He looked upset and I figured we had our man.

"Well?" I asked.

"There is nothing in here which would make me think Dr. Waters is a killer," Dennis said. "But I think you guys might want to get a search warrant anyways."

I looked at Dave, he at me, and we both had the same thoughts. Just what the hell was inside Dr. Waters' black valise?

Chapter Sixty

Dave put in a call to Carl, explained the situation, telling him to get a specific search warrant. Dave described the black valise and how it related to our case. Then he told him to get the warrant and to drive it out to Trask's home.

We had sat around getting to know Trask. I thought he was a standup guy and a war hero. He showed us two medals he had won in the service of our country. He still didn't believe Waters was a killer, especially after seeing the contents of the valise.

The valise was sitting on the coffee table in the living room between us, and I wanted to open it badly. But if Dave or I looked inside before we had a warrant, anything inside would be lost to us as evidence.

While we waited, Trask put on some records and his sound system was fantastic. We listened to some oldies and my favorite, some Frank Sinatra. We were in the middle of listening to Ole Blue Eyes belt out *Fly me to the Moon*, when there was a knock on the door. Trask shut down the record and then answered the door.

Carl was standing there and Trask let him in. Then Carl handed him a copy of the search warrant.

"Dennis, this is Special Agent Carl Walkin, and this is retired Colonel Dennis Trask, Carl," Dave said.

Carl put out his hand and Trask shook it saying, "Might as well call me Dennis."

"And I'm Carl," he replied, "and thank you for your service, Colonel. Where is the valise?"

"Right here Carl, in the living room," Dave said.

We all sat down around the coffee table and Dave said, "Since you got the warrant Carl, why don't you do the honors."

Carl nodded and then slowly opened the valise. He was staring into it and then pulled out a leather strap with a hard rubber ball in the middle of it.

"What the hell is this thing?" he said.

I got up and looked in the valise. There was an assortment of

S&M items inside, including a small whip, a cage which goes around a man's penis, some furry handcuffs, anal beads and a few other things.

"That is a ball gag, used by people involved in S&M, Sadio-masochism," I said. "All of the things in this valise are used by people who either like to inflict pain and humiliation or like it to be done to them."

"Holy shit!" Carl said and dropped the ball gag back into the valise.

"Now this is an interesting situation," Dave said.

"You're not kidding," I said and sat back down.

"Does this change your thinking that Dr. Waters is a serial killer?" Dennis asked.

"I'm not sure yet Dennis," Dave said. "The fact is, Dr. Waters was well within range to kill Max Gardner in Baltimore and at times, he has been everywhere there has been a murder. I'm not sure right now if the dates match up though. Dennis, do you keep a record of dates and times when you fly into an airport, including the times you deviated from your flight plan?"

"Sure I do. I keep a log every time we fly. They are in a file cabinet at the hangar where we keep the jet."

"Would you be willing to give us them or if you want, we can get another warrant?"

"If it helps clear Dr. Waters, I'll give them to you right now."

"Okay, Warren and I will go in our car. Carl, you head back to the office and see about making up a time line of the killings, with the locations. Dennis, if you don't mind, you should drive yourself so you can be free after we get the logs."

"Sounds okay to me, just let me get my keys and we can go."

"One more thing. We are going to take pictures of the contents of the valise, and we want you to keep it here. If Dr. Waters comes to get it, or asks you to bring it to him, do so. But please don't let on about its contents or about us seeing inside. Can you do that?"

"I suppose so, but the second you clear him, as I'm sure you will, you have to let me know."

"No problem."

We all left Trask's home and as we started the drive to MacArthur Airport where the jet and logs were, I called the two agents on surveillance. I told them they were free to go and thanked them. The only thing they requested was to be filled in when we could do so.

We were following Trask since he knew the route to the airport. As we drove I thought about the contents of the valise.

"You thinking about those items Warren?" Dave asked.

"How the hell couldn't I," I replied. "I don't care what tickles Waters fancy, but I would like to know what it means for our case."

"Yeah, kinda threw a monkey wrench into the works."

"I was sure there was going to be rope, and cuffs... but not those kind of cuffs."

We both laughed at that and then Dave continued, "But it still doesn't clear him. Our killer likes to inflict pain as well as death. In a way, the items sort of fit.

 I'm thinking once we get those logs and Carl matches them up, we will know if Waters is our killer."

"But then, if Waters is cleared. Who the hell is the killer?"

"I don't know, and we will be back to square one. Let's hope the logs and the times of the murders match up. Then we will have our man."

I thought about everything we had, and I felt the same old itch in the back of my brain. I had been sure Waters was our killer. Now, although the contents of the valise didn't clear him, it did throw a monkey wrench into the case. But if Waters wasn't the killer, who was? Could it be Trask? He would have been everywhere the doctor was. But if the logs clear the doctor, they would clear Trask as well, so it didn't make sense.

One way or another, I wasn't going to stop till I and the rest of the team caught the killer. If only I knew how.

Chapter Sixty – One

Dr. Waters was still very concerned about the valise. Of course, his son's condition was foremost in his thoughts, but he couldn't shake the need he had to get the damn valise back! He decided as soon as he could get away from the hospital and Jocelyn, he would go to Trask's home and get it. But for now, he and Jocelyn were staying by Brandon's bedside, watching for any sign their son was coming out of his coma.

He and Jocelyn were sitting there, Jocelyn holding onto her son's hand. She was talking softly to him, sometimes crying, sometimes just staring into his face. Dr. Waters had never felt so helpless in all of his life. What good was all his money or his training as a psychiatrist? None of it could help his son, and he would be rid of it all if it meant his son would wake up.

Although he wasn't a religious man, he had walked down to the chapel in the hospital several times in the past two days. He wasn't sure there was a God, didn't know or really believe there was an Almighty Being listening to prayers. But he would go to the chapel and pray.

He was about to go and pray again, when he heard something. It sounded like...Mom. He looked at his son and saw his eyes flickering open. Jocelyn began to cry, and Dr. Waters did too.

"Brandon!" Jocelyn cried out.

"Mom...what happened, where am I?" Brandon said in a weak shaky voice.

"I'll go get the doctor," Dr. Waters said and left the room.

As he walked to the nurses station he found himself thanking God. He spoke to a nurse, telling her his son had come out of the coma. The nurse stated she would get Dr. Patel. He turned to walk back to his son. Suddenly, he stopped and thought to himself a disgusting thought. Now he could go and get his valise. He admonished himself for even thinking of anything but his son. He hurried back to his son's room.

"I'm here too Brandon," Dr. Waters said, taking hold of his son's other hand.

"I don't know what happened Dad, but I'm sorry," Brandon said.

"There is absolutely nothing you need to be sorry for son. All will be well once again."

Dr. Patel entered the room and said, "Dr. Waters, Mrs. Waters, I think you both need to step out for a few minutes please. I need to talk and examine your son."

"Of course Dr. Patel, and thank you for saving our son," Jocelyn said.

Dr. Waters and Jocelyn left the room and walked down to a nearby waiting room. As they sat, they were both deep in thought. Jocelyn was thinking of all the hard work ahead for their son. But anything he needed, anything at all, she would make sure he had. She then said a silent prayer.

Dr. Waters on the other hand only had one thing on his mind, the valise.

Chapter Sixty – Two

Dave and I had followed Trask out to the airport. When we arrived, Trask went to some locked file cabinets on the far wall. I stood and looked at the jet, and wondered how much it had cost. Trask came over with twelve logs in his hand. I assumed each one was for each year he had flown Dr. Waters.

"Here they are," Trask had said and handed them over to me.

"Warren," Dave had stated, "let's put them back in the file cabinets. Then I will take pictures of it all. The cabinets, the logs in the cabinets, Dennis handing them over and each one separately."

I handed them back to Dennis and Dave did just what he had said. Then I finally put them each into our car.

Before we left I had said, "We have a pretty nice jet too Dennis, but I think this one puts ours to shame."

Trask smiled and invited us inside. The FBI jet was great, but this jet was way over the top. I saw a couch, and some comfortable looking chairs. A fully stocked bar and small kitchen near the rear. Trask then moved to a wall and pulled down on a small hook. A full bed appeared as if by magic. There was also a large screen TV and music system.

I was impressed and as we left the jet I had to ask Trask how much it had gone for.

"This is actually a new jet we got only last year," he had replied. "This one is more decked out than the last one. I believe Dr. Waters paid in the neighborhood of fifteen million dollars."

"Holy crap!" I had said and then recovered from my shock. "I suppose it's okay, if you have the money," I had added and then we all had laughed.

We had said goodbye to Trask with a promise of letting him know whether or not he was working for a killer. As we drove away, I thought Trask was a standup guy.

We got back to HQ, and now we were waiting on Carl to deliver the news. Was Waters our killer or were we back to square one.

"I'm still betting on Waters being our guy," Aaron said.

"What about you Warren?" Dave asked. "Do you think we have the right guy?"

"I'm not sure, but all the facts tend to make me think he has to be our killer," I answered. "Did you inform Teller where we are?"

"Yeah, I spoke with him this morning. He wasn't too happy about the contents of the valise when I showed him the pictures. But he said he thinks we are right on the money. He said, don't let doubt creep in, follow the evidence and we would see Waters is our killer."

"I'm glad he is so sure."

We sat around not saying much more, each of us thinking about the case.

"Hey there guys, why the long faces!" Lou said as she walked into the room.

"Lou!" we all called out and bombarded her with questions.

"How is Billy? When did you get back? Where is he? Who is watching him?"

"Whoa guys," Lou said, "one at a time."

Lou sat down and Dave said, "it's good to see you Lou. Why don't you tell us what's going on."

"First off, no donuts?"

"I'm afraid I had the last one Lou," Aaron said.

"And four others," Dave said.

"It's okay Aaron," Lou said with a smile. "Okay let's see. I'm sure you heard about Billy's fall. I thought I was going to die along with him! Luckily we had those two agents watching over us."

"I was happy they were there too. By the way Lou, they both want an update on Billy when you can."

"Sure but you will have to give me their numbers. So, Billy was going crazy in that hospital, and I finally convinced the doctor to discharge him. I got a nice comfortable RV, and we hit the road yesterday. I got him all set up in my apartment."

"Who is watching him while you are here?" I asked.

"You wouldn't believe it. I had been speaking to his mom and dad after the accident. They wanted me to take him to their home in Syracuse. Billy was adamant he wasn't going home. When I told them, they said they were on their way here. They are at a hotel near my apartment, and they are watching over him."

"I bet Billy was thrilled."

"Actually, the big kid cried when they came in. I figured as long as they are staying in town, I could get back to work. I just left Teller, and he was glad to see me...I think."

"I'm sure he was Lou, and so are we," Dave said.

"Okay then, catch me up."

Dave sat down with Lou and brought her up to speed. As he was telling her everything, I left the conference room to call Trace. I wanted her to tell her Billy was back in New York, his parents were here as well, and I had received a text from Coppa.

I called and when she answered I informed her of everything.

"Coppa said he is swamped all week, but they would be able to come over tonight if that is okay," I said.

"I'll have to hustle," Trace replied, 'but of course tonight will be great!"

"They will be over at seven Trace. You don't have to go all out. Maybe we could barbeque?"

"Great idea War! I'll go to the stores and get some steaks and some hot dogs and hamburgers for Brian. I better get going. Give a kiss to Lou for me. Bye!"

I went back into the conference room and saw Lou showing the team pictures of Billy after the fall. It looked to me like he would be laid up in bed for at least a month. Maybe more. We were all talking about the case and Billy and his fall, when Carl walked in with some papers in his hands.

"Hi Lou! When did you get back? How is Billy?"

"She can answer all your questions later Carl," Dave said. "What did you figure out?"

"Here are the facts folks," he said, "and there is no way Dr. Waters is our killer.

"Shit," Dave said. "Are you sure Carl? Of course you are sure, sorry Carl."

"No problem Dave, I have been known to make a mistake once in a while. But not this time. I ran the logs and the murders through three times looking for a mistake. He was nearby in two of the murders, but not in the other four. There is no way he is the Brutal Abuser. I figured we would keep the name after what Billy has been through."

"I guess so. Great. I'll go and inform Teller and then we will have to figure out where we go from here."

Dave left but we didn't say anything. We were all too deflated with the news. I was pissed off, but I was also assured we would find the killer, one way or another. But how was the thing? I kept on waiting for the itch in my brain to make itself known, but it just wouldn't come. I looked at each of the agents sitting around the table and then decided being pissed or defeated just wasn't going to help. I waited for Dave to come back in and when he did, I stood up.

I knew Dave wouldn't mind me saying anything, so I began by saying, "Let's cut out the long faces! We've been in tough situations before. I know each and every one of us will not quit until the Brutal Abuser is either behind bars or dead. So what are we going to do? Are we going to mope around, or catch us a killer?"

"Catch us a killer," Dave said."

"Right," Lou and Aaron replied.

"You bet!" Carl joined in.

I was proud of the team, and I knew we would never stop till we had him. We all sat down and got back to work.

Chapter Sixty – Three

Tuesday, Huntington, LI, My home, 6:45 pm

Trace had bought some great looking thick steaks, some corn on the cob, franks and hamburgers with buns, some Cole slaw and potato salad. We were going to have a feast. She also picked up some wine and beer.

I was getting the grill ready when the doorbell rang. I heard Trace saying hello to everyone and then she led them into the backyard.

Coppa came over and gave me a big hug. Then I gave Debbie a kiss and shook hands with Brian.

"I don't think we have met Brian," I said.

"No sir, I don't think so," he answered.

"Well, you don't have to call me sir. You can call me War."

"War?"

"It's short for Warren and I'll let you in on a secret. There is only one other person who is allowed to call me War."

"Really? Who is the other one?"

"That would be me Brian," Trace said. "How about I put on a movie for you till the food is ready?"

"Can I?" he asked his mom and dad.

"Sure Brian," Coppa said.

Trace took him into the house, and I heard her ask him if he wanted a burger or dog and he yelled out both!

"You want me to cook those steaks, Temple, I would hate to see them ruined," Coppa said.

"I think I have it handled," I answered with a laugh. "Grab yourself a beer and get me one too!"

"Tell me about this serial killer you are hunting."

"That's our cue to go inside, set the table and let the men talk," Debbie said.

Trace gave me a kiss and went inside with Debbie.

"This case has me stumped, Coppa," I said.

"Not the mighty detective Temple!" he replied.

"Me and my team. I have a great group I work with, but we all had thought we had our killer identified. There is a Dr. Waters, a psychiatrist who has his own jet."

"I didn't think those guys made that kind of money."

"I don't think they do, but when he was twenty, his parents died in a car crash, and he inherited in the neighborhood of fifty million dollars."

"Holy cow! I suppose he could afford a jet. Go on, tell me more."

I turned the steaks, and Coppa was looking over my shoulder.

"The steaks are fine. Dr. Waters flies up and down the east coast, treating women and children of abuse. He visits shelters and safe houses. And he usually doesn't charge for his services."

"Sounds like a good guy."

"We have six men killed up and down the east coast in the last four or five years. Each man abused his wife and, or, kids. Now here is the kicker. Dr. Waters saw or was involved with every one of the wives of the dead men. Well, not all six, but the other five.

One guy was murdered recently, but twenty years ago, Dr. Waters and his wife worked with a nurse named Brandy Gardner at Johns Hopkins. The sixth victim was Max Gardner. Twenty years ago he murdered Brandy and just last week he was murdered in Johns Hopkins, after getting paroled."

"No way that is a coincidence."

"Exactly but we just compared the flight logs for the last six years. Compared them to where and when the killer struck."

"They don't match."

"Bingo."

"You're back at square one?"

"Yes we are. But we aren't going to stop till we catch this guy."

"I know you won't Temple. What name did you and your fellow Feebs give to this case?"

"We call him...ummm...the Brutal Abuser."

"You're kidding."

"Wish I was. The kid who came up with the name used to be my partner in the One-Eleven. He got hurt recently and now we feel we can't change it."

"If you need some help, I can always add my brain to the mix, but I think you will figure it out."

"Thanks, Coppa."

I finished grilling the steaks, burgers and hot dogs. We all sat down and talked and laughed about the old days. Trace and Debbie were talking about the adoption and to my surprise, when Brian heard us talking he spoke up.

"War, Mrs. Temple, are you both thinking of adopting some child?"

"Yes we are," Trace replied.

"You know, I was adopted."

"I know."

"I just wanted to tell you it's probably the greatest thing you can do. I remember being in a foster home, and though the people who had me were nice, they weren't a real mom and dad. Some kid out there is praying every night for someone to love him or her. I know I prayed every night. And now I have a mom and a dad. They love me and I love them."

Debbie got up with tears in her eyes and gave Brian a big hug and kiss. Trace was crying, I had tears in my eyes too, and even big bad Coppa grabbed a napkin and wiped his eyes.

Trace cleared her throat and said, "Thank you, Brian, for saying that. You are a very special boy."

We finished the meal and Trace and Debbie ordered Coppa and I out to the deck. He had two cigars, and we lit them up, grabbed a beer and sat down, waiting for our wives. Brian went back to the movie he had been watching.

"Quite the boy you have there, Coppa," I said.

"He is always surprising me, Temple," Coppa replied. "I hope you and Trace will find someone as loving and special as Brian has been to us."

Finally, Trace and Debbie came out and she had a folder with some papers in it. We gathered around and then Coppa and Debbie started to go over the adoption process in New York State.

They showed us the website where we needed to start. It was, ocfs.ny.gov, which stood for Office of Children and Family Services. Then they proceeded to go over the different forms we needed to fill out, and how we had to prepare our home for a child. We talked for over an hour, and by the time we were through, Trace and I had a better idea of what we needed to do.

It was getting late, and they were getting ready to

leave. Trace was talking with Debbie and Brian, and Coppa took me aside for a second.

"You do have another way to adopt, Temple," he said.

"Okay, how?" I replied.

"Have you ever heard of the NYF&BFC?"

"Ummm no. What does it stand for?"

"New York Finest and Bravest Foster Care. It was started soon after 9/11. With so many dads and moms being killed in the towers, some kids were left alone. They started the NYF&BFC soon after. There are still kids today who have lost a mom or dad in the line of duty or from other illnesses. Give them a call. They prefer to keep the kids in the family, so to speak."

"Thanks Coppa, and let's try to keep in touch."

"You bet Temple and good luck. On the adoption and on catching the Brutal Abuser."

Trace and I sat up for a bit, and I told her about the NYF&BFC. She thought it was a great idea. Tomorrow, along with Melissa, she would check it out. We went to bed soon after and I stayed awake for a little while. My mind was on a child being in our home soon. I was also thinking about our serial killer. We would catch him, I was sure. I just wish I had a clue as to how we were going to do it.

Chapter Sixty – Four

Wednesday, FBI HQ, Conference Room, 11:45 pm

We had all been in by 8:30 this morning. We had met up in the conference room and ADD Teller had joined us. We all sat up a bit straighter as he began to speak.

He hadn't read us the riot act, but he was angry because after all the trips to different states, and all the man hours we had put in, we were back to square one. He didn't exactly come out and say it, but he did hint he might have to turn the case over to another set of Special Agents. He gave us two more weeks or the death of another man who abused his wife, before he would decide what to do. He then wanted individual reports written up by us all and on his desk within two hours. The report from Billy could wait, for now. Then he walked out.

Lou, Carl and Aaron got up and went to their offices to write up their reports. Dave was sitting there, staring at the white boards, filled with all of the information we had.

"I'm not seeing anything there Warren," he had said. "Maybe Teller is right. Maybe we can't catch this guy and new eyes looking at it might be able to."

"Bullshit!" I had said. He looked at me and I continued. "No one else is going to see anything different from what we see. We are missing something, but we won't miss it forever."

"We don't have forever. Teller gave us two weeks. Or maybe sooner if the killer strikes again."

"Doesn't matter Dave. You, me and the others will catch this guy. I have no doubt Dave, and you shouldn't have any doubts either. Now, I'm going to my office to write up my report. We need to make copies of the reports, and each of us can read each other's. We will find something. I'm sure of it. See you back here in about two hours."

Dave got up, patted me on my back and went to write out his report. I went to my office and began to put all my notes in order. As I wrote my report, I kept looking for something we missed. Unfortunately, I didn't find a single thing.

Two hours later, I brought my report to Teller. He asked me to shut the door and take a seat.

"I need a truthful answer from you Special Agent Temple," he began. "Do you believe you and the team will be able to catch this killer?"

I took a second to answer, and then I replied, "I've been doing this job for a long time sir. There have been times when a killer falls in our laps. Then there are times when we get to a point where we think we will never catch him or her. It is at those times when you find out just how good you and your team are. Do they give up, throw in the towel? Or do they pull themselves up and start all over if need be. And I have found when you have men and women who can pick themselves up, then you have a team which will succeed no matter what. I think, no, I know the team led by Special Agent Dave Anderson is such a team sir."

Teller looked me in the eye and said, "Thank you Special Agent Temple. You reminded me just why I made Special Agent Anderson the leader of this team, and why I asked for you and Special Agent Groat to be made members of the FBI. That will be all."

I stood and walked out just as Dave was walking in. I just smiled at him and whispered everything was just fine.

Now all of us were sitting back in the conference room, reading each other's reports. After an hour, Dave suggested we call out for food. After giving the order to a local pizzeria, Carl excused himself and went back to his office.

The food arrived and we all dug in. Carl hadn't returned yet, and Lou was just about to get him, when he came in. He had his laptop in his hands, and he had a huge grin on his face.

"What do you have, Carl?" Dave asked and I swear each of us were holding our breath.

"It may not be the answer, but I think it might be!" Carl said.

"Sit down and spill it," I said, feeling excited about the case once again.

"Okay. So I was thinking when I was going over my reports about all the people we were checking backgrounds on. And then I remembered, Jocelyn Waters background only went as far as high school. I didn't really give it much thought then. But today, I said to myself, why? Why didn't it go back further."

"And?"

"I went back in and using a new program the FBI geniuses developed, I finally found out her entire story."

"Okay Carl, you have all of our attention."

"We know that her name before she married was Jocelyn Mason. But she actually was born Jocely Carpenter. She was raised in Philadelphia and her parents were Samuel and Theresa Carpenter. She also had an older sister, six years older than her, named Joyce."

"I assume you found out what happened for her to have her name changed to Mason and have a new family."

"Yes I did, and it wasn't easy."

"You're not getting a raise Carl so just tell us," Dave said.

"When Jocelyn turned thirteen, her sister Joyce killed their parents. Joyce had been abused by their father, starting when she turned thirteen. When Jocelyn turned thirteen, her father had told Joyce she was no longer going to be his special girl. Now Jocelyn would be. Then her father did abuse Jocelyn one time.

Their mother, Theresa, apparently was abused as well and knew about the abuse to her daughter and did nothing. So Joyce decided her father was not going to touch her little sister again. She had taken her father's shotgun and killed them both in their bed while they slept."

"Oh my God!" Lou said. "How awful. What happened to Joyce?"

"Joyce was nineteen, tried as an adult and sentenced to life. But two months after starting her sentence, Joyce hung herself in her cell. Jocelyn was placed in foster care because there were no other relatives, Almost a year later she was adopted by the Mason's."

We were all stunned by this news. We sat there thinking it all over and Dave finally spoke.

"Are you saying you believe Jocelyn Waters is our killer Carl?" Dave asked.

"I don't know for sure Dave," he replied.

I stood, paced the room and then said, "It makes sense, I think. Jocelyn finds out her father was abusing her sister. Her father abuses her. Then her parents are murdered, and her sister commits suicide. She is adopted, has a normal life for a while. Maybe she blocks out her child-hood and the abuse.

Then she becomes a nurse and becomes friends with Brandy Gardner. Brandy is abused and murdered. Years go by, and her husband treats abused women. Maybe she has access to who he treats. Maybe she finds out some-how, who the men are, where they live, and she snaps. She starts killing the men who abuse their wives and kids, just like her father had."

"It tracks but how are we going to prove it?" Aaron asked.

"I'm not sure yet," Dave said. "What we need to do is come up with a plan. So get settled in and let's put our heads together and work out some way to prove it. Carl, you did a fantastic job! I'm going to inform Teller about this new information. You guys get started thinking. Oh and Carl?"

"Yes?" Carl replied.

"I'm going to try and get you a raise."

Dave left and we all started throwing out some ideas. I finally knew what the itch in my brain had been trying to tell me. Until everyone had been cleared, they were suspects. It was Homicide 101 and somehow I had let it slip by. We had investigated Jocelyn Waters but had never really cleared her. Now I knew we were going to catch the Brutal Abuser, even if it had turned out to be a woman.

Chapter Sixty – Five

We had brainstormed for the past few hours and had finally come up with an idea. We weren't sure it would work or blow up in our faces, but we didn't know what else to do. The first thing we did was to contact Dennis Trask. He was told who we thought was our killer. We also told him our plan.

Trask was told to contact Dr. Waters. Even though Waters was some kind of a freak when it came to sex, we thought he was a decent man. We didn't think he had done anything criminal with his sexual preferences. He treated abused women and children, as well as doing it gratis. Even though we thought he was an honest good man, we had no idea if he would turn on his own wife.

We told Trask to arrange for Waters to come out to his home to pick up the valise. We decided the best day would be Friday, in the morning. We knew his son Brandon had come out of his coma, and therefore the doctor would be able to leave his son's bedside. Once Trask was sure Waters was going to be there, Dave and I would get to Trask's home first.

The only thing bothering Trask was the possibility Waters might fire him as his pilot. Trask wasn't worried about the loss of income. He had a pension from the Air Force, as well as money from saving his money and making some good investments. But he still wanted to keep his job because he felt he was helping the abused women and children in some small way. But Trask finally agreed, understanding catching a serial killer was the most important thing.

The danger was if Trask decided to get in touch with either Waters or his wife. We didn't think he would, but to be on the safe side, Carl and Aaron were going to try and get a warrant for Trask's phones. Both his cell and land line needed to be bugged. We knew Trask still had a land line, because when we were over there, we had seen it.

Next, we had to consider Dr. Waters either tipping his wife off or confronting her. Both of those scenarios would be extremely dangerous. Jocelyn Waters might snap and kill her husband if confronted. Or she might kill herself. Then there was the possibility of either Jocelyn Waters trying to escape, with or without her husband.

We decided to call it a night and wait to hear if Waters was going to get his valise on Friday. We would all try to get a good night's sleep and come back in fresh the next morning.

I drove home and for the first time working on this case, I felt optimistic. Of course a lot of things could go wrong. But men and women in law enforcement become very good judges of character. We had all agreed we were reading both Trask and Dr. Waters correctly. We were 95% sure both of them would go along with the plan we had come up with.

And I was certain Jocelyn Waters was our killer. None of us had met her and didn't have a clue as to her strength. Aaron had caught a glimpse of her when he went to the hospital. He told us she was about 5'10" and looked to be of an athletic build. We figured she was using something to disable her victims. The likely thing was some sort of a taser. For our plan to work, we would have to take it into consideration. As to the injuries she was inflicting, we thought she must be using something easily held and very hard.

I had been thinking and driving on remote, so when I pulled into my own driveway I was a bit surprised. I got out of my car, and I had to talk to Trace about something our plan included. I wasn't sure she would be too happy about it, but I would have to convince her.

I walked in through the back door, looked at the water can sitting there, and went to find her. She was sitting in the living room, and before I said a word I knew something was up.

"Hi Honey," I said. I leaned down and gave her a kiss.

Trace said, "Hi, War. I have some news but I'm not sure how you are going to react."

"There is only one way to find out Trace, spill it."

"Okay, but let me finish before you start asking questions or getting upset. Deal?"

"Sure, deal."

"Melissa and I went to the office of the NYF&BFC today. We met with a very nice woman there, a Mrs. Sugarman. She is in charge of the program and happens to be a widow of a firefighter killed in the North Tower. She was a big part in starting the program.

Melissa and I told her why we were there and that we were hoping to adopt a boy or girl, maybe in the age range of five to eight. She listened to us for about an hour, asking us some questions. She wanted to know all about our home, how old we both were, your job and some other things.

Finally, she called in one of the other women who worked there. She asked her to bring in the Davis file. I have to tell you, War, I was so scared and excited at the same time. Maybe the Davis file had the name of some child we could possibly adopt!

The woman came in with a file and handed it to Mrs. Sugarman. Then Mrs. Sugarman told us she had a very special case in her hands. She said she didn't want to get our hopes up, but in her opinion, she thought this might be the answer to our prayers."

Trace stopped talking and pulled out a file. She then said, "I need you to keep an open mind and look at the entire file before you say anything."

I took the file, opened it and began to read. I was a bit shocked, but as I read the entire file and I looked into my wife's eyes, I had pretty much made up my mind.

The file held the picture of a young rookie cop, Adam Davis, and a picture of a pretty young woman, Laura Davis, his wife. They had been celebrating a very difficult pregnancy, by taking a small trip upstate, two months after she had given birth. They were going to go to Niagara Falls and some of the roads had been slippery. They had been killed when their car went out of control, went through a guardrail and plunged over one hundred feet, down into a chasm.

They had left behind identical twin boys. When they went on their trip, they had left the boys with a close neighbor. The Davis's didn't have any relatives at all. The twins, Michael and Gregory Davis, now aged ten months, were in foster care with the NYF&BFC. There was a picture of the two boys in the folder, and I saw why my wife had the look on her face. It was easy to fall in love with the two boys almost at first sight.

I closed the folder and got up to walk around and think. We had agreed on one older child, not two babies. Would we be able to handle two children? I wasn't sure. I thought about both of our ages. I was almost fifty and Trace forty-eight. But we were both in good physical shape and we both had a lot to offer. Still, it was a lot to ask, to raise not one but two children from the age of almost one.

I looked at my wife, the woman I loved, the woman I would die for. She had such hope in her eyes, and I knew there was only one possible answer.

I sat down next to her, took her hands in mine, and said, "yes."

She looked at me and smiled, and then took me in her arms and kissed me. I supposed we were now on a new adventure together, and together we would handle all the ups and downs.

Chapter Sixty – Six

Trace had been overcome with emotions when I had said yes. After kissing me, she jumped up, then sat down, then jumped up again. Then she began reciting all the things we needed to do. We would have to get two cribs, and baby monitors. Of course we needed to get them clothes, but not identical clothes. She never liked the idea of dressing twins exactly alike. Of course we would have to find a way to tell them apart. Then we needed to make the house baby-proof for safety. We would have to tell all our friends, and of course we needed to decide on Godparents. Then she had said how silly. Of course Dave and Mellissa would be the Godparents!

I had finally got her to calm down and we discussed things in a more sane and quieter way. We agreed to keep it quiet, except for Dave and Melissa, until the adoption was finalized. I had asked if we were adopting or fostering the twins. Trace said even though the name of the organization was foster care, they did adoptions as well. Adoptions it would be.

The timeline for the adoption would still take several weeks, but we had a lot to do. Later that night, after we had made love, I told her about the plan we had decided on at work. She was a bit hesitant but then agreed.

The team had all gotten together at 8:30 and had been refining our plan. We had called Trask to find out if he had contacted Dr. Waters yet. He had tried, but the doctor was at the hospital. His cell had been turned off, but Trask had left a message. As soon as Waters called him and confirmed he would come for his valise on Friday, Trask would call us.

Dave had gone to get ADD Teller and now as we waited for him to come in, I went over our plan once again in my mind. I thought it was a good plan and hoped Teller would sign off on it.

Teller came into the conference room, sat down and waited for Dave to go over the plan we came up with. After thirty minutes and answering questions, Teller had simply nodded, wished us luck and then left.

We went over it for the tenth time, refining our plan and then ordered some food. While we were eating, we talked about the plan and then Lou told us about Billy.

"I hate to say it," Lou began, "but Billy is really depressed."

"Why is he depressed?" Aaron asked, food falling from his mouth.

"Chew with your mouth closed big man," Dave said. "Of course he's depressed. He is going to be laid up for a long time, he's going to need a lot of physical therapy, and he is probably worried about his job. Wouldn't you be depressed?"

"Yeah, I suppose I would."

"It's all that," Lou said, "plus a few more things."

"Like what?" I asked.

"How would you feel if you had to be taken care of by your mom and dad?"

"I suppose it could be a bit trying," Carl said. "I mean, I love my mom and dad but having them take care of me as a grown man, yeah, it would suck."

"What else Lou?" Dave asked.

"He feels very left out Dave. He put his life on the line, sort of, doing the climb with Waxman. And then he fell and although we cleared Waxman, he felt he had screwed up. And now because I am back in the thick of things, he feels like he has been pushed to the side."

"Of course he does. I think I know a way to make him feel better."

We finished our food and then all five of us packed into an SUV and drove directly to Lou's apartment. Lou walked into his bedroom first, while we stayed quietly in the living room.

"Hi Billy," we heard Lou say when she walked in. "Hi Mr. and Mrs. Groat."

"Now Lou," I heard Mrs. Groat say, "How many times must we tell you to call us Harry and Gail? And why are you home so early?"

Dave whispered, "At least she didn't say to call them mom and dad!"

We all stifled a laugh and then continued to listen.

"I figured Billy might want some more company... Gail," Lou said. "Come on in gang!"

We all rushed in, and Billy was so shocked and surprised. He even had a few tears run down his cheeks.

"What are you guys doing here!" he cried out.

"We figured you might want to help us refine our plan Billy," Dave said. "We do have a serial killer to catch."

"I think we better let Billy help his team out Gail," Harry said. "We'll be back later son."

Gail gave Billy a kiss, and then surprised Dave by giving him one on his cheek as well.

We spent the next few hours filling Billy in on the case. He actually came up with a few good suggestions.

Then we had to hear all about his climb and how he had fallen.

"It was a great climb," he was saying. "Waxman was really strong and when he made the jump across the crack in the face, I thought he was crazy."

"No, you were crazy for trying to jump it!" Lou said.

"Maybe a little crazy, but I had done similar jumps in the past, Lou."

"Yeah, like ten years earlier."

"Let the man speak," Dave said.

"Right. So, he made the jump and made it look easy. I got into position and made the jump. But my hand hit the outcrop of rock Waxman had grabbed. After I fell, I don't remember much until I woke up in the hospital with this damn thing on my leg!" he said and gave his cast a good pat.

"I think we all need to sign his cast guys," Carl said.

Lou got out a big black marker and we all took turns signing his cast. We had plenty of room to sign because it went from his waist down to his ankle. Before Aaron signed, Lou reminded him Billy's parents would be reading it.

"Oh yeah," Aaron said, and then revised what he was going to write.

We spent some more time with Billy, laughing and telling some war stories, and then Lou said we had better get going. We all shook his hand, told him to get better soon.

"You better get back to work soon Billy," I said. "I need my old partner back."

Dave was about to go, when Billy called him back.

"Boss," he said, "thank you for bringing the team out here. I'm sure you guys will get her."

"Thanks Billy," Dave said. "We will now, because of the help you gave us today, and for all you did on this case. Get well, young man."

Lou was letting us out and she gave each of us a kiss on the cheek.

"Thank you guys," she said. "You really made Billy's day, and I think he will be better from here on. You guys are all angels."

Lou stayed behind and the rest of us talked the whole way back to the office. It had been a great day, and tomorrow might be an even better one. When we got back to the office, there was a message waiting on Dave's office phone. We all listened to it, squeezing into Dave's office.

"This is Trask," the message began. "Dr. Waters will be at my home at eleven tomorrow morning."

"Okay men," Dave said. "Tomorrow Warren and I will meet with Dr. Waters and hopefully he will cooperate. Until then, go home and get some rest. This case is now speeding up and we all better be sharp."

We all left Dave and headed home. I was excited about tomorrow, but I kept on thinking, in a few weeks or months, I would be going home to the love of my life and two sons. Two sons. Wow.

Chapter Sixty – Seven

Friday, Lake Success, Trask's Home, 9:50 am

Dave picked me up at my home first thing in the morning. He had stopped at McDonalds to get some bagels with egg, ham and cheese, and two cups of coffee. He wasn't sure if Trask was going to offer us any food as he did the first time we had showed up. It was sort of out of the way for Dave to come all the way out to Huntington, but he had insisted. He wanted to go over our plan again and the ride back to Lake Success would give us time.

We got into Dave's G-ride, a government car, and we began the trip. We ate along the way, refining what we were going to say to Dr. Waters. At first, we were going to threaten him with the exposure of his sexual preferences. But Billy had suggested we should not even mention the valise, unless absolutely necessary. He thought because Waters treated abused women and children, he would do the right thing. Both Dave and I had agreed to do it the way Billy thought we should.

We arrived at Trask's house and parked up the block. We didn't want Waters seeing another car parked out front and get spooked. We knocked on Trask's door, and he opened it and was wearing slacks, an open neck golf shirt and running shoes on his feet. He invited us in, and he had a very somber look on his face.

"I'm still not sure this is such a good idea," Trask said. "What if Waters gets pissed and just leaves? What if he breaks down and what if he tells his wife?"

"Look Dennis, we know this isn't easy for you," Dave said. "But we have six dead men who we are very certain were killed by Mrs. Waters. Six men who were animals, abusing their wives and children, but still should not have been murdered, and brutally, I might add. Do you think we shouldn't try any and everything we can to stop the murders?"

"Of course not. I guess I'm just nervous about hurting Dr. Waters with the news."

"You won't be hurting him at all. We've decided not to bring up the contents of his valise to him, unless he refuses to cooperate. So you don't have to let on at all that you know the contents either."

"I'm glad you decided to not reveal your knowledge of the valise. It will make things a bit better. Although hearing your wife is a serial killer will be devastating enough."

"Just let us handle it. When he knocks on the door, I want you to bring him into the living room where we will be sitting. You will introduce us as FBI agents. Then Warren and I will take over the discussion. You can leave the room if you want to, but I think it will be better if you stay."

Dennis checked his watch, seeing we had only fifteen minutes till Waters was going to arrive.

"Do you both want some coffee or anything else?" Trask asked.

"Coffee would be great, but I think we will take it in the living room, if that's okay with you," Dave replied.

Trask left the room, and I said, "What do you think Dave? Is he going to be okay?"

"I'm not absolutely sure but we are here, Waters will be here soon, so we will have to see how it goes. Remember, you are going to take the lead this time and if necessary, I will be the bad guy bringing up the valise."

"Okay, but I hope we won't have to say anything about the contents of his bag."

Trask brought out the coffee and we were just sitting there waiting for Waters. Finally there was a knock on the door, and Trask got up to answer it.

"Come on in, Dr. Waters," we heard Trask say. "I'm afraid I have some company."

"Oh, well, I just want to get my valise and be on my way Dennis," Waters said.

"Let me introduce you to them and I will get the valise sir."

They walked into the living room, and we got our first look at the doctor. He was taller than I expected, standing about 6'2" or 6'3". He had on a blue three piece suit, had a full beard and black hair, with some gray. If we hadn't cleared him, I would have thought he was big and strong enough to have committed the murders. Dave and I stood and put out our hands.

Trask said, "Dr. Waters, these gentlemen are from the FBI."

As he shook our hands, Dave said, "Dr. Waters, my name is Special Agent Dave Anderson, and this is Special Agent Warren Temple."

"The FBI?" Dr. Waters said. "Is there something Dennis has done? Are you here for me for some reason?"

"Please have a seat Doctor and we will explain," I said.

Trask didn't sit down and said, "I'll get your valise, Dr. Waters," and left the room. I really didn't blame him for not wanting to be here when we spoke to Waters.

I began speaking clearly but in a soft voice saying, "Dr. Waters, we have been conducting an investigation into the murders of six men for the past month or so. All of the men murdered were abusers of their wives and in some cases, their children."

"What could that possibly have to do with me? Obviously you know I treat abused women and children, but you can't possibly think I'm involved in these murders?" Waters said.

"We don't Doctor, at least not anymore. Because of certain things which I will explain, you were a suspect, but you have been cleared. Perhaps if I give you the names of the six victims you will understand better. Listen to the names and then you might be able to tell us if they sound familiar."

"Please do."

"Robert Heller, Jerry Baxter, Dr. Cary Tomlinson, Anthony Blake, Stuart King and finally, Max Gardner. Do those names sound familiar to you?"

Dr. Waters stood and began pacing. He was rubbing one hand through his beard, and took out his pocket watch, glancing at it several times. Finally he sat back down.

"I am pretty sure most if not all of those names are the same as women I have treated. But Max Gardner... that's a name from the past. He killed his wife Brandy Gardner. She was a nurse who worked with my Jocelyn and me at Johns Hopkins. But that was close to twenty years ago. When was he murdered?"

"He was killed about a week ago in Johns Hopkins. He was a janitor who had been placed there by his parole officer. He was released after twenty years in prison."

"And he was killed...in the hospital?"

"Yes he was. Let me ask you a question. Do you know anything about your wife's childhood?"

"I know she was raised in Philadelphia."

"What about her birth parents and her sister?"

"What do you mean, birth parents? I've met Jocelyn's parents, the Masons. And Jocelyn was an only child. Look, this has gone far enough. Just why are you here and what do these murders have to do with me or my wife?"

"Sit back Dr. Waters."

Dennis came back into the room with the valise. Dr. Waters showed obvious interest in it but tried not to show it.

"Dennis can you get Dr. Waters a glass of water," I said. "Take a deep breath and I will tell you exactly why we are here sir."

Chapter Sixty – Eight

Dr. Waters was now standing at the doors to the patio, staring out without saying a word. He was sipping on some 18 year old scotch Trask had gotten for him. He had sat and listened to me as I told him about his wife's childhood. About the abuse she and her older sister had suffered, about her mother, also abused but doing nothing to protect her children, and of how her sister had killed them both. I told him how her sister had committed suicide in prison and then about her being adopted by the Mason's.

He hadn't asked any questions and had asked for the drink and a moment to think. We had sat patiently waiting, knowing everything we had said so far was quite a shock. Dr. Waters finished off his drink, and then sat back down.

"What you have told me is almost unbelievable," Waters began. "I think my pulling Jocelyn into my work could have been a trigger. Mind you, I still don't believe she has killed anyone. But then again, I will explain what I mean."

"Thank you Doctor," I said. "One of the things we have been confused about is just how your wife would know about the husbands. Their names and where to find them?"

"That is the trigger I mentioned. You see, I would record all of my sessions with the women and children at the shelters and safe houses. Then I would record my recommendations for treatment. At the beginning of my sessions I would ask the victim of abuse for her name, her husband's, where they live and employment. Jocelyn would be given all the recordings as well as my recordings of suggested treatments. She would then transcribe everything for me. She has been doing so for many years."

"So your wife knew about the abuse each patient had received, as well as the names, addresses and employment of all the husbands."

"Pretty much, although sometimes their home addresses and the husbands employment didn't come up. But their names and obviously the states they lived in was always recorded. It is possible, seeing how Jocelyn had been abused and suffered the loss of her parents and sister, something she heard could act as a trigger. But all I'm saying is it *could be* a trigger. Not necessarily a certainty."

"When you go on your trips, does your wife go with you?"

"Sometimes she does, but when she stays home, she is very busy being on the board of several charities, and our golf club. I'm not sure she would have the time. Still..."

"Yes Doctor?"

"I don't keep a watch on what she does or where she goes. But our son Brandon has said she has gone off for a day or two at times when I am gone. It never concerned me; I trust my wife as she trusts me. But none of this is proof. I need proof."

"As do we, Doctor, which is why we are going to ask you to do something. It will either clear your wife..."

"Or send her to prison. What is it you want me to do."

We spent the next few hours going over our plan. It was complicated and would involve Lou. Dr. Waters listened to our plan and even revised it a little bit. He was being cooperative. Whether to clear his wife or to find out the truth, I didn't know. But at the end of our discussion, Dr. Waters agreed to do exactly what we said. Then we would spring our trap and see if we could catch a serial killer. I was just hoping it wouldn't backfire in some way. As was once said, *'The plans of mice and men often go awry.'*

Chapter Sixty – Nine

Saturday, Great Neck Home, 11:00 am

Dr. Waters and Jocelyn had just finished picking up Brandon from the hospital. Dr. Patel had only authorized his release after Dr. Waters assured him how they had prepared their home. They had purchased a hospital bed and a wheelchair. If he needed surgery on his knee, he wouldn't be able to use crutches with his broken arm. They had also purchased physical therapy equipment and hired a full time nurse to stay at their home. Then they contacted a physical therapist who would come every day as recommended by Dr. Patel.

Dr. Patel had relented, and they had just arrived at home. The nurse was standing by and assisted in getting Brandon into his new bed. He would now be on the first floor since climbing steps was one thing he certainly didn't need. The pain in his knee was bad but he was dealing with it. An MRI had been set up in two weeks, unless the pain became too much for him to bear.

When he had been put in bed and set up, he had asked if he could talk to his mother and father alone for a minute. The nurse, a middle aged woman named Claire, had excused herself.

"First, thank you for doing all of this, I don't think I could have stayed in the hospital one more day," he said.

"Of course son," Dr. Waters said. "We will do anything to get you fully recovered."

"Ummm, did you guys go to the funeral?"

"We did son, and the funeral was as lovely as a funeral for someone so young, could be. I don't think Jake's mom had any bad feelings toward you. In fact she wanted to know when she could visit."

"Thank God, I thought because Jake died and I didn't, she would be angry with me. I'm sorry I missed it, but when I am better I will visit the grave. He was a good friend, and I want to say goodbye."

"You don't have to worry about it Brandon," Jocelyn said. "Your only concern will be to get better. Your school work will be sent to you and done on a laptop. And you will have to get an MRI on your knee, in two weeks, unless the pain gets too much for you. Now, is there anything you want right now?"

"How about a much younger and prettier nurse!"

"Brandon! I think Claire will be able to take perfect care of you. Now rest."

Dr. Waters and Jocelyn left Brandon, and Claire returned to sit by his side. They went into the den and sat down.

"I'm so happy to have Brandon at home again," Jocelyn said.

"Yes," Dr. Waters replied, "I am happy too. I suppose now that he is home and being cared for, we can get back to our usual routine."

"I do need to check in with some of the charities. And there is a vote coming up at the golf club. But do you think we should leave him alone here with just Claire?"

"We hired her for that very reason, Jocelyn. I'm not going to go out of state, but there are several safe houses and shelters I can visit here, in Connecticut and in New Jersey. Just local so I won't be too far away."

"I suppose you are right Malcolm. I know Brandon was very happy to see us both by his side when he came out of the coma. Do you think it will have affected his brain in any way?"

"I doubt it. He was well taken care of while in the hospital. Dr. Patel did a great job, and I trust his skills and opinions on Brandon's care. If he needs anything done with his knee, we will make sure he has a top orthopedic surgeon. So stop your worrying. Brandon will be back to his usual self soon."

"I suppose you're right Malcolm. How about some lunch?"

"Yes, lunch will be fine, but I need to go over some of my patients' recordings. Because of his accident, I haven't completed my recommendations for their treatment."

"When you are finished, I will get them transcribed right away."

"Thank you Jocelyn."

Jocelyn went into the kitchen and began to put together a nice lunch. Dr. Waters went into his office and closed the door. He felt like Judas, betraying his wife instead of Jesus. But he needed to know the truth. Had he been sleeping with a killer? He still didn't believe it, but he wasn't as sure after thinking it over.

The FBI agents had said he had been their prime suspect. And of course he would be. He travelled to all the states the murders occurred in. He treated or knew of all the abused wives and children. And he was strong and big enough to have committed the murders.

But could Jocelyn have carried out the murders? The agents told him all about the murders after he had insisted. The thought of his Jocelyn, beating men so badly and then cutting their throats didn't seem possible to him.

Then again, Jocelyn could outdrive him on the golf course. And she also never asked him for help in lifting anything. She always said she could handle anything. She was strong, powerful and she was the type of person who when she made up her mind, she followed through.

Monday he would receive a call and head out to one of the safe houses. At least it was what he would tell Jocelyn. He was actually going into the city, to the FBI building. There he would meet with Anderson and Waters, and a female agent. They would read from a script prepared by them. He would read it first to be sure it contained the proper triggers. Then, after giving the fake recordings to Jocelyn, they would wait.

Would she take the bait and go to kill another man, someone she thought was an abuser of a wife and children? He didn't know for sure, but he had to find out.

Jocelyn called from the kitchen saying lunch was ready. He said a quick prayer, asking for the truth to be known. Then he went into the kitchen to eat lunch with his wife. He tried hard not to let on he knew she was a killer. Or maybe, hopefully, she wasn't.

Chapter Seventy

I was grilling once again. We decided to have the team, as well as Melissa out for a barbeque to make sure of our plan. We all sat around having a good time, eating some hotdogs, burgers and a few steaks. After we all ate... and had a few beers, Trace and Melissa began to go inside to talk about the adoption away from everyone else. Meanwhile, the rest of us, minus Billy, were going to go over the plan once again.

Everything was going just fine until Aaron, Carl and Lou stood up facing us. Trace and Melissa didn't get inside, and they looked at me to ask what was going on, but I just shrugged. I had no idea. Melissa sat back down next to Dave, and I moved next to Trace.

"Ummm, something you guys want to say?" I asked.

"Do you know who you work with Warren?" Lou said.

"I believe I am pretty sure. Unless the three of you work on the side as mob hitmen or something."

"No, we do not go around killing people. But we are investigators. Good investigators...no, forget good. We are great investigators, the best."

"Okay, I wouldn't argue with you. But, so what? What are you all standing there like you are about to cut our heads off. What did we do?"

"How long were you guys going to wait before you told us about the twins?"

Trace looked at me, me at Dave, Dave at Melissa and then back to me.

"Which one of you spilled the beans?' I said to Dave and Melissa. "Did you tell them Trace?"

Dave, Trace, Melissa and I were speaking all at once, when Lou let loose with a loud whistle. We all stopped talking and looked at the three of them standing there.

"Didn't you hear what I said?" Lou asked. "We are great investigators and there was no way you four could have hid this from us. So, are we going to open some champagne or what?"

There was no point in trying to deny it, so Trace and I stood up, getting hugs and kisses. There were congratulations all around even though Trace and I told them it wasn't a done deal. They didn't want to hear anything negative and demanded to see pictures of the twin boys. They wanted to hear their names and anything else about them.

Finally after a lot of hugs, kisses, ooh's and aah's, I was able to get their attention.

"I'm afraid we don't have any champagne here usually, so what will you all have?" I asked.

Aaron was laughing and produced not one, but two bottles of champagne from somewhere. He promptly opened them both up with a loud pop, while Trace and I got some glasses. Then when the glasses were filled, I made a toast.

Lifting my glass I said, "I want to say I have the best friends a man could have. And of course the best wife who will soon be a momma. Here's to the future and whatever it brings. With all of you, I know we can weather any storm, but let's all hope for days filled with sunshine, good friends, and love."

We all said cheers and drank down the champagne,

except for Melissa who was pregnant, and really beginning to show. The party went full tilt for a few more hours and we never did get to go over anything about the case. But for some reason, I didn't care at all.

Chapter Seventy - One

Monday, FBI HQ, Conference Room, 1:10 pm

The team all met at 8:30 and as usual, Aaron had brought in donuts. Dave had splurged and brought in bagels, some croissants, cream cheese, butter, lox and some tarts. After making coffee, we all sat around stuffing our faces.

As we were finishing up, I asked Lou if I could speak to her about something. We excused ourselves while the others gave us some puzzled looks. Then we went into my office, and I closed the door.

"Okay Lou," I said, "talk."

"Talk about what Warren?" she asked with an innocent look on her face.

"There is no way Aaron or Carl would have been able to find out about the twins. So talk."

"Okay, okay. Remember the woman who brought in the file to Mrs. Sugarman when you went to the NYF&BFC?"

"How the heck do you know about who brought in a file? And how did you know we went to the NYF&BFC? Do you have a tail on me? Are our phones bugged?"

"Calm down Warren. There really is a simple explanation but before I tell you, you have to promise to take no action. Do you promise?"

"Yeah, sure. Now spill it."

"The woman who brought you the file is my first cousin Lucy. She knows who I work with and when she heard your name, and you said you wanted to adopt the twins..."

"She called you."

"Yes she did. At first I wasn't going to say anything till you and Tracy told us. But after the way this case has been going and Billy getting hurt, I figured we all needed something to celebrate. I'm sorry, but I couldn't help it."

"You do know your cousin could be fired for revealing something like this?"

"Yeah, but you promised."

"Okay, I would never get your cousin fired. We better get back to work. Buy your investigation skills had nothing to do with finding out about the adoption. I suppose you're still a great investigator."

That earned me a light punch on my arm, and a big smile. Lou and I joined the others who had cleaned up the table. Then we sat down and began to go over the script Lou and Dr. Waters would be reading from.

"I think we shouldn't read the script," Lou said, "at least not while we are making the recording."

"What do you mean?" Dave asked.

"I don't mean we shouldn't follow it, I just meant reading it out loud would sound fake. Dr. Waters and I should get the jist of it memorized and then play it as it goes."

"I think you're right Lou," I said. "But I suggest you both have it in front of you just in case. It's almost 9:30. I'll make the call to Dr. Waters."

I had dialed the doctor and since he was waiting for the call, he wasn't surprised. He played his part, saying he would be over to the safe house as soon as possible. When I hung up, I gave the team the ok sign. Now all we had to do was wait for him to show up.

We had been sitting around, wondering where the doctor was. It was just after 1:00, and we were all getting nervous. Maybe he changed his mind or told his wife what was going on. I didn't think so but...

Just then an Agent knocked on the conference door and escorted Dr. Waters in.

"Sorry about being late, but traffic from Great Neck into the city was terrible," Waters said.

"No problem Dr. Waters," Dave said. "Let me introduce you to the rest of the team. This is Carl Walkin, Aaron Devlin and Louise Carmichael. She will be acting as your abused victim."

"I suppose I could say it is nice to meet all of you but obviously it is not."

"Let's sit down Doctor. Would you like some coffee or something to eat?"

"Coffee would be fine. So, were is my script?"

Lou and the Doctor decided it would be better if they read the script alone for a while. We all left them and went into our offices, except for Dave and me. We went to tell Teller we were proceeding with the plan.

"Do you believe this will work Special Agent Anderson?" Teller asked.

"I do sir," Dave answered. "We wrote the script with some suggestions from Dr. Waters himself. Knowing his wife's past, he gave us some specific triggers to put into the script. We believe Jocelyn Waters will not be able to ignore them. She will be compelled to act, and then we will have her."

"And the Doctor is willing to do this? He is basically going to be the one who puts his wife in prison."

"Dr. Waters is a decent man sir," I replied. "I'm sure it isn't going to be easy for him. But he treats abused women and children. He is a law abiding citizen and he believes in right and wrong."

"Okay Special Agent Temple, I just hope he doesn't cave and tip off his wife. Do we have eyes on the house and his jet, just in case she is tipped off or figures something is wrong?"

"We do sir. We have a full team watching the house and her. They will stay on it till she makes her move, one way or another."

"Okay then, get to it."

After we left Teller, we all went back to our offices. We had no idea how long it would take Dr. Waters to memorize his end of the script. But it shouldn't be too difficult. He would be playing the role with a great deal of experience. He would really only have to be his natural self.

There was a knock on my door and Lou came in, saying, "We're ready Warren."

I got up and went into the conference room. Dave and I would be in with Dr. Waters and Lou. Carl and Aaron had told Dave if they were there as well it might throw the doctor off.

Lou was sitting across from Waters with his tape recorder between them. He was ready to start and asked us to remain quiet. If there was something we needed to tell him, we would write it on a white board we had set up.

He didn't look nervous and neither did Lou. I was a bit nervous but not about them doing a good job. I was just worried this wouldn't work.

Dr. Waters nodded to us, cleared his throat, turned on the tape and said, "This is Dr. Waters at the Midtown Safe House in New York City. Today is....

Chapter Seventy - Two

Monday, FBI HQ, Conference Room, 4:30 pm

Dr. Waters and Lou just finished their session, and Waters turned off the recorder. He stood up, stretched and asked if we might have something a bit stronger than coffee. Dave left the room and returned with a small bottle of bourbon and a glass.

"Will this do Dr. Waters?" Dave asked.

"Yes, perfect," Dr. Waters replied.

Dave poured him two fingers in a glass and handed it to him. Dr. Waters sat back down and took a sip.

"You know, ever since you told me my wife was a serial killer, I haven't slept at all," Dr. Waters said. He took another sip and continued, "I have thought about the timeline for all of the murders. Where I was and where I thought my wife was. Unfortunately, I have come to the conclusion she could mind you, could have been at all of the crime scenes. I still have some hope it isn't her, but... but I have come to believe she is probably guilty of these horrendous crimes. Of course, it really isn't her fault. We all are shaped by our past gentlemen, and she was shaped at an early age."

"I'm very sorry it has come to this Dr. Waters," Dave said, "and I realize how hard this is for you. All I can say is she won't be hurt. I promise you."

Dr. Waters finished his drink, stood and said, "I suppose it is all I can ask for. I will go home, and Jocelyn will transcribe this tonight or tomorrow morning. If she is the killer, she will be triggered by the tape. I guarantee it. Goodbye gentlemen."

Dave escorted Dr. Waters to the elevator and then returned to the conference room. Carl and Aaron joined us, and we all sat down.

"I could use a drink of that bourbon myself," Lou said.

"Not while on duty, but I'm sure you can find some when you get off," Dave said.

"How was the doc?" Aaron asked.

"I think he was shaken and extremely upset, but wouldn't show it," I replied. "Honestly, if I were in his situation, I doubt I could do what he is doing. I don't think I could ever do that to Trace."

"You could Warren if you truly believed Trace had killed six men," Carl said. "The Doc knows she is guilty in his heart, if not in his mind. It's the only way he can go through with this."

"I suppose you're right Carl. I feel for him. He's a decent guy, no, more than decent. He believes in right and wrong, and he is doing his duty, no matter how hard it is for him."

We all sat around for a bit more and then called it a day. The agents watching the house would report if Jocelyn Waters left the house. They would easily be able to follow her because we had gotten a warrant to put a tracker on her car.

We all said our goodbyes and I went home to get ready. It might take a day, or a week for Jocelyn Waters to plan her attack. But we would be ready for her. The waiting for her to make her move would be the hardest part.

I drove home and kept thinking how all of this would be over soon. Then Trace and I could really start the process of adopting the twin boys. I smiled and thought, I'm going to be a dad. I couldn't wait.

Chapter Seventy-Three

Dr. Waters had left the FBI building and slowly driven home. The entire way home he wrestled with himself. Could he do this to his loving wife? Could he turn her over to the FBI as Judas had turned over Jesus? The thought crossed his mind to get her out of the house and fly somewhere safe. But he needed to know the truth and the only way he would ever know, would be to go through with the plan.

What if she was the killer? He knew it really wasn't her fault. She had been abused as a child. Seen her parents murdered by her own sister, and then suffered her sister's death, by her own hand. Yes, she had been adopted by a loving family, but those memories, though buried deep, had resurfaced.

When Max Gardner had murdered her friend Brandy, those old memories had probably returned. But she didn't act on them. Not until I had her transcribe the sessions with women and children who had been abused. I had triggered her pain and suffering, and she had to act. But I didn't know about her past. How could I have known it would cause her to go on a murderous rampage, killing six men?

Six men! She had brutally killed six men!

As he pulled in front of his house, Dr. Waters made a decision. He would go through with the FBI's plan. But when she made her move, if she made it, he would follow her. If he could, he would get her away. He had a gun he kept for reasons of security only. Could he actually use it though? After all the years of love they shared, he owed it to her. Somehow he would have to take her and disappear. He had enough money, and he could send for Brandon once they had settled somewhere safe. He would treat her mental disease himself, cure her, and then they could live out their lives in peace.

He entered the house with a new determination.

"Jocelyn," he called out, "I'm home."

Jocelyn came out of the kitchen and said, "Oh I'm glad you are home. Dinner is just ready. Go say hello to Brandon and then come down to eat."

She gave him a kiss and he turned to go to say hello to his son. He steeled his nerves not wanting to appear afraid. He might let on just how troubled he was to his son. Brandon didn't need to worry about any of this, he had enough on his plate.

He entered his son's room, happy to see him sitting up and playing cards with Claire.

"Hi Dad," Brandon called out. "I think Claire is more of a card shark than a nurse!"

"Don't believe a word this young man says Dr. Waters," Claire said. "Would you like me to give you some time alone?"

"No Claire, you keep playing and taking as much money from him as you can," Dr. Waters said. "I just wanted to say hello. I'm going to eat dinner with your mother, but I'll be back after."

"Okay Dad," Brandon said, and he and Claire resumed their card game.

Dr. Waters washed his hands and face, looking into his own eyes in the mirror. He was determined to act his normal self. He went into the kitchen and sat down at the table.

"Something smells delicious," he said.

"I figured after the past week and then you having to run out this morning I would make you your favorite Malcolm," Jocelyn said.

"Veal cutlet parmigiani, with rigatoni and small potatoes?"

"You guessed it!"

"Wonderful. Thank you Jocelyn."

"Just dig in dear and tell me about your day."

"Let's not talk about my day, you will hear all about it on the tape. How was your day?"

They ate their meal and made small talk. After eating, both cleaned up the meal and then went to spend some time with Brandon. After an hour, they said their goodnights to their son and Claire. Then they sat down in the living room together on the couch. After a few minutes, Dr. Waters stood.

"I think I'm going to go up to bed Jocelyn," Dr. Waters said. "Today has worn me out. Thank you again for the splendid meal. Are you coming up?"

"I'm not really tired Malcolm," Jocelyn replied. "I think I will get started transcribing today's tape. I would like to get it done because I might have a busy week ahead of me. You go up and I'll be up as soon as I am finished."

Dr. Waters gave her a kiss and went up the stairs to their bedroom. Jocelyn poured herself a little white wine and then went into the office. On the desk was sitting the tape. She sat down, got comfortable and hooked up a set of headphones to the recorder. She always listened to the tape all the way through before she began to transcribe it.

She pressed play and began to listen. After the initial part where Malcolm gave the date, time and place, and other essential information, she listened more carefully.

Dr. Waters was saying, " Just relax Mrs. Temple. May I call you Louise?"

A shaky female voice replied, "Everyone calls me Lou Dr. Waters."

"Very good Lou. First can I get you anything? Has someone treated your eyes and lips yet? And any other injuries?"

Jocelyn thought to herself the bastard must have done some number on her.

Lou continued, "It doesn't hurt much Doctor, I'm... I'm used to it."

"Alright then," Malcolm continued, "in your own words tell me what happened."

"Okay. Me and the girls...I have two girls. Teresa is 19 years old and Susan, we call her Susie, had gone to the mall to shop. We went out to dinner after, and I had forgotten to call Warren. So we got home late. When I walked in the door, he grabbed the packages we had bought. He tore them open and saw the two new dresses I had bought for the girls."

Jocelyn heard Lou sobbing and Malcolm offering a tissue. Jocelyn was getting angry thinking about Lou's bastard husband!

"Thank you Dr. Waters," Lou said.

"Take your time and continue Lou," Malcolm said.

"War, I call him War, took the dresses and walked into the den. Then he took some scissors and cut them to shreds! He told Teresa to go up to her room and get ready for daddy. That's what he says when he...he goes up to her room. But then he said Susie should do the same! Susie is only thirteen!"

"Does your husband abuse Teresa when he goes up to her room?"

"Yes he does, and I haven't been able to stop him! The girls went up to their rooms, crying, and then he turned on me. He hit me in the face, knocking me down. Kicked me a few times and then he...he..."

"Calm down Lou and tell me what he did."

"He raped me! Right there on the floor. Then he told me to get to our room and stay there or else. I knew I should do something, but I couldn't. I went to the room and heard the girls screaming! In the morning while War was sleeping, I grabbed the girls and ran. I came here. War works from home; he never leaves except to go to the bar. I don't know what he is going to do when he finds out I've left and taken them."

"Have you contacted the police yet?"

"No! Please no! I just want to get the girls and me away before he kills one of us. I can't go to the police. I have a sister who lives in California. I just want to get the girls there for good."

"We will talk about it but don't worry. Now..."

Jocelyn was so angry she picked up her empty wine glass and threw it against the wall!

"That bastard!" Jocelyn said to herself. "He...he raped those girls! And his wife!"

Jocelyn slowly got control of herself. She started to pick up the broken glass and began planning in her head what she would do. She wasn't going to wait too long before taking care of Lou's husband. The bastard needed to feel the pain he had inflicted on his own wife and children. And then he needed to die so he would never cause pain again.

She sat back down after cleaning up the glass, then turned on the tape from the beginning again. This time she had a notepad and pen. She wrote down their names, and where they lived. She listened, still angry but now under control as she thought about what she would do to Mr. Warren Temple.

Chapter Seventy - Four

I was starting to feel like a prisoner in my own home. Dr. Waters had called us on Tuesday, saying his wife had transcribed the tape. He said she wasn't acting any different, as far as he could tell. He assured us if she was this killer, the triggers on the tape would have her seething. She would have to act, and she wouldn't, no couldn't wait too long.

I hated having Trace leave the house until this whole thing was resolved, but *my wife*, Lou, was in the safe house, supposedly. If Jocelyn Waters did any surveillance, we couldn't take the chance she would see Trace. Trace was staying with Melissa, and Dave had moved in with me. We had also set up Carl and Aaron in one of the neighbors' homes. They were good friends of mine and were actually excited by the whole thing.

I made a show of looking like a mean slob, walking outside to throw away the garbage with an old cigar stuck in the side of my mouth. I wore a pair of ripped shorts and a stained tee shirt. I had also taken some old clothes belonging to Trace and thrown them on the lawn. Dave had even purchased some girls clothes along with some little things *my girls* might have owned. They were on the front lawn too.

Dave and I were sitting at the kitchen table with all the window curtains drawn. No one could see in.

"You think today might be the day Warren?" Dave asked me.

"I certainly hope so," I replied. "Don't take this wrong, but I prefer having Trace here with me."

"Understood. I'm sure she must be getting ready to strike. The agents watching her have said she has gone out to their golf club. She also made some stops at her son's school and charities she works with. Nothing out of the ordinary."

"You don't think we are wrong do you?"

"No way, I'm positive Jocelyn Waters is the Brutal Abuser. I still can't get used to the name Billy came up with."

"I agree, but hopefully, she will try to get to me and then we can close this case and forget about the name. What about Dr. Waters? What has he been doing?"

"We have an agent watching him too. He has not visited any shelters or safe houses, but he has been out of the house every day. He has made a few visits into the city, visited a few banks and some offices in Manhattan. He is following our instructions, giving his wife the opportunity to come and kill you."

"Ummm, let's make it...try and kill me."

"Right. Try and kill you. Feel up to another game of gin? I want to try and win back some of my money."

"I'll get the cards. But don't think I'm about to go easy on you."

I got the cards, refilled my cup of coffee and pulled out the pad we had been keeping score on.

"Looks to me you owe me just a hair over two thousand dollars Dave," I said with a laugh.

"Yeah, I know but thank god we aren't really playing for money. Right?"

"I don't know. I'm going to have two more mouths to feed soon. I might need some extra money."

"Don't forget I'm going to have one more mouth to feed soon too. Plus, you wouldn't want your godchild to suffer because you are taking money from their father, would you?"

"Uh huh. But you would be taking money out of both your godchildren."

"Just deal, Warren."

We played for the next hour and once again I was crushing Dave. The tally was up to almost three thousand. I only needed fifteen more points to win another game.

Dave picked up a card and slammed them down yelling, "Gin!"

Then the phone rang. I got up and answered it and then sat down and put the cards back in their box.

"She's on the way," I said.

"Is the agent tailing her sure?" Dave asked.

"She got on the L.I.E. and is heading east. She is close to the Huntington exit and if she takes it, he will call back."

We didn't have to wait long. The phone rang, I picked it up and said, "Okay."

We had everything basically prepared, as much as we could. But preparation only goes so far. Somethings you couldn't plan for. I went upstairs to get myself ready. Dave called Aaron and Carl to inform them Jocelyn Waters was on her way. Dave had a good spot at the side of the front door. I came downstairs and sat down in the living room. The curtains were wide open in case Jocelyn Waters wanted to look in before ringing the bell. She wouldn't be able to see where Dave was hiding. We were ready.

The phone rang and I figured it was the agent telling us she had turned onto my street. But when I answered it, it was a different agent on the phone.

"Yes?" I said.

"This is Special Agent Dixon," I heard him say. "I was assigned to follow Dr. Waters, ummm, but somehow he gave me the slip. I have no idea where he is right now. Sorry."

"Okay, don't sweat it. Mrs. Waters is almost here so I don't think it matters. Let us know if you reacquire him. Bye."

"Who was that?" Dave asked.

"Dr. Waters gave our guy the slip."

"Do you think he might have changed his mind, maybe trying to stop his wife?"

"I don't know Dave. I suppose we will just have to be careful and see how this thing plays out. She should be here any minute."

I sat back down, Dave got out his weapon, and we both waited. I turned on the television and made like I was drinking a beer. Of course the can was empty. Five minutes later I heard the front bell ring. I took a deep breath and stood up.

Then I yelled out, "Hold your damn horses! I'm coming damn it!"

I opened the door and saw Jocelyn Waters with a wild look in her eyes, a taser in her hand and then her pushing it into my stomach.

Chapter Seventy - Five

Thursday, Huntington, LI, the Temple home, 12:45 pm

All hell broke loose!

I didn't go down from the shock of the taser and grabbed the hand holding it. On the steps next to her was a large bag. Dave jumped out with his gun, pointing it directly at her. I tried to get her to the ground but couldn't move fast enough, due to what I was wearing. Dave tried to get around me, grabbed her other arm, and got her down on the ground.

Dave said, "Stop struggling Mrs. Waters! It's over and you are under arrest!"

He was trying to get cuffs on her while I wrestled away the taser.

"He has to die!" Mrs. Waters was screaming and flailing around. "He is a rapist! He has to die, and I will kill him!"

Carl and Aaron appeared from my neighbor's house, running toward us. Then the agent who had been following her was on the scene as well. It was almost over, Dave had gotten one cuff on her wrist, when Dr. Waters calmly walked up and put a gun to Carl's head!

"Let her up, Agent Anderson," he calmly said. "Do it or I will be forced to kill Agent Walkin."

Dave let her up, still holding onto her cuffed wrist. I stood as well, and we all stayed still. Aaron was slowly moving forward. The other agent was trying to slowly flank him.

"Dr. Waters," I said as calmly as possible, "you really don't want to do this."

"Stop moving! All of you stay still. I needed to know for sure and now I do. But I still love her. Get the handcuff off of her, now!"

Dave uncuffed her and took a step back.

"I don't understand Malcolm," Jocelyn said. "Why are you here? Why are these men all here?"

"I will explain once we have gone Jocelyn," Dr. Waters said. "For now, just walk next to me toward the car. Everything has been arranged."

Dr, Waters pushed Carl toward the street where his car was waiting.

"Let me get my bag."

"Hurry dear, we must get going."

Mrs. Waters grabbed her bag and began following behind her husband. Before any of us could do anything, she opened the bag, withdrawing a large knife and thrust it into her husband's back!

We all moved at once. Dr. Waters dropped his gun, Carl spun and knocked the knife from Jocelyn's hand. Dave tackled her, and I got to the doctor, putting pressure on his wound. Aaron got on the phone and called 911 for an ambulance.

Jocelyn was finally cuffed and she was screaming, "You fucking traitor! You set me up! I'll kill you Malcolm! Do you hear me? I'll kill you all!"

Dave got her up and into the Agent's back seat. He would keep her there until we had the scene under control. We could still hear her screaming through the windows of the car.

Dave looked at everyone and said, "Is anybody else hurt?"

We all said no, and I stayed where I was, holding pressure on Dr. Waters back. I wasn't sure if he was going to make it. He was having trouble breathing and his color was pale.

Aaron leaned down and felt his pulse.

"He's not gonna make it unless the ambulance shows up soon," he whispered to me.

"Damn it!" I said. "Get your car up here Carl! Now! Dave, we are going to Huntington Hospital. Give them a heads up!"

Carl drove his car onto my lawn and together we got Dr. Waters into the back seat. Aaron jumped into the front seat and Carl peeled out. I gave him directions to the hospital. It was only five minutes away.

Dave got the number for the hospital and had made the call. When we pulled up, a full team was there to grab Dr. Waters. When they had him, I finally took a deep breath.

"Good driving Carl," I said.

"Yeah, well he was bleeding all over my car and I wanted him out as soon as possible." Carl said.

Aaron and I looked at him, and then we all cracked up. Cops all around the world always knew what to say to relieve the pressure from a situation. Anyone who heard Carl would be shocked, but it was the way cops handled the crap we dealt with every day. I supposed FBI Special Agents did the same thing.

"Aaron, you stay here with Dr. Waters," I said after catching my breath.

"Got it Warren," Aaron said and walked into the hospital.

"Let's get back to my house Carl,"

"You got it Warren," Carl said. "Do you want me to drive a bit slower getting back there?"

"I think it would be a good idea Carl."

I got into the car and soon we were back at the house. Dave was standing there waiting to hear how Dr. Waters was.

"Is he going to make it?" Dave asked me.

"Not sure Dave," I replied. "Let me get changed and call Trace. She will want to know we are safe, and it is over. Then we can get Jocelyn back to the city."

"You got it Warren. Make sure Tracy tells Melissa I'm safe too."

I went into my house and upstairs to the bedroom. I had to sit down on the bed for a second to let the adrenaline rush pass. I was suddenly very tired, but I knew there was still a lot of work to be done.

I stood up and thought for a second about Dr. Waters. Would I have done the same thing, or would I have never turned on my own wife? I wasn't sure what the answer was, but I was going to do everything I could to try and get Dr. Waters free from prosecution. I felt as if I knew why he had done what he did. Maybe he wasn't responsible for his actions, just as he had said his wife wasn't responsible for her actions. I shook my head and began to get changed.

Chapter Seventy - Six

We transported Mrs. Waters to FBI HQ, where she was checked for weapons and any injuries. She had finally calmed down and was put in an interview room. Her hands were cuffed to a solid steel ring in the center of the table. Even though we had enough proof to put her away, we wanted a confession if possible. Carl stayed with her in the room, while Dave and I went to tell Teller everything which had occurred.

"Please sit down," Teller said when we entered his office. "I know a bit of what occurred, but I would like to hear a quick rundown on the arrest."

We sat and Dave began, "We thought we had everything covered but Dr. Waters threw us for a loop. We were informed Mrs. Waters was on the way. Then right before she showed up, we got a call telling us Dr. Waters had slipped his tail."

"Not much time to deal with it. Go on please."

"Warren was ready. He was wearing a full body suit made of rubber. We figured she was using a taser and so we prepared for it."

"And did she use a taser? Were you affected, Warren?"

I was shocked he had called me Warren, but I answered saying, "I felt nothing sir. I think she was a bit astonished when I didn't go down and grabbed the taser and her arm."

"Then I went to grab her other arm, and get her on the ground," Dave continued. "I had one cuff on, Special

Agents Devlin and Walkin were approaching, as well as the Special Agent who had been tailing Mrs. Waters. Unfortunately, Dr. Waters showed up and put a gun to Agent Walkin's head before we could do anything."

"Well now, we will have to deal with him soon. Go on please Dave."

"He was walking Carl to his car, with Mrs. Waters next to him. She had grabbed a bag which had fallen on the lawn. We were unable to do anything at the moment when she opened the bag, took out a large knife and stabbed her husband in the back. She was disarmed, cuffed and Warren, I mean Special..."

"Warren is fine."

"Umm, Warren put pressure on the wound and then Carl and Arron lifted the doctor into the car and drove him to the hospital."

"Is he going to make it?"

"Unsure at this time sir. Aaron is staying at the hospital and will call us as soon as he knows."

"Excellent job men. You all did an outstanding job. You are going to do the interview now."

"Yes sir."

"Then if there is nothing else..."

"Actually sir, I have something I would like to run by you," I said.

"Yes, Special Agent Temple?"

Uh oh, we were back to Special Agent.

"I don't believe we should charge Dr, Waters with any offense."

"He put a gun to the head of a Special Agent of the FBI. Why shouldn't he be charged."

"I agree with Warren sir," Dave said. "I believe he was under tremendous stress and made a... a terrible mistake. But the only person hurt was the doctor."

"I will think about it, but you will have to make your case to a Federal Judge. But I will let you know what I decide about it. Now go do the interview."

"I didn't know you were thinking the same thing Dave," I said as we made our way to the interview room.

"I was just thinking about what you had said," he replied. "Remember, you said you didn't think you could turn in Tracy. I was thinking if I could turn in Melissa. And Dr. Waters did cooperate with us. He brought the murders to an end."

"Hopefully we can talk to a judge, if Teller lets us, and get him off with no time served."

"I believe once we tell a judge about Dr. Waters treating abused women and children for free, and the fact he has an injured son at home and the stress of turning in his wife, I think we can convince a judge. Now, let's get back to work."

We entered the interview room where Carl was waiting. The camera and microphone had been turned on as soon as she had been brought in. Dave and I took our seats. And Carl stepped out. We knew Carl, Lou and Teller would probably be watching.

Dave introduced us both and then read Jocelyn Waters her rights under Miranda. She answered she understood them, and she was willing to talk.

"First Mrs. Waters, I..." Dave began but was stopped when she tried to hold up her hand.

"I see no reason for formalities, please call me Jocelyn." she said.

"As you wish. First I would like to know if you killed Robert Heller, Jerry Baxter, Dr. Cary Tomlinson, Anthony Blake, Stuart King and finally, Max Gardner."

"Yes I did. They all needed to die. They abused their wives and children. They were scum. They needed to be put in the ground like rabid dogs."

"Besides the fact they abused their families, why did you feel the need to be the one to murder them? I'm sure you know murder is wrong."

"Is it? One night after Brandy was murdered by Max Gardner, that pig, I remembered what my own father had done. He had abused my mother and sister, and finally me. I had blocked it out for a long time, and then suddenly, I remembered it all.

But I didn't decide to kill anyone then. I just blocked it out once again. I married Malcolm and then we had our son, Brandon. We were very wealthy, and I had everything I could ever want. But then Malcolm asked me if I would like to transcribe his sessions. I agreed, and at first it was fine. But every time I heard another woman crying, every time a woman told him how she and sometimes her children were abused, it got harder not to do something.

I began having nightmares. Then headaches every single time I listened to his sessions. One day, I couldn't stand it. I had just finished listening to the wife of Anthony Blake. I knew I had to act, and I did. It wasn't hard. When you look through my little bag of tricks, you will find some lead weighted gloves. I'm not a weak woman, but with those gloves on, I could hear bones breaking with every punch. And then I would slit their throats after they couldn't take another punch.

After Tony, it got easier. I started inflicting more and more pain. But the best was Max Gardner. I read he had been released, and using my husband's contacts, I found out where he was living and working. It couldn't have been better. He was working in the same place where my best friend Brandy had worked. I dressed as a nurse and snuck in way before Max even got to work. Killing him was the best thing I ever did.

Now I have confessed. May I ask you a question or two?"

"Of course, ask away Jocelyn."

"How did you figure out it was me? And why would Malcolm cooperate with you? I now know the last taped session was just a ruse. He was in on it, and I'd like to know how. Oh, and if he is dead."

"Originally we figured Dr. Waters was the killer. But after checking his flight logs, we eliminated him. His pilot, Dennis Trask, also was eliminated. We had one other suspect who was cleared. Then when we found out about your childhood, it all fell into place. As for your husband's cooperation, you will have to ask him if he survives."

"Why didn't my taser knock you down? It has quite a wallop you know."

"I was prepared, wearing a rubber suit Jocelyn," I replied.

"Very smart. Well, I'm tired now and would like to be brought...I guess to a cell. It was all worth it, every single one of them I murdered deserved to die."

We signaled Carl to come in and bring her to a holding cell until she could be moved to a proper cell. Of course she would be able to plead not guilty, but somehow I believed she was accepting her fate. She would plead guilty.

As she was being brought out, she turned and said, "Please let me know if Malcolm dies or survives. Funny, I'm not sure which would make me happier."

Dave and I watched her go, shaking our heads. He went to his office, and I went to mine. The Brutal Abuser case was finished, except for the paperwork. There was always paperwork.

I sat back and thought about the case. I supposed it really had begun with Jocelyn's own father. If she hadn't been abused, would any of this ever have occurred? I didn't know the answer.

I began to write out my report, but then closed my laptop. I was too tired to think and all I wanted to do was to hold and kiss my wife. I shut the light, closed the door to my office and headed home.

Epilogue

Saturday, Huntington, LI, Our Home 11:30 am

It was close to two months after the arrest of Jocelyn Waters. She had pleaded guilty, just as I thought she would. She was sentenced to life in prison, without the possibility of parole. She never got the chance to ask her husband anything.

Malcolm Waters had survived his stabbing, but once he was able to talk, he stated he never wanted to see or speak to his wife again. He hired an excellent lawyer and was sentenced to probation for three years. Dave and I were happy with the result. I wasn't sure ADD Teller was, but he dealt with it.

Brandon Waters made a full recovery after having arthroscopic surgery on his knee. He was doing physical therapy with his dad right by his side. Dr. Waters decided he needed to be more present in his son's life. He stopped flying around the country and seeing abused women and children. Instead he got himself into a practice near North Shore University Hospital, with two other psychiatrists. He was working only three days a week. The rest of his time he spent either with his son or at his home. He also threw away his black valise.

As for Dennis Trask, Dr. Waters had given him his jet. Trask was overwhelmed with the generosity. Dr. Waters had told him if it hadn't been for him, he would have never been put in touch with the FBI. Trask then started his own business, flying executives around the country. He was doing well the last time I had checked with him. He even offered a free ride anywhere Dave and I wanted to go. Maybe one day we will take him up on it.

As for Trace and me, we had adopted the twins. When we adopted them, we had been told we could officially change their names because they were so young. Trace and I knew we wouldn't do it. They had been named by their mother and father, and the names they gave them were going to stay. Michael and Gregory Temple had come home to our house a few weeks ago. It had been a trial of errors for both of us, but the boys were doing fine now. And we figured out how to tell them apart. Michael had a small heart shaped mole on the back of his neck. Gregory did not have it, but he did have a mole on his left ankle. I supposed somehow they got them to help us tell them apart by an act of God. I thanked him for it.

Today was their one year birthdays. We were having a huge party for them and the guests were arriving. The two detectives, Maguire and Robles, were there, and Robles had brought his wife and four kids. My old captain, Terry Jackson, came with his wife. It would have been great if my old partner Tom Delaney could have been there.

Lou arrived with Billy, walking with crutches. He had been working at the office on light duty, and in a month or two when the cast came off, he would start training for his physical. He wanted to get back to work. I hugged Lou and looked down to the engagement ring on her finger. Billy had asked her, and she had said yes. Dave was still trying to figure out how it was going to work with them married and working on the same team. But he was determined to keep the team together.

Next to arrive was Carl and Aaron, with Aaron carrying not one, not two, but three large boxes filled with donuts! Somehow, it figured, and I was sure he was going to eat the majority of them. He also had a stunning redhead hanging on his arm. He and Cassandra had been flying back and forth to be together. Maybe there would be two marriages in the near future.

Dave and Melissa came onto the back patio, with Melissa carrying their new baby girl. They had named her after Dave's mother, Gloria. They started calling her Glory right away. I thought it was a perfect name.

We were all sitting around the back patio when finally the guests of honor arrived. Trace came out holding both of them in her arms. She wasn't holding them for long. Everybody tried to have a minute holding each boy, taking turns passing them around.

I was a bit nervous and asked Trace if we should get them back to their cribs.

"Oh War, our sons couldn't be in safer hands," she said. "Now go inside and bring out the cake. And don't forget to light the candle."

She handed Maguire a video camera and everyone had their phones out as well. I walked out and placed the cake on the table. Then Trace got hold of Gregory and I took Michael out of Terry Jackson's hands. He really didn't want to let go of him.

I looked around at my friends and colleagues. I didn't think anyone was as lucky as I was. Then Trace nodded at me, and we were ready.

We both held the boys and together, everyone blew out the candles after we all sang happy birthday. I looked around at my friends, my colleagues, my wife and my boys. I was the happiest man on Earth!

THE END